I0637123

GOING OVERBOARD

PORTIA MACINTOSH

Boldwood

First published in Great Britain in 2025 by Boldwood Books Ltd.

Copyright © Portia MacIntosh, 2025

Cover Design by Alexandra Allden

Cover Images: Shutterstock

The moral right of Portia MacIntosh to be identified as the author of this work has been asserted in accordance with the Copyright, Designs and Patents Act 1988.

Every effort has been made to obtain the necessary permissions with reference to copyright material, both illustrative and quoted. We apologise for any omissions in this respect and will be pleased to make the appropriate acknowledgements in any future edition.

A CIP catalogue record for this book is available from the British Library.

Paperback ISBN 978-1-80426-759-2

Large Print ISBN 978-1-80426-760-8

Hardback ISBN 978-1-80426-761-5

Ebook ISBN 978-1-80426-758-5

Kindle ISBN 978-1-80426-757-8

Audio CD ISBN 978-1-80426-766-0

MP3 CD ISBN 978-1-80426-765-3

Digital audio download ISBN 978-1-80426-763-9

This book is printed on certified sustainable paper. Boldwood Books is dedicated to putting sustainability at the heart of our business. For more information please visit https://www.boldwoodbooks.com/about-us/sustainability/

Boldwood Books Ltd, 23 Bowerdean Street, London, SW6 3TN

www.boldwoodbooks.com

For Joe
Thanks for always being there

1

'Cheer up, love, you might have marked the days wrong in your calendar.'

Ugh. Gross. And way to make an already misogynistic phrase just that little bit worse. You've got to hand it to some people, going above and beyond like that.

I suppose (some might say) it's my own fault, for sitting on the side of the pub garden next to the pavement, like I was just asking to be talked to by one of the drunk men pub-crawling past.

I am smiling now, to be fair, but not because he told me to, because the man who said this to me was dressed like a T-Rex. Peak dinosaur behaviour, as expected.

I swirl my drink around in my glass, watching the ice melt under the afternoon sun. I'm trapped somewhere between heaven and hell. Well, you can't beat a Saturday afternoon in a pub garden in sunny Headingly... it's just a shame that some of the people doing the Otley Run are so worse for wear at this point that they're in that annoying stage of drunkenness where being a bit of a dick seems like the funniest thing.

I know, I sound grumpy for a thirty-two-year-old, and I was no stranger to an Otley Run – the infamous fancy-dress pub crawl – when I was a student in Leeds. It's just that today I'm trying to vibe in the sunshine, now that it feels like summer might finally be well and truly here after a few false starts, and that vibe is being killed by things like handing back a rogue inflatable banana to a twenty-something Minion with a beer stain down the front of his dungarees.

Don't get me wrong, I love that Headingly is a social Petri dish, but I'm feeling kind of stressed today, and coming here was supposed to relax me and cheer me up, and yet I find myself sitting on my own watching the world go by – literally, I just saw someone dressed up as a globe.

I smile to myself as a gaggle of girlies dressed as bowling pins trot by in their heels. I have a lot of time for that – that respect for style, even when it feels impossible. I don't envy them navigating the pavement flags though, which I always seem to trip on, even when I'm in my trainers.

It's been a long time since I went on a pub crawl with Kelsey, my bestie. Isn't it weird how you sort of reach an age when you decide you're too grown-up for such things... but then one day your perspective shifts and you start feeling like you might be old? Maybe I'll ask her if she's up for it, one of these days – perhaps we'll even dress up for old times' sake.

At least it's sunny. The entire street is bathed in a warm glow – and my legs are getting their first official outing of the season. Shorts seemed like a great idea, for keeping cool, but it has to be said that my legs are looking alarmingly reflective. Maybe I should have stuck some fake tan on, just to not be such an obstacle to traffic should the light bounce off my ghostly-white legs and blind a driver, but to be honest with you I was so eager to get out of the flat and feel the sun on my skin that it's a miracle I even bothered shaving them.

I'm scrolling aimlessly through Instagram, busying myself with something, when a shadow falls across the table. It's not a cloud – it's a man.

'All right, princess,' he says, his voice a mixture of swagger and slur.

And there he is. Super Mario himself. Super-*drunk* Super Mario.

His hat is kind of flat and sad and his stick-on moustache is clinging on for dear life, but he's got the full outfit on – even the white gloves. Well, I assume they were white when he put them on.

'Erm... hi,' I say, polite but cool, already turning back to my phone, pretending like I'm doing something very serious, very urgent, very... none of his business.

He doesn't take the hint.

Mario plonks himself onto the bench opposite me, causing it to creak under his weight – almost like it's protesting his intrusion on my behalf.

'What's a lovely lass like you doing sitting on your bill?' he asks, leaning across the table with the kind of smile that makes me think either this has worked for him before, or he has an over-whelming level of self-confidence. I'm certain it's the latter.

'I'm with someone,' I tell him. 'My b—'

'You dressed up too, yeah?' he asks, squinting at me as he talks over me. 'What are you meant to be?'

I blink at him. I'm wearing denim shorts, a white vest and a pair of sandals. My long blonde hair is in loose waves – nothing fancy. Who or what on earth could I possibly be? Other than a millennial thirty-something starter pack.

'I'm not dressed up,' I say flatly.

He grins.

'Not dressed, eh? Even better. You can be my Peach. I wouldn't mind takin' a bite out of that.'

I feel a wrinkle form on my forehead at his choice of words. Well, one word in particular – *that*. I don't know whether to cry at the sheer bleakness of it or burst into flames.

'Charming,' I say under my breath.

'Come on, princess, what do you say?'

Ugh, and then he winks. Honestly, like that was going to help.

'Don't you have a drain to jump down?' I ask, briefly confusing him with my smile.

He leans over the table, too close for comfort, the overwhelming stench of stale beer and cheap aftershave overwhelming.

'My boyfriend will be here in a minute,' I tell him, starting to feel uncomfortable.

'Oh, your *boyfriend*,' he says mockingly. 'Suddenly she's got a *boyfriend*.'

'Yep,' I say weakly.

I glance around, looking for a friendly face, or even the unfriendly face of a bouncer, but I'm not on anyone's radar right now.

Mario smirks – so much so, his moustache is hanging by a thread now.

'You don't seem like you've got a boyfriend, princess.'

I furrow my brow involuntarily, because what does that mean?

He shrugs like he's just said something deeply profound.

'I'm just saying... if you were mine, I wouldn't leave you sat out here alone. I'd be by your side, holding your hand, feeding you chips... maybe whispering something dirty in your ear...'

And they say romance is dead.

Mario reaches across the table and takes my hand in his. I try to snatch it away but he keeps tight hold of it.

'Okay, seriously, I'm not interested,' I say plainly, because politeness is getting me nowhere.

'Come on, don't be like that,' he says, shaking my hand in his. 'Just one drink, come on, say you agree – look, you're shaking my hand, that's binding.'

'I'm really not, and I'm really, really not interested,' I tell him. 'Can you let go of my hand, please?'

The word please leaves my lips like a reflex, like muscle memory I've been trying to shake my entire life.

'Why, are you worried your fake boyfriend will get jealous?' he asks.

He clearly doesn't believe me on that one, which is infuriating, because I do have a boyfriend, and I am waiting for him.

'Sorry I'm late, babe.' A voice snaps me from my thoughts as I feel someone sit down next to me.

As I turn to look instinctively I'm greeted by a peck on the cheek – well, mostly the cheek. His lips ever so slightly graze mine on one side.

I just look at him and blink at the absurdity of the situation.

Super Mario somehow stumbles to his feet – that's the only way I can think to describe it – as panic sets in.

'Shit, sorry, mate, sorry,' he babbles. 'She said she had a boyfriend. I thought she was joking. Sorry, sorry. My bad. No hard feelings, eh?'

'We're trying to have a nice day, if you wouldn't mind pissing off...'

'Yeah, of course, mate. Sorry,' Mario replies.

Stunning, really, that Mario wouldn't take no for an answer from a female, but when a man rocks up he gets not one, not two but – let me just count them quick – five sorrys.

'Sorry,' Mario says again – taking it to six.

I don't know what to say so I just glance back and forth between the two of them.

'Just... go, yeah? Get back to your mates. Have a good time.'

He leans over to give Mario an encouraging pat on the arm. He's so cool, calm and collected. It's a move that somehow seems friendly and low-key threatening. It works.

'Yeah, okay, you too,' Mario replies as he makes a move. 'You're a legend, by the way.'

Mario practically runs away, his moustache finally falling off, landing on the floor next to us.

Wow, just like that, gone as fast as he arrived, and it didn't take magic words, as such. Just any words spoken by a man. Bro code – ugh. Still, at least he's gone.

I turn to look at my hero. My tall, dark, handsome hero. He has messy brown hair and eyes hidden behind mirrored sunglasses, giving nothing away. His cheeks dimple as he smiles, showing a gentler side – I suppose something has to offset those bulging muscles and tall frame. Even sitting down, it's impossible not to notice.

'Hi,' he says, grinning.

'Hi,' I reply, unable to keep a matching smile from my own lips.

The sunglasses, the tight black t-shirt – I can't tell if he's giving secret agent or Balenciaga model or both.

'He seemed nice,' he replies.

I let out a short, breathy laugh.

'Yeah, no, not at all,' I say. 'Thank you for that. He was... persistent.'

'That's polite,' he replies. 'What are boyfriends for?'

'True,' I say, my smile widening by the minute.

'Anyway... I'd better get going...'

I can't form sentences in time to stop him in his tracks. He's gone, disappearing into the crowd, leaving me feeling like I've had too many cocktails (or not enough) or like a little heat-stroke made me hallucinate the whole thing. I can't help but stare into the crowd, waiting to see where he's gone, if he's coming back...

'Oi, Jessa.' A voice snaps me from my thoughts.

I turn to see Todd standing there with a beer in one hand and a piña colada in the other.

'Wow,' I blurt at the sight of the huge glass, overflowing – probably due to the sheer volume of garnishes and various other bits in it (two umbrellas feels like a bit much).

'You said surprise you,' he says, sweat dripping from his brow.

'Consider me surprised,' I reply. 'You were ages – I didn't realise it was so busy.'

'Ah, no, I got distracted, watching the match on one of the big screens,' he confesses. 'Your drink might be a bit melty. I'd drink it ASAP.'

'You're a bit melty,' I tease him.

'Well, that's no way to speak to your boyfriend,' he jokes. 'Any-way, who was that, sitting next to you? Someone you know?'

'Oh, no, I don't know him,' I reply. 'He was just...'

'...Just after our table, eh? Did you tell him to piss off?'

'I didn't need to. He just left,' I reply simply.

'This is why we think you women are so mysterious, FYI,' he tells me. 'You never say what you really mean.'

'I am always telling you wh—'

'So mysterious,' he says again, turning his phone sideways, giving away exactly what he's doing. Putting the match on. From where I'm sitting it looks like football – but by that I mean I can see a lot of green and a lot of men. It could be anything.

I drain the last of my sea breeze before making a start on my piña colada. Wow, even though it's melting, it still gives me the most intense brain freeze.

With Todd immersed in his sport, I feel just as alone as I did before he got back. Well, minus my brief encounter with my heroic yet mysterious stranger.

I can still feel his kiss on my face, like the ghost of it is still hanging around. It was just a peck – and only 10 per cent of it, tops, on the lips – but it really feels like it's left a mark.

I'm really grateful for him stepping in and saving the day like that. I wonder who he is, who he's here with, who he was dressed up as... I wouldn't have thought he was dressed up but Mario clearly knew who he was supposed to be because he called him a legend. Then again, Mario was incredibly drunk.

I suppose I'll never know who he was, it was just a random man right when I needed one – maybe that's why my imagination is running away with me, because life feels a little boring these days, so why not project a bunch of wild scenarios onto a blank canvas of a man?

He was something exciting... someone interesting... someone other than Todd who noticed me for a moment.

But now the moment has gone and it's back to reality.

Still, better to be sitting at a table with a boyfriend engrossed in a football game than a drunk fake plumber.

But only just.

2

ONE YEAR LATER

I never knew you could fall in love with an en suite until I met this one – and it's a love that intensifies every time I step in it.

I love feeling the heated tiles underneath my feet, even on a warm day like today. When Todd was designing this place, he put so much thought into so many things, like which rooms should face south and be bathed in sun, and which rooms would do well to be on the cooler side of the house. I love his attention to detail with things like that.

In here it's all smooth marble and soft lighting, with gold taps that gleam like they have a dedicated cleaner who shines them every day, and then there's the double sinks – a sink each, both big enough to wash a medium-sized dog in at least (but you wouldn't, because there is a dedicated sink for that in the utility room).

And then there's the bath. Oh, the big, big bath. It's free-standing and sits next to a floor-to-ceiling window – but not one with frosted glass, like you might think, nope, one that looks out over the West Yorkshire countryside, with uninterrupted views and – best of all – no one around to peep in at you while you're soaking the day away.

I walk over to it and trail my fingers across the edge of it, thinking about how I'd love nothing more than to get in it, relax, have a glass of wine, maybe light a candle and just allow my brain to empty. Bliss.

But I can't do that right now, for so many reasons.

Back in the bedroom, the cloud-like mattress calls my name in a similar way. It's a super-king, super-squishy bad boy loaded up with at least eight pillows and cushions. It's the kind of bed you could just dive right into... were it not for the perfectly laid-out tray of breakfast sitting on top of the duvet. Croissants, glasses of champagne, cute little jars of jam. Waking up to this on a morning – that's the life, right?

I carefully adjust the rolled-up napkins, angling them just right, and polish one tiny missed smudge from the silverware. Okay, now it's perfect.

'It's ready,' I call out.

James walks in, his camera hanging from his neck, ready for action.

'It looks great,' he tells me.

'Thanks,' I say with a smile. 'Oh, wait, one last thing...'

I grab the small vase with one single rose inside from the sideboard and place it on the breakfast tray.

'Okay, now it's ready.'

I watch James as he cracks on, snapping pictures of the room before zooming in on the cute little details that make all the difference.

'Love what you've done with the place,' he jokes as he photographs the breakfast.

'This old thing?' I reply, batting my hand playfully.

James and I have really got things down to a fine art. He's a photographer, for a luxury estate agents – which is a genuine art form, from the bonus lifestyle pictures to the twilight shoots. All things that make so much difference when it comes to not just selling a house but selling a home – selling a way of life.

God, imagine waking up to this every morning. Imagine owning this house. I often wish the houses I worked in were my own, but this one is really something else.

'Oh, wow, I wish it always looked like this,' Joanne, the actual owner, says as she joins us.

Joanne is in her late forties, early fifties maybe. She's wearing white – all white – the volume of white that only comes with having enough money to not need to worry about destroying it. Her tan gives away that she's been on holiday recently – and the photos dotted around the place give away that she goes on holidays often. I can tell just by glancing at her shoes that they cost more than my weekly food shop – then again, you don't live in a house like this, custom-designed by a luxury architect, without being super rich.

'Jessa!' she says warmly, giving me the sort of smile I would usually reserve for cute dogs. 'The place looks simply divine. I'd seen your work but... wow. You've really outdone yourself.'

'Thank you,' I say, genuinely pleased with how it's turned out. Sure, it's a beautiful house (although maybe I'm biased, because I know the architect who designed it, obviously) and gorgeously decorated, but my little touches are really helping it shine. 'It's easy when the bones of the house are this good,' I reply. 'I just dress it up a bit.'

'Come,' she insists. 'Let's go downstairs, while James works his magic. I have so many questions, and I've made coffee.'

'Sounds great,' I say with a smile.

I follow Joanne downstairs, running my hand along the polished curved banister as I admire the hallway window. The front door sits below two storeys of glass, allowing light to pour into the property – and that's on the north side of the house. In here it's like an art gallery – or the set of a contemporary murder mystery – with so much to take in it's almost too much, but it just works. There's something new to notice every time I pass through.

'So, do tell,' she says as we arrive in the huge open-plan kitchen. 'How did you get into this line of work?'

'Oh, it was just sort of... a natural progression,' I explain. 'I worked in a showroom, when I was younger, then for an interior designer. I fell in love with the idea of making homes perfect, but it was dressing them, rather than decorating them, that really appealed to me. So I started doing some jobs here and there, and then I started working with your agent and here we are.'

'So is it always the same things you add, or do you tailor it to the house?' she enquires.

She seems genuinely interested, so I'm happy to talk about it.

'Everywhere I go it's slightly different. It's all about emotion,' I say, smiling to myself as I talk about my favourite subject. 'You're not selling a house, you're selling the idea of a better life. The right scent in the hallway. The exact throw on the sofa. Books on the bedside table or a coffee on the kitchen island. The details make people feel something – or fantasise about something, even. That's what gets them. They walk in and think, "This is exactly where I'm supposed to live."'

We step through tall glass doors and into the garden.

Ugh. This garden, honestly.

There's a pool. A full-size, heated outdoor pool with mosaic tiles and submerged steps like something you would expect to see at a spa or a resort. Next to it, an almost unused-looking outdoor kitchen sits under a pergola, with a marble countertop, built-in appliances and a wine fridge – because who wants to trail inside for a glass of white? There are loungers arranged around the pool, perfectly spaced. A firepit. Fairy lights strung between the trees. Everything's so perfect it almost doesn't feel real.

Joanne gestures for me to sit on one of the linen-cushioned outdoor sofas. She cradles her mug in her hands – a mug that perfectly matches the marble countertops, it's like even the crockery knows how to coordinate effortlessly here.

'So,' she says, tucking one leg under the other, 'is it fun? Your job, I mean. Dressing up houses like this to help them sell?'

I smile.

'Oh, absolutely,' I reply. 'It can be hard work, but it's a fun challenge. My car is always packed full of things like plants, candles, fake lemons – all sorts, but I love it. It's like playing house for grown-ups.'

She laughs.

'So what exactly do you do? Like, what's the process? I'm fascinated.'

'Well, I usually walk through the property first, get a feel for the place,' I explain. 'Then I create a mood board based on the architecture, the target buyer, the light, even the postcode some-times. There's a big difference between styling a city apartment for a young professional and dressing a place like this.'

Joanne nods along, clearly captivated. I always worry about boring people, when I bang on about my job, but she seems genuinely curious.

'Then I source things – it can be big things, like furniture, artwork sometimes, rugs, plants, textiles, or small things like bottles of wine and candles – whatever the space needs. It's about finding balance and creating an atmosphere. Making it feel aspirational but also possible. Like, "Okay, this is how I live. I casually have fresh peonies in my kitchen and perfectly misaligned coffee-table books about Scandinavian design."'

She laughs again. 'I do love the peonies.'

'I know,' I say with a grin. 'They're fake. Don't tell anyone.'

'So what actually sells a house?' she asks, leaning forward. 'I mean, aside from having it all. What gets the potential buyers on the hook on the day?'

'Honestly? Details,' I say. 'It's all in the details. Smells, for example – they make a huge difference. People walk in and if the place smells dusty or like last night's dinner, they're already turned off. But if it smells like fresh linen or warm vanilla, suddenly it feels like home.'

'Oh, I've got a cupboard full of diffusers,' she says proudly.

'Perfect,' I reply. 'And if you've got time before a viewing, baking something – like cinnamon rolls or even just warming some cookie dough – works a treat. It sounds cliché but it really taps into the cosy home vibe. I did it once at a house just outside York and everyone made an offer on the day – it was a beautiful house, sure, but you never know. Maybe it helped.'

I laugh, to let her know I'm sort of joking, but things like that do make a difference.

Joanne raises her brows, impressed.

'Wow. Okay. I can do that. Anything else?'

'Music,' I tell her. 'Something soft and ambient. Nothing distracting – no vocals, no guitar solos, nothing too upbeat. Just something to smooth the edges. It fills the silence in a way that makes people feel comfortable.'

She nods thoughtfully, sipping her coffee.

'And tidiness, I assume?'

'Absolutely,' I say. 'And I mean extreme tidiness. Like... ruthless. Clear all the surfaces of almost everything, pack away the kids' and pets' toys, remove anything personal or cluttery. People think they want to see a "lived-in" house, but actually, they want to see their future life. Not yours. So the less stuff, the better. Sometimes it's worth getting a storage unit for a few months. Even if the buyers are going to come in and immediately fill the place with their own clutter, they need to believe they're starting fresh. Like they're going to suddenly become minimalist overnight just by moving in.'

'I can do that,' she says, shaking her head. 'Wow. I really feel like I've already got my money's worth. You should do workshops.'

'Maybe,' I reply. 'But then who would need me?'

Again, I'm sort of joking, but it's true I suppose.

We both laugh and look out at the pool, sunlight glinting off the water making it sparkle.

I sigh. It is lovely here, the colours, the smells, the attention to detail.

'This,' I say, almost to myself, 'is the dream.'

Joanne smiles knowingly.

'It is, isn't it?' she replies. 'They tell me your husband designed the house for the previous owner.'

'Boyfriend,' I reply. 'Yes.'

'Perhaps he'll build you one, one day...'

He has the skills, sure, we just don't have the budget.

I would say this is the house I want to live in when I grow up but, being in my early thirties, surely I'm already there? But I know that what I have now isn't as good as it gets.

I'm building up my business and Todd is climbing the ladder at the firm of architects where he works, and the goal is to have all of these things... someday.

Until then I'll just continue to daydream as I fluff pillows and arrange throw blankets and decide whether a ficus or a Swiss cheese plant will emotionally seduce a buyer into a £2.3 million home.

I'll keep selling the dream, telling the story, until one day I can buy it myself.

Here's hoping that day isn't as far away as it seems.

3

The sunshine hits me in the face as we step out of the church, temporarily blinding me as the church is bathed in some kind of heavenly light from above.

Now that my eyes have adjusted, the light is warm and golden, the kind that makes everything look prettier – hair, dresses, the flowers. The bells ring out, celebrating Kelly and Logan on their big day, almost as loud as the cheers from their friends and family.

Todd squints beside me, tugging at his collar, his suit jacket already slung over his shoulder. He's always warm, I'm always cold – and isn't that just a recipe for the perfect couple?

He looks like he's suffocating, and melting, but he smiles anyway. We linger on the old stone steps for as long as we have to, waiting for our moment. Then we line up until someone shouts, 'Go on then!' and we all start tossing confetti at Kelly and Logan as they emerge for their photos. They look ecstatic, completely swept up in it, and it's such a well-choreographed moment, I bet the photos will look amazing.

We clap and cheer, take a few photos, then start the slow

trickle back to the car park with everyone else. Todd opens the door for me and I slip in, the leather already uncomfortably warm from the sun. He gets in on the driver's side, and the second the door clicks shut, he exhales like he's been holding his breath since the first hymn.

'Well,' he says, starting the engine. 'That was a very long hour of pretending we're in Year Four again. I half expected someone to pull out a recorder and start playing "He's Got the Whole World in His Hands". It was like primary school assembly. They're not even religious.'

I laugh.

'Some people like to do the church thing regardless. It's traditional,' I remind him.

'It just feels so... inauthentic,' he replies.

'The church, the bells, the stained-glass windows – it's a vibe people want for their big day, even if they're not very religious, I guess,' I reply.

'Well, that won't be me,' he says firmly, glancing at me sideways. 'When I get married, it's definitely not happening in a church. Not a chance.'

I don't say anything to that. Just smile a little to myself and watch the countryside roll by through the window.

We've talked about marriage before, Todd and me. It's always been in that semi-serious way couples do – a case of when, not if – but it still hangs in the air like a maybe. And I hate that the tradition is still so one-sided. Like it's his decision to make as the man, he gets to call the shots. He gets to plan, pick the ring, pop the question. I just have to wait. I mean, yeah, it's 2025, that definitely needs a revamp, but at the same time there's no way I'd want to ask him. I couldn't do it. I'd probably mess it up – and what if he said no? I wouldn't want to chance it, not when I'm happy now.

Todd snorts beside me, dragging me back to the present.

'And did you catch that thing the vicar said? About them being childhood sweethearts?' he says. 'Together forever – except for that one year where they broke up and they both hooked up with other people. They clearly skipped that detail.'

I can't help but laugh again.

'You are so cynical,' I point out.

'I'm just observant,' he says with a grin. 'And realistic. They can say what they like, but half the people in there know the real story.'

This is one of the things I love about Todd. He's a classic Yorkshire lad through and through – he says what he thinks, usually with a dry smile, never too harsh, just honest. He thinks musicals are embarrassing, yoga is a scam, and any meal that doesn't include meat is to be glared at in disbelief. It sounds awful when I say it out loud, but somehow, it's charming. He doesn't say things to hurt anyone; he just doesn't see the point in pretending. Thankfully everyone finds it charming, and he keeps more in than he lets out, believe you me.

I'm so glad that we're doing this, it feels like I've hardly seen him recently, he's been so busy with work. I have too, but my workload is nothing compared to his, so I don't want to complain, but I have been feeling a little lonely. A night or two away, even if it is for a wedding, is just what we need to get a little of the magic back.

I look at him now, still grinning about the newly-weds' carefully curated love story, and I wonder what the vicar (or non-religious equivalent) would say about us. Maybe marriage is on the horizon, somewhere closer than I thought. I could almost get excited...

But I don't. Today is about Kelly and Logan. My relationship can wait.

As we pull into the venue car park I feel like I've stepped into a postcard. East Riddlesden Hall sits in front us, this gorgeous old building with light shining through its structure. It's framed by thick, leafy trees, and everything's so green it almost doesn't look real. There's a lake just off to the side with a weeping willow dipping its fingers into the water. It's the kind of scene that makes you feel like you're in the middle of a period drama – like someone's going to ride up on horseback, a Mr Darcy type, and mumble something utterly charming.

Todd whistles low under his breath as we get out.

'Wow, it's nice here.'

He's not wrong.

We walk down the path toward the barn where the wedding reception is being held, and it's like walking into a dream. Twinkling fairy lights are strung from beam to beam overhead, and flowers – what looks like actual fresh ones, not your standard wilting supermarket bouquet – hang in glass jars and twist up the wooden columns. White curtains are draped over the stone walls to soften them, and they flutter slightly with the breeze coming in from the open barn doors. It's romantic and beautiful and kind of ridiculously perfect.

The tables are laid out beautifully, like something from a bridal magazine, with flowers and gold cutlery, elegant name cards and more candles than a ninetieth birthday. It smells like fresh flowers and champagne, and I don't know if that's because both are here or they have a special diffuser made to smell like dream weddings hidden somewhere.

It's stunning. But... it doesn't scream Kelly and Logan to me. It's not them. Not really. It's like when I stage a house for clients – everything styled to perfection, everything beautiful, just a little bit detached from reality. But why not, right? They'll look back on the photos from this day, no matter what happened, and see all of the beauty. The things they wanted to remember. Anything negative – anything not quite right, any stains on clothes, or dodgy smiles – will all be fixed by the photographer in post. Like it never happened.

We spot the bride and groom near the entrance, beaming in that way only newly-weds do. Kelly's cheeks are flushed – she's literally a blushing bride – and Logan's smile is wider than I've ever seen it. Todd wraps Logan in a hug and tells him how amazing it all is, how happy he is for them both – completely backtracking on everything he said in the car, but with Todd it never feels fake. He means what he says, he just leaves out the negative stuff. I give Kelly a hug and tell her she looks beautiful, because she really, really does.

After chatting for a bit we head to our table. I'm instantly relieved when I see I'm next to Kelsey. It's such a blur of weddings this year, and we all share so many friends, I've actually started to forget who belongs to which friend group, but Kelsey is my bestie, and her fiancé, Neil, is Todd's – not that they would ever refer to themselves as besties, of course.

Kelsey beams with similar relief when I sit down next to her.

'Can you believe how gorgeous it all is?' she says. Then she lowers her voice. 'Not very "them" though...'

'And did you hear that stuff about them being together forever?' Neil asks in similarly hushed tones.

They're so like us.

'Don't get me started, mate,' Todd replies as he pours himself a glass of water.

'I know,' I say, pulling out my chair and taking my seat. 'It really is beautiful though. It's like a wedding Pinterest board come to life.'

Kelsey laughs, tucking a long brown curl behind her ear.

'Not long until your big day now,' I say – not that she will have forgotten, of course.

'Big week,' Neil says under his breath.

Kelsey glances at her engagement ring and then back at me, unable to hide the mix of excitement and nerves surging through her body.

'I know. I'm excited. And terrified. But mostly excited... I think.'

I reach for Todd's water, to take a sip.

'It's going to be amazing,' I reassure her.

It really is. Out of all the weddings this year – and there are so many – the one I'm looking forward to most is hers. Kelsey and Neil are doing something different. Something... very them though.

'She's got a plan for everything,' Neil tells us. 'Everything that could go wrong, she's got it covered. Not that she's made it easy for herself.'

'Erm, what I've made is a hopefully beautiful wedding week – for both of us – thank you,' she replies.

'We're having our wedding at sea,' he claps back, deadpan. 'If Mother Nature kicks off, there's nothing your scrapbook can do about that.'

'He's clearly not seen inside my scrapbook,' Kelsey tells me with a wink. Then she turns to him. 'The actual wedding isn't at sea. You do know that, right?'

She knows he knows that, but this is their thing: playful bickering.

Neil grins like the wind-up merchant he is.

'Yeah, yeah, I know, I'm kidding. But come on, a five-day cruise before the wedding? You're practically asking for a storm.'

'A cruise *to* a wedding,' she corrects him. 'Because one

member of the wedding party doesn't like flying – just let me check my notes, see who that is, oh, yes – you.'

'But you're the one insisting we get married in Sicily, my darling,' he replies.

Honestly, I could watch this all day.

Kelsey rolls her eyes and mutters something under her breath about how she could insist they don't get married at all.

I just laugh. This is peak them. Their banter, their easy rhythm – it's why I always feel happy when I'm around them. Todd seems a bit distracted – he's probably still seething over having to sing, because that makes his life a little too much like a musical.

Kelsey really has taken destination weddings to a whole new level. She's not just getting married abroad. No, no. Too simple. She's sailing into her wedding like the queen that she is, turning the journey into a sort of pre-party at sea for the important names on the guest list. A five-day cruise through the Med, docking in Sicily where the actual ceremony will take place. That's a movie-worthy wedding, surely?

Am I mad that I need to take a week off work for it? Absolutely not. Todd and I have been talking about needing a holiday for months, but we're always too busy – one, the other or both of us. This way, it's all rolled into one – a holiday, a wedding, an escape from day-to-day life. I've been trying to find a way for the two of us to spend more time together, so this is our chance. And we get to watch our best friends tie the knot too, so even better.

Luckily the expense isn't something mere mortals like us need to worry about, because Neil is from one of those old-money families, and his family in particular just loves keeping up with the Joneses. Hilariously, their last name is Jones, which means they're keeping up with themselves, and that seems accurate to me. I haven't spent much time around Neil's family, or his friends outside our mutual group, so I'm hoping it isn't going to be an overly stuffy thing full of rich people who eat crumpets and play polo.

Kelsey might not be old money, but she's always dreamed of a big fancy wedding, and she deserves this. Cruising to her perfect wedding. Love that for her.

The food is unbelievably good – all three courses of it. We've just finished dessert which was a dark chocolate tart with something citrusy and suspiciously addictive. I ate mine and half of Todd's. Well, he did leave it unattended, so I assume he wasn't planning on finishing it.

It's a good job I've had Kelsey to chat with all day because Todd can't seem to sit still for more than five minutes. He's been up and down all through the meal – getting drinks, wandering outside, probably taking photos of the grounds or the old hall. He does that sometimes when he's overwhelmed, he retreats to nature and architecture, so I just leave him to it.

'I'm just going to nip to the loo,' I tell Kelsey, pushing back from the table.

'Don't get lost,' she replies. 'I hear it's a trek.'

Okay, she's not kidding, you do have to 'travel' to the loos, but they have a golf buggy if you want a lift. I think that's Kelly's mum, kind of drunk, hanging off the back of it, so I make the short journey on foot, admiring the lake as I walk alongside it.

I step into a cubicle, and that's when I notice it – someone crying in the one next to me. Not just quiet crying either. Full-on sobbing, with this weird, wobbly pitch to it. It sounds like yodelling. Like someone's messing with the volume dial on a sad song. I've never heard anything like it.

'Are you okay in there?' I ask, knocking gently on the wall between us.

'I'm fine,' the woman says quickly. A sniff, a pause – then she starts up again.

She doesn't sound fine.

'Are you sure?' I call back, torn between giving her space and not wanting to leave her having a breakdown on her own. 'I can get someone for you, if you want.'

'No,' she replies quickly. 'I'm okay, it's just... weddings. And my boyfriend. And... and I'm giving someone everything. Every part of me. My life, my future, my happiness – it's all in his hands.'

I nod, even though she can't see me.

'That's good, though,' I say softly. 'You have an open heart. That's how love gets in.'

She gives this half-laugh, half-sob.

'My boyfriend is never going to propose to me,' she tells me. 'He won't commit. I don't think he can. All he cares about is his job and having a good time and bloody sport – above everything. There's someone better for me out there, someone who really cares about me – not about sport.'

'Ugh, sport,' I groan playfully. 'My boyfriend looooves football.'

'For mine, it's cricket,' she says, sniffling. 'He loves it more than he loves me.'

'I'm sure that's not true,' I reply – it can't be, can it?

'It is,' she insists. 'He'd marry cricket if he could. But he won't marry me. And I guess I need to accept that. But breaking up... moving on... it's so final. And I can see us having a great life together. Why can't he?'

Her voice cracks again, and the yodelling sobs return, louder this time. I feel awful for her. It must hurt, so much, to love someone who can't see the future you're trying to build with them. And honestly? Cricket might be the most boring sport out there – I thought football was bad, but cricket? Although, to be fair, I've never watched golf. It's a close one to call.

I pause for a second, thinking about what to say, about how much to stick my beak in. This isn't my problem, or my business, but the urge to help her is one I can't ignore.

'You have to be happy. That's the thing,' I tell her. 'That's all that matters. If he isn't making you happy – and only you know whether that's true or not – then do what you need to do. Dump him. Be with someone who makes you feel loved and chosen and not like you're waiting to be picked.'

'I feel bad dumping him,' she says, softer and calmer now. 'He obviously has issues. Commitment stuff...'

'That's on him,' I reply without a moment of hesitation. 'You're his partner, not his therapist. Like my granny used to say: fuck around, find out.'

She laughs – really laughs this time. It bursts out of her.

Almost everyone knows that's just a joke, that my granny didn't really say that, but it always gets a laugh. It's a good phrase to have in the tool belt, especially when you're trying to cheer someone up.

'Thanks,' she says eventually, her voice much stronger now. 'You've given me a lot to think about. You're right. I should dump him. Go for what makes me happy.'

'You deserve to be chosen,' I remind her. 'Take care of yourself, yeah?'

'Yeah,' she replies. 'Thanks again. I'll sort myself out and be right out.'

I step out of the cubicle, wash my hands, and leave her to it. My work here is done.

Back at the table, Todd is nowhere to be seen. Neither is Neil.

'The boys have gone again then,' I say, taking my seat again.

'I'm starting to wonder if there's a football match on or something... Do you think they're in the car watching it?'

Kelsey laughs. 'They're a funny double act, those two. Honestly, if Neil hadn't picked one of his oldest mates to be his best man, I think he would've chosen Todd.'

'Boys don't sweat that stuff, do they?' I say, scanning the crowd near the bar and the sweet cart. 'They don't overthink it.'

'You looking for someone?' Kelsey asks.

'Yeah,' I say, having no luck. 'A girl I spoke to in the bathroom. She was crying. Like, really crying.'

'What did she look like?' Kelsey asks, leaning in a little. 'I probably know her, I know almost everyone here.'

'I didn't see,' I reply. 'She was in a cubicle so I only heard her voice.'

Before Kelsey can respond, Neil strolls back to the table, looking far too pleased with himself.

'Oh, here he is,' Kelsey says with faux sweetness. 'You look sheepish. Were you in the car, watching some silly sport?'

'Guilty,' Neil says, grinning. 'But I have to. You're marrying a rugged manly man, remember?'

You can tell he's laying it on thick, joking around, trying to charm his way out of trouble. It's definitely working. Kelsey rolls her eyes but smiles, clearly amused.

'Is Todd still there?' I ask.

Neil blinks.

'Oh, erm... no, I was on my own.'

'Oh,' I say simply.

Kelsey's already scanning the room, her eyes quick and sharp.

'He's over there,' she tells me, nodding toward the far end of the barn.

I follow her gaze. Todd's at the bar, talking to the barman, who's gesturing with his hands like he's giving directions. Probably to the toilets.

'If he gets looking at the old house, he might not come back until it gets dark,' I joke.

Eventually, the lights dim and the music starts to shift. The crowd parts slightly as the DJ introduces the first dance, and the bride and groom step out together, ready to tick off another wedding to-do.

Kelsey and I fall quiet, watching them sway together in the middle of the barn.

'Unchained Melody' by the Righteous Brothers – sort of what I expected for a classy affair like this. Something classic but crowd-pleasing.

When it's time to join the happy couple, everyone starts reaching for their partners and takes to the floor.

I glance around, hoping Todd's made it back in time. For a moment I can't see him, and I'm just about to feel disappointed when I spot him in the doorway to the barn.

Just in time.

I hurry over to him, weaving through the tables, dodging chairs and flower arrangements, and take his hand without thinking. His palm's warm but stiff, like it's braced for something. I pull him toward the dance floor, smiling up at him.

I know he's not a big fan of dancing, but he usually makes an exception for first dances at weddings.

'I thought you'd abandoned me,' I say with a soft laugh, trying to keep it light and not sound like I'm criticising him, but he does seem a little more awkward than usual today.

Todd doesn't laugh. Doesn't even fake a smile.

'It was just a joke,' I say, a little quieter now. My stomach twists.

Still nothing.

'What's wrong?' I ask, keeping my voice low, aware of all the people around us swaying and smiling, lost in their own little bubbles. We're just another couple dancing.

Todd opens his mouth, but nothing comes out. His jaw clenches, like he's having to wrestle with his words.

'Todd?' I press.

He's scaring me now.

'It's not working,' he says eventually, not even looking me in the eye.

'What's not working?'

'Us. We're not working,' he replies.

Now he's the one glancing around the room like he's looking for someone, although I don't think it's a person he's looking for, it's an escape.

I just stare at him. I can't have heard that right.

'What do you mean "not working"? What are you trying to say?'

'I'm trying to say,' he starts slowly, like it's something he's building up to, 'things haven't felt right for a while. And being here, at this wedding, it's just... reminded me that I can't see a future where we do this. You and me. Getting married.'

My chest goes tight.

'I don't care if we get married,' I say quickly, not doing the best job of hiding the panic in my voice. 'That's not the point. We're happy. Or... I thought we were.'

He sighs, and it's worse than if he'd shouted.

'I don't want to be harsh, Jessa. But I want to be honest,' he says and I know I'm not going to like this. 'I do want to get married. Just... not to you.'

There's so much I want to say, and I have so many questions, but I can't make my voice work. I'm not even sure if I'm breathing – still dancing though, of course.

'I've been thinking about it for a while,' he continues.

I laugh, but it's not a real laugh, it's a sarcastic laugh, the kind that helps my voice come back.

'You're breaking up with me? At a wedding?' I check.

'There's no point pretending everything's fine. That's more dishonest,' he says, and there's something frustratingly calm about his voice. Measured. Like he's rehearsed this. Perhaps he has been thinking about this for a while but, damn, it would have been nice to know.

'You want to talk about dishonest?' I say, still keeping control of my tone, given that we're – y'know – at a wedding, on the dance floor. 'Try pretending you're happy for God knows how long. Sitting through a three-course meal and smiling at people like everything's fine.'

Around us, everyone keeps dancing. No one notices us bickering. We're literally dancing through a break-up, it's absurd.

Is this karma? For telling that girl in the loos to dump her boyfriend? Then again, I'm not him. I'm not the one refusing to commit. I'm not the one choosing something else over someone who loves them. If anything, Todd is the one who should be getting dumped.

'We should talk about this in the car,' Todd says quietly.

'It should've been a conversation for the car from the beginning,' I practically hiss. 'But it's too late now. You've made yourself clear.'

'Jessa, don't be like that,' he pleads – in fact, he sounds almost annoyed that I'm not taking this break-up as he had hoped, the idiot.

'Like what?' I snap. 'Furious? Shocked? Embarrassed? You're lucky we're at a wedding, because if we weren't, I'd be reacting very, very differently right now.'

And then the song ends. There's nowhere to hide now.

The music fades and applause erupts around us, and I let go of him. Too quickly. I style it out by clapping for the happy couple, a smile firmly fixed to my face so that no one suspects anything is up.

Inside, though, I'm screaming.

I suppose with one beautiful beginning comes a savagely brutal end.

This is the last thing I expected to happen today. It's going to take a lot more than a bit of airbrushing to forget this bad memory.

4

I'm in the bath. Because of course I am.

It's practically a post-break-up cliché at this point – a sad sack of a girl, scented candles, an inconvenient amount of bubbles, and a tub of chocolate ice cream teetering dangerously on the edge – sort of like myself, if you'll allow me a little joke in the middle of my emotional breakdown.

I'm even listening to a playlist called 'Sad girl songs' which I originally made as a joke, for all the soppy ballads I love, but now that just feels like a pathetic prophecy. Like I knew I was on the chopping block when I put all those Lewis Capaldi songs within easy reach.

I scoop another spoonful of ice cream into my mouth and sink deeper into the water, bubbles creeping up over my collar-bones. The steam curls around me, warm and comforting like a blanket.

You know what, I think I'm in shock, because I really, truly wasn't expecting Todd to dump me. If you'd told me something was going to happen, as pathetic as it may sound, my money would have been on him proposing. How tragic is that.

God, it really was such a shock.

One minute I was pulling him onto the dance floor, laughing, thinking he looked handsome in his suit. The next, he was looking at me like I was a problem he needed to solve, not someone he loved.

We were together for over a year. We'd talked about moving in together. Had actual conversations about locations, mortgages, how we'd decorate. I'd started mentally dressing the house, even though I didn't know what it would look like. We'd even fantasised about building our dream house when we could.

Yikes. What if we had moved in together? We'd be scrapping over furniture and Netflix accounts – it would be much messier. I should count my blessings.

So by my count that's one blessing. Nice.

I guess I just didn't think we were broken. Not even close. I thought we were... normal. Happy, even. I know I was.

Some chocolate ice cream slides off my spoon and lands with a little plop in the bath. I stare at it as it floats, the water turning brown around it.

I'm not pathetic enough to scoop it up and eat it. Obviously not. But I am pathetic enough to just leave it there, bobbing among the bubbles like it belongs. Like some kind of dessert bath bomb.

I sigh and close my eyes. Out of sight, out of mind.

The worst part is, I know I'll still have to see him. Todd. Because we share so many friends. Everyone's tangled together – my friends are his friends and his friends are dating my friends, we're in the same group chats, we go to the same events – he's going to be at Kelsey and Neil's wedding, for God's sake.

I've managed to avoid him since Kelly and Logan's wedding. That feels like a small win. And he's stayed away too. Left me alone. Well, of course he has, he doesn't want to be with me, or have anything to do with me, so what would he say? 'Hey, just checking in on the person I savagely dumped mid-slow dance?'

No. He's long gone. I need to accept that. But first I need to wallow in the bath for the foreseeable future.

My phone rings, well, it vibrates on the side. I groan softly, almost in sync with it, lifting one arm from beneath the luke-warm water to grab it from the windowsill where it's balanced precariously between a mostly drained glass of wine and a candle that's seen better days.

I grab the phone carefully, my fingers slippery from the bath-water. One slip and it's over – for both of us. It would be so like me to dunk it in the water. The only thing that could make today worse would be sobbing over a bag full of rice with my soggy phone somewhere in the middle.

It's Kelsey. She's probably the only person in the world I would answer to right now.

Well, her or maybe Tom Hardy, or Zac Efron, or pretty much anyone willing to sweep me off my feet and make Todd reconsider his life choices.

'Hey,' I say, my voice already softer, quieter, like the harder I try to sound okay the more I confirm that I'm not.

'Aw, Jessa,' she says. Her voice is like a hug. 'How are you doing?'

'Oh, you know,' I say, letting my head fall back against the bath pillow. 'As you'd expect.'

'You're in the bath, aren't you?' she says, and I can hear the smile in her voice. It's half-amused, half-concerned – 100 per cent Kelsey. She knows me so well.

'Of course I am,' I reply.

'Are you at least changing the water?' she asks. 'You were in the bath the last time I called. Tell me you get out to pee…'

I laugh, a real one, bubbling up from somewhere below the pain. It surprises me.

'I'm spending time outside the bath and running fresh ones, I've not had a total breakdown. Not yet, anyway,' I reassure her. 'Although... I did just drop some chocolate ice cream in the water. I've made peace with it though.'

'Chocolate ice cream? I'll believe you,' she replies.

I laugh again. It's good to hear her voice.

'So. I was calling to ask – do you want a lift to Al and Kira's wedding this weekend?' she says, cutting to the chase.

'Thanks,' I reply, 'but I think I'm going to drive. Just in case I want to make a quick getaway.'

There's a beat. I know what's coming next.

'Are you sure you'll be okay... seeing Todd there? It's only been two weeks.'

'Of course,' I reply, and I make it sound so casual, like I'm just talking about what a sunny July we're having. 'I'm actually handling it really well.'

There's another pause. Then...

'Is that... is that Lewis Capaldi I can hear?' she asks gently.

'Just a bit,' I reply. She's got me there.

'Thought so.' She doesn't laugh, bless her. Kelsey never laughs at me. 'Look, it is going to be okay, even if it doesn't feel like it. I'll be right there. I won't leave your side. We'll get you through it. Consider it a dress rehearsal for my wedding. Survive your ex-boyfriend once, you can do it again, and each time it will get easier.'

I smile, even though my stomach has twisted into something tight and knotted.

'Yeah,' I say – maybe if I say it, I'll believe it. 'Don't worry about me. I promise, I'll be fine. Nothing is going to ruin your wedding.'

There's a pause. One of those loaded ones, where you can feel the other person hesitating on the edge of something.

'Are you sure you're okay?' she asks me.

'I will be,' I say. I've said it so many times now it barely feels like a lie. It's something to say. A reflex. Like 'bless you' when someone sneezes. 'Plus, I'm chief bridesmaid, so I have jobs to keep me busy.'

'Speaking of,' she replies, holding on each word for a little longer than normal, like she's stalling for time. 'I know you said you'd handle it, but are you sure you don't want me to talk to the wedding planner? We can sort out your new room situation. Obviously you won't be sharing with Todd now, and—'

'Kels,' I interrupt gently. 'I've got it. Really. Let me sort it, it will be therapeutic for me.'

She hesitates again. I can almost hear her thinking, biting her lip like she does when she's trying not to fuss. I'm not sure whether she believes me or not, but what can she say?

'If you're sure...'

'I'm sure,' I lie again.

The last thing she needs is anything extra on her plate.

We say our goodbyes and I set my phone back on the windowsill, still careful not to drop it. I lean back, close my eyes and try to relax.

The bathwater is starting to feel cold now. The bubbles are gone. I glance down at the rogue chocolate chips still bobbing by my knee. At least I can pick them out now.

This sucks. This all sucks. So, so much. I have to convince Kelsey that I'm okay though, because fuck Todd, for doing this right before her wedding. I'm not saying he should have stayed with me, I'm saying that if supposedly he's been feeling this way for a while, he should have spoken up much sooner.

I'm not sure I will be okay, if I'm being totally honest with you.

I need to stop telling people that I am – especially myself. But not Kelsey, not little more than a week before we set sail for her wedding. I'm not going to let this ruin her day. I'll show up. I'll wear the dress. I'll fix her veil and help her go to the bathroom and make jokes during the photos. I'll smile like my heart hasn't been ripped out of my chest, even though it really, really has been.

I will do it... I'm just not sure how yet. That's all.

5

I key in the phone number for Emma, the wedding planner (or is she the wedding coordinator – I can never remember which one is which).

I stare at the number for a second before pressing call, taking a deep breath like I'm about to jump in at the deep end. I suppose I am, in a way. I just need to get this over with, ask her to sort it out, to wave her magic wand or iPad or whatever it is she uses and make it all okay. Kelsey will have made sure there was a back-up plan for this. Well, not specifically me getting dumped right before her wedding, but the need for an extra room here and there.

I don't even care who keeps the cabin Todd and I were meant to share. He can have it. I don't care if his has the better view, the fluffier towels, the minibar stocked with champagne. Hell, he can sleep in a penthouse suite with a hot tub and his own butler for all I care. I just want a door between us. The more the merrier.

All I care about – the only thing – is not sharing a room with my ex at Kelsey and Neil's wedding. And it's not even simply a room, is it? It's a cabin, on a ship, that will be at sea for multiple days, multiple nights. It's bad enough I have to share a ship with him – I mean, it's bad enough I have to share a fucking ocean with him – but the cabin, that's the pressing matter. That's what I need to get sorted.

But I've spoken with Emma before and she's... what's the opposite of a breath of fresh air? The opposite of 'nothing is too much trouble'? Because her attitude stinks, and literally anything you ask of her is too much trouble.

Ah, well, here we go. I sigh and finally hit 'call'.

Two rings and she picks up.

'This is Emma,' she says, in a way that sounds like she believes it just cost her money, having to explain that to me.

She sounds like someone who irons her nighties and judges people for drinking Prosecco instead of champagne.

'Hi! This is Jessa, I'm Kelsey's chief bridesmaid. She suggested I call you as we just need to make some changes to the cabin set-up, for the boat.'

Silence. Not the sort of silence where someone's writing something down. The kind where you can hear the frown. A silence just long enough to suggest I've already inconvenienced her.

'And what sort of change would that be?' she asks.

'Well, it's—'

'And it's a ship, not a boat,' she can't help but interrupt me.

'Isn't a ship just, like, a really big boat?' I ask.

'I don't have time for this, Jessa,' she snaps back.

Ha! She was the one who started it. Anyway...

'Right, well, as I was saying, we just need to make some changes.'

'You said that,' she replies. 'What changes?'

If she could stop interrupting me for five seconds, I could tell her.

'I am currently down as sharing a room – a cabin – with Todd,' I say, quick to self-correct, before she chimes in with any more fun facts. 'We need separate rooms. Cabins! We need separate cabins.'

Another silence, this one even frostier than the last.

'You want me to help you with that?' she asks.

'Well, yes, please, Kelsey said to call the wedding coordinator, or the planner – you, basically.'

'I suppose you think they're the same job,' she says, sounding offended.

I absolutely do. But I don't know the difference between a boat and a ship, so...

'And why are we making such significant changes when the wedding is imminent?' she asks.

'We've broken up,' I reply, keeping it simple. No need to unpack it too much, not when I'm trying to stuff my emotional baggage to the back of my mind.

I have a tendency to overshare when I'm anxious, or trying to justify myself, or make myself easier to relate to. If I start elaborating, I'll end up telling her about the slow dancing, being savagely dumped in public, and the rogue floating ice cream in my bathwater. No one needs that visual.

'Are you drunk?' she asks.

'No,' I reply – although I have had a couple of cocktails. I thought it might help, give me a bit of Dutch courage, to make the phone call I've been putting off.

'Are you high?' she asks next.

'Look, I know it's late in the day, but I wasn't expecting to need my own room, or for Todd to need his own room...'

'Late in the day? Do you know how long I've been planning this wedding, young lady?'

I try not to snigger at her calling me a young lady, because I'm pretty sure she's not much older than I am.

'You should have let us know sooner,' she informs me. 'We're very close to the event, and cabin allocations were finalised weeks ago. We might have something in reserve, but no promises.'

I inhale slowly, doing my best to hold back the sarcasm that wants to burst out of my body, *Alien* style.

'Right, yeah, sorry about that. I didn't plan on getting dumped, you know? Bit of a surprise for me too.'

So, not keeping it all in too well then.

She makes a noise, one of those little huffs of annoyance, not so subtly letting me know that she's not at all impressed.

'I'll also need to confirm with the other guest on the booking,' she continues. 'Todd, is it? Make sure this is what he wants too.'

Of course.

'Right, yeah, let's make sure Todd's comfortable,' I reply. 'We wouldn't want Todd – who surprise dumped me – not being comfortable.'

'You say he dumped you?' she replies – when I literally just told her that. 'Surprising.'

Lovely, she's being sarcastic. Just what I need right now.

'Yep,' I reply, popping the 'p'.

Emma sniffs. 'Well, as I said, I'll see what I can do. But we're under quite a bit of pressure, so next time, a little more notice would be appreciated.'

'Okay, Emma, thanks so much, yes, next time I'll tell you sooner,' I reply with faux enthusiasm.

'Thank you,' she replies, not picking up the tone I'm putting down.

I hang up before one of us says something we will regret.

I fling my phone onto the bed and flop down next to it, groaning into the duvet.

None of this is going to be easy, is it?

6

You really can't beat the Yorkshire countryside. The rolling green hills, the trees, the drystone walls – it's iconic.

I'm noticing, as I'm driving to Al and Kira's wedding venue – a hotel just outside York – that the cows are lying down. They say that means rain, don't they? I don't know who 'they' are, or if it's true, but I really hope it isn't because I'm going to a wedding under a marquee in the hotel grounds.

Al and Kira are great. She's kind of a rock chick, he's a former Mr Universe (or similar – one of those where you layer on the fake tan and pose in tiny trunks, rather than the one where you throw a washing machine while pulling an HGV), and you would think they wouldn't work together but they really do. I think it's good, sometimes, when you have two people in a couple who are so different. Although with Todd I always used to say that my weaknesses were his strengths, and vice versa. You know, my weaknesses like maths, and his weaknesses like staying in our relationship.

Ugh. Every bend I drive around – and this is one windy road –

pisses off the butterflies in my stomach, and they're not in a good mood today as it is.

Unsurprisingly the thought of seeing Todd has me feeling like I'm going to throw up. My brain is going here, there and everywhere, thinking about what will happen, running all these different simulations – Will he talk to me? Will he ignore me? Will he be rude to me? I'm actually arguing with him, in my head, imagining him saying horrible things and thinking about how I'll reply. To be honest with you, it's making me even more mad at him, and it's not even a real conversation.

Glancing at the satnav, I can see that I'm only ten minutes away now.

It's just a reception, without a ceremony, because Al and Kira got married on a beach somewhere (and didn't demand everyone they know join them), but they still wanted to have a traditional wedding so it will have everything else. The outfits, the cake, the speeches, tossing the bouquet – probably to me, because I'm not even sure who else we know who isn't coupled up. Maybe I'll hide in the loos for that part of the proceedings.

My palms feel sweaty – it's an extra effort to keep them in place on my steering wheel, and driving my Fiat 500 through a drystone wall is not going to make today any easier. Then again, I'm sure it will get me out of the inevitable moment towards the end of the night when I find myself sadly swaying to 'Mr Brightside', all on my own, in the middle of the dance floor.

Still, it's not all bleak, I'll probably get some cake. Let's focus on that... Except I can't focus on that, because it's only been two weeks. That's just fourteen days, since he dumped me in such a spectacularly cruel fashion. I know, there's no ideal time to dump someone, but surely on the dance floor at a wedding is the worst? I'll never understand why he did it, then and there, and as much as I want to ask him to satisfy my curiosity, I don't think any good can come from me having an answer to that question.

Well, I'm here now, there's no turning back, I suppose.

Wow, the hotel is picture perfect, like something out of a bridal mag with a headline above it saying: *Most perfect wedding venues in Yorkshire.*

It's an old stone building with those tiny windows you often see in older properties, but then there's an ultra-modern extension that seems more practical. Still, with it being all glass, it reflects the countryside around it, making it appear almost invisible. That's one of Todd's favourite tricks. Fuck, it annoys me so much that I keep talking about him, like he's still mine.

There's a large fountain (that looks oddly inviting on a scorcher like today – not that I plan on getting in it) that acts as a sort of turning circle for cars, and with no idea which car park I'm supposed to go in I decide it's best I drive up to the hotel entrance and see if there are any signs, saying where wedding guests should go.

Oh, okay, this place really is fancy because it has valet parking. There's a man standing in the doorway, next to a sign that says 'wedding parking' and has an arrow pointing right at him. He's wearing a jacket with a name badge on, not that I can make it out from here. I've never had anyone park my car for me before so I'm suddenly self-conscious of all the empty food wrappers (never turn up at a wedding hungry, you will never eat enough to last to the end of the day otherwise) and the fact that Busted is playing on the stereo. Perhaps we'll turn that off.

I jump out of my car and walk up the couple of steps to where the man – Ryan, I can see from his badge – is standing, but just as I reach the doorway I notice him, Todd, standing in reception. Oh, and he looks infuriatingly good in his suit. He looks mentally good too, like this break-up hasn't affected him in any way. Looove that for him. He's talking to a hotel employee, laughing his head off, clearly having the time of his life.

He looks great and I probably look like crap from the sweaty drive. My plan was always to go to the loos and touch up my make-up so he absolutely cannot see me until I have done that, because I need to look good too, like I have my shit together, not like I'm losing it.

Okay, let's not panic, let's just give the man the keys and then make a shifty dash to the toilets before Todd sees me, because right now I'm a sitting duck out here. Getting in the fountain might actually be a good option for me.

I practically thrust my keys into the valet's hands. He looks taken aback by my abruptness – I'm not surprised, I'll bet the clientele here is usually much less flappy.

'Sorry, I'm in a rush,' I explain, because I just offloaded my keys to him like they were a grenade with the pin pulled. 'I'm with the Al and Kira wedding party. The wedding. I think I'm late so I'll just grab the keys from reception later, yeah? I'm Jessa, by the way, if you need to put a name to them. Again, sorry, just rushing – and don't worry about the light that comes on when you turn left, it's been doing that for ages, no one knows why.'

The man blinks at me as the corners of his mouth twitch into a smile. Okay, yeah, he's never had to deal with a hot mess like me before.

'Yeah, sorry,' I say as I dash off.

'Enjoy the wedding,' he calls after me.

Ha. Chance would be a fine thing. At least I've managed to get away from Todd though, even if it is just for now, if it means I can top up my warpaint then great, anything that might help. Perhaps I could nip to the bar too, seeing as though I do actually have time to spare. I could have a drink now, take the edge off – well,

I'm going to be here all day, so it will be long out of my system by the time I can get away with ducking out.

Yep, a hasty makeover, a cheeky cocktail – then all I need is Kelsey, my wingwoman, and I'll be fine.

It will all be fine.

7

Okay, so I didn't have one drink, I had two, from the bar inside the hotel, and lucky for me I did my make-up before I ordered them, so no adverse effects from drinking and eye-lining thankfully.

The crisps and biscuits I ate in the car have done little to line my stomach because I feel tipsy as hell, slightly unsteady on my heels, a little lighter in two ways. First of all, being tipsy makes me feel emotionally lighter, like it might all be okay, but physically lighter too, like maybe I'm floating slightly.

Bottom line, the drinks are strong, so I might have to see if they have a free room I can check into, or spend a similar amount on a taxi back to Leeds. Either way, unless the valet is also a taxi driver, or I eat enough cake to sober up in time, I don't think I'll be making the early exit I thought.

Still, better to do this with a little liquid courage than without. I just want today to go well, to be here for my friends, to not make a scene. A gentle cocktail buzz might be my ticket to letting it all wash over me. Here's hoping.

It's nice, out here in the marquee, because even though it's sunny outside there's a nice breeze dancing through the tent, just enough to take the edge off the heat. I've been to marquee weddings that were basically like sitting inside a plastic oven, being slowly cooked – my friend Josie's dad actually passed out doing his speech at her wedding, and we all thought it was the heat. No one so much as looked at the dance floor until the sun had gone down that day.

They've done a great job with the summer flowers and the elegant table settings. Round tables are dotted around, forming a sort of circle around the dance floor in the centre. Not many people have taken their seats yet, they're all congregating in the middle of the room, everyone chatting, kids running around the place excitably. I like to see kids at a wedding, it always makes me feel a little sad, when they're not included. Or maybe I just don't want to be the only one throwing a tantrum later.

I'm more than relieved to have been moved to sit with Kelsey and Neil at the table they're on, but I'd be lying if I said I didn't feel like their third wheel, the child they couldn't find a babysitter for – not that they're making me feel like I'm crashing or anything, but poor Kelsey is mummy-ing me, just a little, checking on me, making sure I'm okay. I do appreciate it though. This would be a lot harder without her by my side.

The happy couple are here – and they really do look happy. Kira looks stunning in her dress. I don't know how she's managed to make a white bridal gown look gothic but she's nailed it some-how. Then there is Al, a genuine mountain of a man, who has already ditched the jacket that was most likely preventing his muscles from flexing. While Kira floats around effortlessly, meeting and greeting, Al breaks out his usual party tricks like lifting people up on chairs and miraculously managing not to get any of his fake tan on his white shirt collar. I don't know which one impresses me more. I can get foundation on my collar by simply picking out what I'm wearing, never mind letting it rub against my skin as I go about my day.

I haven't seen Todd since I spotted him in reception, not that I'm looking for him (I'm absolutely looking for him, I can't help myself), but that suits me just fine. If he were to vanish, would I even care? I mean from the wedding but, to be honest, it would be much easier for me if he ceased to be a part of my world. I've never dated so close to home before, it's always been a case of breaking up, parting ways, and healing and moving on in my own space. Bloody Todd though. He's integrated in my life in a way that is inescapable. Although I was friends with Al and Kira first, so really the decent thing for him to do would be to give me custody of this wedding, and space from him – and then the same for Kelsey and Neil's wedding too. Kelsey is my best friend, I've got more right to be there than him, he should just let me enjoy it, allow my friend to have a stress-free day – I wouldn't say he had to disappear forever, but it's only been two weeks.

'I hope he has left,' I mutter to Kelsey, having just told her all about how I spotted him earlier. 'Wouldn't that be nice.'

'I kind of hope he has too,' Kelsey replies. 'I hate seeing you so stressed.'

Neil nods.

'Yeah, if it were me who had broken up with Kels, I don't think I'd have the balls to come here,' Neil adds.

'Erm, can we not talk about breaking up when we're less than two weeks away from our wedding, please,' Kelsey practically ticks him off. 'Your cousin has already been freaking me out with her musings on what she would do if she was jilted at the altar.'

'Well, I guess if I were to jilt you, you would either know before we set off, or I'd be trapped on a ship or an island with you so...'

'So you're talking about it again – stop,' Kelsey claps back, laughing a little this time.

'That's cousin Caroline?' I check. 'She keeps staring at me. I wasn't expecting to see her here.'

'Well, she's here with her new boyfriend – Owen,' Kelsey says, raising her eyebrows for effect.

Owen is one of Neil's friends. Now that is dating too close to home – letting a member of your family date one of your friends. Imagine trying to consciously uncouple that one.

'She's very proud to be "no longer single",' Kelsey tells me with a look that says it all. 'I'm sure she wants to tell you alllll about it.'

Caroline is one of those people who always finds the wrong thing to say in every scenario. She's sure that she's right – even if she changes her mind, which is a spectacular skill when you think about it. She's also one of those people who makes herself feel better by making other people feel worse, because apparently the best way to detract from your own insecurities is to highlight someone else's – and if they don't have any, don't worry, they will by the time Caroline is done.

Finally everyone starts shuffling towards their tables, finding their seats, and as the crowd clears I'm finally able to pick Todd out again – but he's not alone.

He's got a woman with him – a petite brunette bombshell. The kind of girl they whip out on *Love Island* to make all of the female islanders sweat. I know what you're thinking, maybe she just happens to be walking in next to him, maybe they're just friends – no, no, no. For the avoidance of doubt they are holding hands. The message they are sending is loud and clear. They're a couple.

It's been two fucking weeks.

'Wow,' Kelsey blurts, following my line of sight. 'Talk about moving on fast.'

'That's Brody's ex, Nikki,' Neil tells me, one eyebrow raised.

'Wait, who's Brody again?' I ask – not that it matters who she used to be with because she's with Todd now, clearly.

'My mate Brody,' Neil replies. 'You must have met him!'

'Oh. Maybe.' I pause. Maybe I have, maybe I haven't. It's hard to care right now – I can't even think straight. 'Okay, so we really – as a group – need to start dating outside our friendship circle.'

I sigh, my eyes fixated on them as he gives her a playful twirl on the dance floor.

'It wouldn't be so bad if he wasn't parading her around like a trophy,' Kelsey adds. 'Brody's hot. Todd is... well, yeah, no offence, but he's just Todd. No offence to either of you.'

'Some taken,' I say with as much of a laugh as I can muster right now.

'I'm not offended, Brody is my hottest friend,' Neil jokes – maybe half jokes.

'Anyway, it's fine, because me and Todd are over, and so what if he moves on today or next month or next year – we're done, and I'm fine,' I insist.

'Is it really fine?' Kelsey checks, sounding like she doesn't quite believe me, and very obviously reading my mind.

'Absolutely, all good, he's over me, I'm over him, he's moving on – I'll move on too,' I rant.

'I could introduce you to some of my single mates,' Neil suggests. 'A few of them are here today...'

'Yes, please, I want all of them,' I say immediately. A little too quickly, perhaps, and it does sound a little bit like I want to get it on with multiple men at this wedding, so maybe I need to watch my phrasing when I'm tipsy and hurt. 'But first, I think I'll go get a drink,' I suggest.

'Shall I come wi—'

'No, no, all good,' I interrupt Kelsey. 'Back in a sec.'

I stand up, steadying myself on my heels. I love these shoes – big chunky white pumps with a monster heel, but as a rule I only wear them if I'm not planning on drinking, because it takes just that little bit of extra concentration to stay steady in them. Sober, absolutely fine, tipsy like I am now is asking for trouble. Drunk... being drunk in these shoes is like turning up to your job drunk – if your job is an acrobat at the circus.

I skulk around the edge of the marquee like a crab, walking sideways so I can keep an eye on the room, making sure Todd doesn't spot me, because the last thing I want is to meet his new bird. I'm not mentally prepared for that, not today, the rug has been fully pulled. I need a minute – and a drink – to compose myself.

When I reach the bar, I grip it like it might run away if I don't.

'What's the strongest drink you've got?' I ask the barman.

He raises an eyebrow, but doesn't hesitate.

'A Yorkshire Rose,' he replies, grinning. 'If you have two of them.'

'Then I will have two Yorkshire Roses – thank you,' I inform him, my voice all la-di-da.

He slides them across the bar. I immediately down one while he's still prepping the card reader.

'You looked like you needed that,' he says, with a laugh. 'Don't you like weddings?'

'This one, not so much,' I reply. 'Actually – could I get one more, please? For my friend.'

My friend being, of course, me.

'For your friend,' he replies. 'Of course.'

He doesn't even blink. My kind of guy.

Back at the table I can feel Kelsey eyeballing my two drinks.

'Jessa... are you really okay?' she asks.

'Absolutely fine,' I reply brightly – too brightly, like staring-at-the-sun bright.

'I know you're not great when you have multiple drinks,' she says quietly, leaning in towards me so no one else at our table can hear now that everyone is sitting down.

'They're just really good drinks,' I reply. 'I could go get more, if you fancy one?'

'Back to the bar already?' Neil teases me. 'Do I need to confiscate your car keys?'

Hilarious. Like I would ever be so stupid to drink and drive. I'm obviously going to have to book a room, or get an expensive taxi home – I'll do whichever (ideally the cheaper of the two though).

'Don't worry, the valet has them, and after a few more of these I can't imagine him giving them back to me, can you?' I joke.

'What?' he replies, clearly not getting it.

'The valet has my keys safe and sound,' I tell him.

The part of the gardens where the marquee is looks over the fountain, and the entrance where you drive in. Neil glances that way then back to me.

'The valet,' I say again. 'The guy who parks your car for you.'

'Jessa, there is no valet here,' Neil informs me, suddenly completely straight-faced. 'Have you... have you given your car to a random man?'

Oh, shit.

'Jessa, are you sure you're okay?' Kelsey says again.

'Yes, of course, I was just joking,' I say, nudging Kelsey, laughing. 'Oh, the looks on your faces.'

I take a sip of my drink to try and hide the look on my own face. Because I did, I absolutely did, I gave my car to a random man. But he was standing by the sign, wearing a name badge –

Ryan, that's it! And he took my keys. Of course he did. I practi-cally thrust them at him. Can you report a car as stolen if you, erm, gave it away? Right, no, okay, let's just... no one can find out about this. No one here. They'll all think I'm pathetic and that I'm having a breakdown – they might even think I'm doing it for attention, having someone 'steal' my car so that I can make a fuss and get sympathy. No, no, no. I'll park it for the moment, no pun intended, and then slink off to reception when I can do it under the radar.

Okay, I'm definitely going to need more of these drinks.

And presumably a new car.

I can't believe I've done this – on today of all days.

8

Longest. Meal. Of. My. Life.

It's such a shame, because the food was amazing, but I absolutely wolfed it so that I could slink off to reception, to fess up to my stupid mistake.

It was a buffet of sorts. Everyone went up, a table or two at a time, to help themselves to the hog roast, potatoes, salad, bread – all sorts. I thought, by getting a smallish plate, I could eat it as quickly as possible and make my excuses, but Neil very kindly said he would get me mine, so that I could continue hiding from Todd, which I guess is my number one priority. If I can get to the end of the day without him seeing me – or at least without the two of us having to interact – then I might come out of this relatively unscathed. Well, publicly unscathed, I'm sure when I'm alone in bed tonight I'll have a different take.

Well, at least I've eaten – although I have had a couple more cocktails, so I'm definitely what you would call more than tipsy. Now it's time for the wedding tradition of going to reception to report your stolen car. What do you mean that's not tradition?

I'm inside the hotel now, walking past where the toilets are. As I pass the gents, a man walks out and... it's him! It's Ryan! The not valet.

I halt my horses, stopping dead on the spot, almost bumping into him.

'You!' I say, pointing at him just in case there was any question mark around who I'm talking to. 'You stole my car!'

'Me?' he says with a chuckle, pointing at himself.

He isn't wearing his jacket now, so no name badge, but I know it's him. Deep brown eyes, muscular frame, tall, handsome – which I am loath to admit, now I know he's a car thief.

'Yes, you!'

'I didn't steal your car,' he corrects me. 'You gave me your keys.'

'Because I thought you were the valet...'

'Why? Because I'm a man?' he asks accusingly. I think he's joking around, but I've no time for it.

'What the fuck?' I blurt. 'No, because you were standing next to a sign that said "wedding parking" and it had an arrow pointing at you.'

He laughs at me. I want to punch him.

'It was pointing towards the wedding parking,' he replies, talking to me like I'm an idiot.

Am I an idiot? No, because...

'But your jacket had a name badge on!'

'I'm part of the wedding,' he replies. 'A groomsman. We all have our names on our jackets. It's what Al wanted.'

'I didn't see a name badge on Al's jacket,' I tell him, because I would have noticed that, surely?

'How many Als could you see when you were talking to him?' he jokes – obviously implying I'm drunk.

'I'm not drunk, I'm serious,' I snap. 'I didn't see a name badge on Al.'

I fold my arms like a pissed-off bouncer, refusing to let any of his bullshit in.

'It's Al,' he says with a shrug. 'We're lucky he still has a shirt on at this point. He hasn't been wearing his jacket, none of us have, it's too warm today.'

I mean, that's a good point, Al does love to take his top off for virtually no reason.

'So... why did you take my keys?' I ask after a few seconds of bemused silence – unless you count the volumes his smug grin and his stupid dimples speak.

'Because I've just always really wanted to drive a Fiat 500,' he says, deadpan. Then his grin returns. 'To help you out, obviously. I knew you were with the wedding so I figured I could get them to you later. They're in my room, for safekeeping.'

'I want them back now,' I insist.

'Are you sure?' he checks. 'It's not like you'll be driving anytime soon, is it?'

'What do you mean?'

'You're pickled,' he says with a snort.

'I am not... pickled,' I protest. 'And I'm not planning on driving, I just don't trust you.'

'Well, I don't trust you, you've got a bit of an intense vibe about you,' he says. 'So I'll go get them later, how about that?'

Ryan walks back towards the wedding. I follow him, unwilling to back down.

'You can't hold my keys to ransom,' I say, following him as fast as my heels will allow.

'Whoa, who said anything about a ransom?' he asks. 'I'm just keeping them safe. The night is young, the wedding has hardly gotten started. I'm planning on getting pickled myself, actually.'

'All the more reason to – whoa!'

My ankle wobbles and I stumble. Ryan is around like a shot, catching me in his arms, saving me from face-planting my way back into the marquee.

'Erm, thanks,' I tell him, the gratitude genuine but it still tastes bad in my mouth. 'That was...'

'Seriously impressive,' he says, finishing my sentence for me. 'I've made some good catches in my time, but a whole drunk woman falling for me in gigantic shoes might be a personal best.'

'I fell towards you, not for you,' I correct him, shoving him off. 'And another thing—'

'There you are!' Kira says.

She practically floats in my direction, in her beautiful dress.

'I'm about to toss the bouquet and I thought, with you being, you know, newly single, you should be there,' she tells me, taking me by the arm.

Kira is such a genuine person so I know this is coming from a good place but, honestly, I'd rather get up on the makeshift stage and tell everyone I gave my car keys to a random man.

'Oh, right, erm...'

What can I say?

'You two know each other?' Kira says, surprised.

'Not really,' I reply.

'Princess was just ranting about how there's no valet parking here,' Ryan says – I'd call it our own little joke but only he finds it funny.

'That's not like you,' Kira says as she drags me across the marquee, out onto the lawn where the toss is happening.

'No, it's not, is it?' I reply. 'He's just joking. It's just, you know, not funny, so I get your confusion.'

Kira is a woman on a mission, so she pretty much ignores

whatever it is we're doing here. And for some reason Ryan is following us.

'Are you coming to catch the bouquet?' I ask him. 'Seeing as though you're just sooo good at catching things.'

'No, but I can give you some pointers, if you like?'

'Go on then,' I reply.

'Have five less drinks two hours ago,' he teases me.

I seethe.

'Okay, everyone, all the single ladies, line up, get behind me, it's bouquet-tossing time,' Kira announces.

It becomes very quickly apparent that I am the only one standing here. Incredible.

'Erm, Jessa,' Kira says, shuffling awkwardly back towards me. 'I hadn't realised you're the only single girl here so... do you just want to take them? It seems daft, to throw them to you.'

This whole scenario has daft written all over it.

I mean, it's hard to say which is more embarrassing, being the only person trying (and potentially failing) to catch the bouquet or just being handed them like a loser, by default, as the only one here who has no one.

I know what the smart thing is: just say yes, grab the flowers – the participation ribbon – flash a grateful smile, get it over with. But before I can even muster a polite, dead-behind-the-eyes nod of agreement, another voice chimes in.

'I want a chance to catch it,' she says.

The whole group turns like we're in a school play and someone just missed their cue.

Oh, and here she is, Nikki – Todd's Nikki, I guess – here to terrorise me some more.

Kira blinks.

'But... you're not single?'

Kira nods towards Todd so she doesn't have to say it.

'I'm not married,' Nikki replies with a shrug. 'Not yet. There's a difference. I like the sound of wedding bells though, so I want in.'

I might not be able to muster a smile but my poker face is staying intact at least.

Kira practically winces as she looks over at me for my approval. Well, what else can she say? She can't exactly say no, I'm rigging the bouquet toss so my sad single friend can get it because you have her boyfriend now. And I can't really say anything other than...

'It's fine,' I say brightly, even though it's far from fine. What I want to say is: Can this girl not? What kind of psychotic power play is this? You'd think she would show me mercy.

Kira takes her place, ready to throw her flowers.

Well, I can't back down now, because if there's one thing worse than participating in this ridiculous nonsense, it's refusing to, because that would make me look sad and pathetic and like I don't wish them well (even though I truly don't).

I can see Kelsey, next to us, watching me anxiously like it's the final showdown of *The Good, the Bad, and the Ugly.* I'm not sure which one of the three this whole mess is supposed to be – it can't be good though.

Kira flings her bright red flowers over her head, sending them hurtling towards me and my rival.

I glance at Nikki – who is fully committing, clearly, with her arms out, knees bent, like a professional athlete. I reach out too, not to win exactly, more just... to not lose.

And that's when my ankle rolls in my big stupid heel that was not designed with sports (if we can call this sports) in mind.

Suddenly I'm stumbling sideways, crashing directly into Nikki, sending us both down onto the grass. So, I guess if this were a sport, wrestling would be the one, and if we're calling good, bad or ugly, this has ugly written all over it.

Nikki must have landed in a muddy patch of grass because it's all over her cream dress. She screams as though it were blood.

'Did you do that on purpose?' she shrieks at me, scrambling to her feet. Todd rushes over to help her – of course.

I blink up from the grass, stunned. Of course I didn't!

I notice Ryan, standing next to me, holding the flowers, which means he either caught them himself, or he picked them up from the floor to redistribute. God knows to whom.

I look over at Todd and, boy, does he look angry. His nostrils are flaring. The last time I saw that was when Leeds got knocked out in... I want to say a cup final but I also don't really know what that entirely means. Just that it makes grown men who opt to hide their emotions cry.

'We need to take this outside,' he says, reminding us of our surroundings.

'We are outside,' Ryan jokes.

'Come on, over by the fountain,' Todd says, ignoring him.

I try to stand, only to realise I've hurt my ankle. Oof, that stings. I hobble forward two steps before Ryan ever so helpfully scoops me up in his arms. He must be at least 6'2" and he's clearly strong, so he makes it look and feel easy – not that I want him to carry me, of course.

'They want you to follow them,' he tells me. 'I'll give you a lift.'

'How much would I have to pay you to run in the opposite direction right now?' I ask him, not feeling like I have much choice in the matter.

'I wouldn't miss this for all the money in the world, princess,' he replies with a chuckle.

Oh, I bet.

We reach the fountain area where Todd and Nikki are already waiting. Ryan gently lowers me onto the stone edge so I can sit down and take the weight off my ankle.

Todd turns to Ryan.

'Look, man, I respect you, but stay out of it,' Todd tells him. 'But thanks for helping.'

Ryan holds up his hands.

'I'm just helping my new best friend,' he tells Todd. 'To be her feet in her time of need.'

Todd frowns. Nikki huffs behind him like a tiny angry puff of smoke.

Todd turns back to me.

'What the hell are you playing at, Jessa?' he asks, those nostrils of his practically having a mind of their own. 'You pushed her. I knew you'd be jealous, but I didn't think you'd get violent.'

Joke's on him, because if he continues accusing me, I could be tempted.

I glance back toward the marquee. We've got an audience now. Even the happy couple is watching. Great. Just what every bride dreams of: a side-plot at her wedding stealing the limelight. I feel awful. It was an accident though.

'I didn't push her,' I say through gritted teeth. 'I didn't even want to join in. I fell. It was an honest mistake. I'm very sorry. I hope you're not hurt, Nikki.'

'You hurt my couture,' Nikki snaps, peering out from behind Todd, like the small kid shouting insults from behind the safety of the big bully.

'Is that a bone or a muscle?' Ryan asks with a cheeky laugh.

'Shut up, Brody,' she snaps back.

Wait – Brody? Neil's friend Brody? Nikki's ex Brody? Oh, this just gets weirder and weirder.

'You're obviously not over me and it's embarrassing,' she tells him.

He shrugs, seemingly unbothered.

'I would have thought it was more embarrassing to be over someone after two weeks,' he says. 'But you do you.'

'Wait. So let me get this straight,' I start as I put all the pieces together. I look to Todd first. 'You left me for her. And Brody, she left him for Todd?'

Nikki rolls her eyes.

'Glad you're finally getting it,' she replies.

'So we're supposed to believe there was no overlap?' I ask.

'No,' Todd says firmly.

Brody frowns a little.

'There had to be emotional cheating, at least,' I reply. 'We're supposed to believe this is all just a big coincidence.'

'Erm, the only emotional thing around here is you,' Nikki tells me.

Todd sighs.

'She's not emotional, Kiki, she's drunk,' he tells her. Kiki? 'Too much to drink always makes her mean.'

'I'm not drunk!' I snap, standing up to prove it, except I forget about my ankle, and—

Splash. Into the fountain I go. Bum first. It isn't deep but I'm soaked – and kind of stuck.

Out of nowhere Al appears – shirtless, of course – to lift me out of the water like the superhero he is.

'Don't worry, I've got you,' he reassures me, smiling his face off, clearly happy to get to be heroic and topless. 'And you can have my shirt, to wear as a dress.'

I bet I can.

Brody – because that's actually his name, it turns out – appears at my side.

'Come on,' he says, helping me limp off towards reception.

'Are you okay?' he asks.

'I'm fine,' I mutter. 'Just wet and shocked.'

'Normally I'd make a joke,' he tells me. 'But I meant about... all the other stuff.'

I know he did.

'Yeah. I mean, no. But, whatever. It is what it is. I suppose we're in the same boat.'

'You look more like you're out of it,' he teases. 'Well, if you're drunk, no reason not to get drunker, right?'

'An excellent point,' I reply. 'But first I need to book a room.'

'Did you say a room?' a hotel employee who happens to be passing asks.

I nod.

'Fully booked, sorry, love,' he tells me.

'Ah, wonderful,' I blurt.

Brody rummages around in his pocket for a second or two.

'I've got a room,' he reminds me. 'Go shower. Get changed into your new gigantic shirt dress. Rejoin the party when you're ready and I'll buy you a drink.'

'Really? Are you sure?' I reply.

'Absolutely,' he says.

I'm about to thank him when he glances over my shoulder and bursts out laughing.

'What?' I ask.

He gestures behind me.

'I still can't believe you thought that car park sign was pointing at me,' he chuckles.

I narrow my eyes.

'And I can't believe your name's not Ryan.'

'Well, it is in a way,' he replies. 'Ryan's my surname. Brody Ryan.'

'Erm, okay, good for you,' I say, not sure what else he's expecting.

'Don't worry about it,' he reassures me. 'I'm not that sharp when I've had a skinful either.'

'I told you, I'm not... oh, fab, you're winding me up, again.'

Brody is teasing me. Al is shirtless. I'm embarrassing myself. It seems like the balance at this wedding has finally been restored.

9

I stand awkwardly in the middle of Brody's hotel room, dripping water onto the very expensive-looking carpet. I cannot believe this is my life.

In my job it's all about appearances, the optics, and all of that out there was just... everything you don't want. I mean, come on, first of all I'm dumped, then it turns out my ex is here with his new girlfriend, then it seems like I'm going to be the only one catching the bouquet (maybe she should've just handed me it), then my ex's new girlfriend rocks up to compete with me, then we're on the floor, then I'm in the bloody fountain... and now I'm here, about to change into a XXL shirt, with a party full of gawping guests to head back to. It's not a great look, that's all I'm saying.

Brody disappears into the bathroom, rummaging around for towels, while I stand there like a naughty dog that jumped in the lake. My dress clings to me in all the wrong places and the smell – my God. I blow a strand of hair off my face and silently thank the universe that at least my hair and make-up survived the fountain incident. Small mercies and all that.

Brody reappears, handing me a thick, white, fluffy towel with a grin that says he's still trying very hard not to laugh.

'You'll feel better once you're dry,' he promises. 'You'll smell better too.'

I scowl at him.

'Maybe, but I'm not sure it's going to rescue my dignity,' I reply as I start towelling off the sludge from my legs.

Brody holds up Al's shirt. It looks like it might swallow me whole. I must pull a face at it.

'If this said Balenciaga on it you'd pay a fortune for it,' he tells me. 'Just... embrace the oversized look.'

'Hey, I'm more than happy to wear anything that can double up as a tent to hide in,' I reply. 'But could you, er...'

I turn my back to him, hoping it's obvious I need him to do my zip.

'Oh, yeah, sure,' he replies.

He places one hand on my hip as he slowly unzips my dress for me, his knuckles lightly grazing my back. Once it's down to my waist, he hovers in place for a second.

'I've got it from here,' I point out, a little short with him.

He chuckles and, like a gentleman (or a man who's very aware he'll get punched if he's caught peeking), he heads for the door.

'See you outside,' he tells me.

Finally alone, I fumble with my soggy dress, peeling it from my body, the fabric sticking to my still damp skin.

I head to the bathroom, to shower off my lower half, before I pop Al's shirt on.

Brody's room is weirdly neat. No stray socks. No crumpled-up clothes. Not a thing out of place. Just a neatly made bed, an after-shave bottle and a toothbrush in the bathroom, and nothing else. Nothing to give anything away. Then again, he probably only arrived here today, so he hasn't had time to fill the place with booze, bras and bad decisions. I know, I know, I don't know a thing about him, but he's clearly a very good-looking guy, with a very annoying sense of humour, and they're always the ones who know how to have a good time.

Finally cleaned up – well, as good as it's going to get – I button up my shirt dress and zhuzh my hair and take a long hard look at myself in the mirror. If only I knew how I got here. What was I doing so wrong with Todd that made him want someone else? And how could he have wound up with such little respect for me that he would bring someone new to our friends' wedding so soon? I sigh. Ah, well, time to go back out there and face everyone. Can't wait.

I open the door and find Brody waiting behind it.

'I thought I was seeing you outside,' I tell him.

'I thought I'd wait for you, make sure you haven't nicked anything,' he jokes.

Well, I assume it's a joke, I don't find it funny.

'Actually, now that you mention it, you don't have a spare belt, do you?' I ask.

'For the trousers you're not wearing?' he replies with a smirk.

'Hilarious – no, to cinch this shirt in at the waist, make it actually pass for a dress,' I tell him.

'Ah, that's a good idea,' he says. 'Here you go...'

Brody starts undoing the belt he's wearing.

'Whoa, no, that's okay,' I tell him.

He laughs at me.

'Don't be daft, it'll be fine,' he replies. 'They'll stay on – plus, I figured they'd come off at some point tonight anyway.'

Charming.

I take the belt – which I am grateful for – and it does make Al's shirt look more like a dress on me. Not the kind of thing you'd wear to a wedding, but it's better than nothing. To be honest with you, the greatest wedding gift anyone could give Al would be the opportunity to be shirtless.

'You good now?' Brody asks.

'Oh, I'm just fab,' I reply sarcastically as I examine my soggy shoes. 'As good as I get.'

He just laughs.

'Wait there,' he instructs me.

He disappears into his room for a second and emerges with a pair of flip-flops. I mean, Brody is at least 6'2", so he's got a pair of feet to match. They're way too big for me but also my best option right now.

'Thanks,' I tell him.

'It's no bother,' he replies. 'I thought I might hit the gym tomorrow, and the pool, so I brought them just in case. But the chances I won't have a hangover are slim.'

'Yeah, me too,' I reply.

'Well, the first one is on me,' he says. 'We'll figure out the other fifty as we go along.'

I smile, just a little.

I suppose I should have more sympathy for Brody, he's in the same boat as I am (despite me just looking like I had fallen out of it), and I know it's not a nice place to be.

We step into the hallway, heading back toward the party. I can already hear the thump of music and the distant roar of laughter. Perhaps now that the party is in full swing no one will notice me slink back in. I just want to blend in, to have a bunch of drinks, and have a nice time. I don't want any more surprises.

God knows what else this day has in store for me. Is it weird that, as terrified as I am, I'm ever so slightly excited?

10

I don't know what wakes me up, the throbbing pain in my head, the cramping in my back, or the war drums banging in my ears. I think it's a little bit of everything and it's a very rude awakening when you've got the hangover from hell.

My brain feels like it's full of broken glass – or maybe it's just booze and regret, but it doesn't feel pretty at all.

I groan as I wriggle to try and get more comfortable, and then I realise all at once that the room I'm in is cold, echoey and the bed is rock-hard. Because I'm not in a bed, I'm in a bath. It's a big Jacuzzi bath, with a duvet in it instead of water, but it's a bath nonetheless.

I shift upright, my headache intensifying, but I can't lie in here a second longer. Everything hurts.

Everything hurts more when my arm takes out a neat line of spa products lined up along the edge of the bath, causing them all to clatter to the tiles below.

Shit.

I freeze, caught halfway out of the tub like a raccoon with its paw in the bin. For a moment, there's silence. Beautiful, hopeful silence. Maybe no one heard. Maybe I'm alone. Maybe I can pretend this didn't happen and slink out of here without embarrassing myself any more because, frankly, I filled my quota for the year yesterday.

Then the door bangs open.

'Jessa?'

It's Brody, looking concerned, wearing nothing but a tight pair of boxer briefs. Wow, I don't mean to sound like a sleaze, I'm not meaning to look, I promise, but Brody looks like his body has been carved from a chunk of marble and designed to stand in some museum in Greece to show everyone how jacked the gods were. No one just wakes up with a body like that (much as I'd like to – ha ha), it comes from years of crunches and planks and eating foods that are not beige or cheese. I think I'll always prefer having a pizza to having a butt that doesn't jiggle when you slap it. Not that that is a legitimate indicator of fitness, I don't think...

Brody laughs at me, now that he knows I'm okay, mid-bath escape, limbs flailing, my hair and eye make-up probably all over the place, making me look like a haunted Victorian doll.

'Oh,' he says, laughing. 'It's just you being chaotic again. At least you fell in something dry this time.'

'Good morning to you too,' I mutter, climbing the rest of the way out like the creature from the black lagoon, if the black lagoon had been filled with gin. 'So,' I start, 'last night was...'

'Fun,' he says, finishing my sentence for me.

'Yeah. From what I remember,' I reply.

Which, to be honest, isn't a whole lot. I recall sitting with him. Talking. Laughing. A few other guests drifting in and out. Drinks multiplying mysteriously. At some point I must've stumbled back here, with nowhere else to go, Brody taking pity on me once again. And then I guess I slept in the bath, in Al's shirt (although it's covered with booze stains now) but that's preferable to sleeping in Brody's bed because can you imagine if we'd slept together? Not that he's suggested it was on the cards, I think he thinks I'm too silly to be sexy, but that would have made an already messy situation even messier.

'Thank you,' I say sincerely. 'For letting me crash in your bath. That was kind of you.'

He shrugs.

'You seemed pretty desperate, so...'

A jibe. I expect no less now.

'It's okay, women are always desperate to stay in my room. Just usually in my bed,' he jokes.

Ugh.

I can think of one who isn't – Nikki – but I'm not mean enough to say Nikki out loud, even if he is trying to wind me up.

'Well,' I say instead, 'I should get going. I promised Kelsey and Neil I'd meet them for breakfast. I think they arranged it to check I'm still alive.'

'Like that?' he asks, eyeing Al's crumpled, booze-scented shirt.

'It's this or my stinky fountain dress,' I remind him.

'Yeah, you did proper stink in that,' he confirms unnecessarily.

'Thanks,' I reply.

He disappears into the bedroom and reappears a moment later with a bundle of grey.

'Here,' he says, tossing it at me. 'My tracksuit. Take it. I brought it in case I wanted to hit the gym but I'm knackered after last night.'

If he literally hit the gym he would punch a hole through it, hungover or not, it's those bulging biceps.

'Oh, are you sure?' I check.

'Yeah. I've got other stuff to put on,' he replies.

I hold up the hoodie and spot a small emblem on the chest. Yorkshire County Cricket Club.

I raise an eyebrow.

'Big cricket fan?' I ask.

He shrugs.

'Sort of.'

Ugh, men and sports, why do they have to be such a cliché? Then again, here's me, doing the most to prove I'm Bridget Jones.

'Thanks,' I mumble, because honestly, it is actually kind of him. He has these weird little flashes of decency, and I do vaguely remember having a good chat with him last night, too – about something. Not enough to shift my general stance, which is: he's attractive, but he annoys me. Isn't it always the way? If hot people had good personalities too, they'd be unstoppable. Society would collapse.

'I'll leave you to change,' he says, strolling off – still strutting around in his boxers, of course. He could have grabbed himself a robe, while he was getting something for me.

Once I'm alone, I do my best to smarten up. I use the bits of make-up from my bag, doing my best to patch up yesterday's face, and run my mini brush through my hair. Then I pull on the hoodie, sleeves dangling past my hands. The joggers are massive too – I have to yank the drawstring until they're practically cinching my organs to keep them up.

Then I head into the bedroom, adjusting my waistband to make sure it's secure, only to find Brody lying back on the bed, his arms behind his head, flexing his biceps in a way that just has to be intentional.

'Thanks again,' I say, trying to sound casual. 'I'll give this stuff to Neil, to get back to you at some point.'

'It suits you,' he says, with a lazy grin, clearly enjoying the absurdity.

'Erm, thanks, well, bye,' I babble.

I step out, close the door behind me, and exhale.

What a night. What a wedding. What a mess.

I turn to head for the lift but before I can escape to stuff my face with breakfast, I hear a familiar voice.

'Jessa!'

Oh, no. Not Caroline.

I can see her looking at my tracksuit, clearly trying to work out where I got it from. She's smiling like the cat that got the cream and the hottest gossip of the wedding.

'Oh, Jessa, hello! What a day you had yesterday!' she coos. 'I just feel so sorry for you. I really bloody do. After what Todd did to you. Do you think you'll ever get over it?'

I open my mouth to form a polite – or maybe not polite, because why would she say that like that? – reply when Brody's door opens.

He steps out. In boxers.

He's got something in his hands that he wiggles at me.

'You forgot your car keys,' he tells me.

Caroline's eyes light up, twinkling practically, as she puts the pieces of the puzzle together in the only way she can make them fit.

'Okay, wow, well, I'll leave you two to it,' she says, her voice brimming with implication.

Brody looks mildly apologetic but mostly amused.

'Sorry,' he tells me. 'I just didn't want you to forget them.'

'It's fine,' I reply. 'But now everyone at breakfast is going to think we—'

'You've got to stop caring what people think,' he says, annoyingly chill about the whole thing.

I frown at him.

'Bye, Brody,' I say, finally, loudly and clearly.

'Bye, Jessa,' he says with a smirk. 'Until next time...'

'Har-har,' I call back as I head for the lift.

That's enough of him for one morning – that's enough of him for this lifetime, to be honest.

Plus, I'm so, so hungry. I'm edging into hangry, even. You won't like me when I'm hangry.

Yep, I was right, Storm Caroline has blown through the breakfast room and told everyone about exactly what she saw – or thinks she saw, at least.

As I walk in, it feels like every head turns. Not in a 'wow, who's this beautiful woman?' kind of way – more of a 'that's her, the one who fell in the fountain, spent the night with a man she just met, and is now wearing his tracksuit' kind of way. Which, to be fair, is almost accurate.

The sleeves of Brody's hoodie flop over my hands again so I push them back up. Chances I'm not going to dip a sleeve in my breakfast? Slim.

I spot Kelsey waving me over with a grin that is way too smug for this early in the morning.

I sit down beside her, trying to act casual (and pretending like I didn't notice Todd and Nikki on the table behind her) like this isn't the most theatrical walk of shame in history. Kelsey leans in immediately, barely containing herself.

'Caroline's already done the rounds,' she tells me.

I blink, feigning innocence.

'Rounds about what?' I ask.

Kelsey tilts her head, clearly unimpressed by my performance.

'Jessa, please. I might not have believed her, were you not currently dressed in Brody's clothes.'

I glance down at my outfit. Yeah, fair enough, it does look exactly like what Caroline has been telling people, but I can feel

Todd and Nikki behind us, probably listening in because they're definitely within earshot.

I could tell the truth, I guess. Set the record straight that I slept in a bath because I had nowhere else to go, and Brody took double pity on me, giving me clothes to borrow... but wouldn't it be delicious to lean into the story? To let Todd and Nikki think they're old news. That Brody and I are so over them we spent the night together, and it was the best.

And maybe, just maybe, it'll go some way to convincing Kelsey that I am okay with all of this. That I can handle this and her wedding will go without a hitch.

So I sigh, lean a little closer, and say, 'Okay, fine. Just between us... I spent the night with Brody.'

Kelsey's eyes go so wide I'm briefly concerned they might never go back to how they used to be.

'Oh my God, really?' she squeaks.

I nod. 'Yes,' I confirm, because it's technically true.

'How was it?' she asks curiously.

I smile, slow and cheeky.

'So good,' I reply. 'I spent most of the night in his Jacuzzi.'

Also true. Technically. Deeply pathetic, sure, but semi-factual nonetheless.

Kelsey fans herself with a napkin.

'I knew there was something between you,' she says. 'It's a good sign if he's giving you clothes to wear. Boys only do that when they really like a girl.'

Or when the girl smells like a pond. I just smile and nod instead.

'I'm starving,' I say, standing up. 'Let me get some food and then I'll give you the rest of the horny details.'

Well, my stomach is grumbling, and it will buy me some time to make some things up.

As I stand up, I notice movement from the table behind. Todd and Nikki, mid-fake conversation, turn away quickly to pretend they weren't listening in. You can tell by their body language that they heard me though.

Good!

I saunter over to the breakfast buffet with a little spring in my step.

Okay, yes, it was petty. Absolutely. But it was so, so worth it to bring them down a peg or two.

Plus, it's not like anyone is ever going to find out the truth, is it?

11

I really, really hate calling Emma the wedding... whatever she is, I'll only get it wrong. Now more than ever though, I need the wedding cabin situation sorted, because I want to be around Todd as little as possible.

I'm a grown woman, I'm smart, I'm brave – I'm obviously deluded – but we move. I just need to suck it up, to call her, and then I'll feel better.

'Yes?' Emma answers, clearly annoyed, and it makes me wonder if she might have saved my number under something like: 'annoyance' or 'pain in the arse'.

'Hi, Emma, it's Jessa,' I say brightly, hoping my cheery demeanour might be catching. Well, if I'm faking it, surely so can she.

'Jessa,' she says.

I don't know if she's wondering who I am, confirming that she knows it's me, or what.

'I'm just calling to check if the whole cabin situation is sorted yet?' I say, all easy-breezy.

She exhales so hard it distorts the sound for a second.

'Jessa, I have told you, I will sort it,' she says through gritted teeth.

'Oh, I know, I just wanted to check...'

'I will sort it, Jessa, but you need to stop calling me, okay?' she replies.

Bloody hell, what's her problem?

'I just wanted to check,' I continue, trying to explain myself, but obviously only making it worse.

'Jessa!' she snaps. 'I told you, I'll sort it. I do have other jobs, you know. Other clients – and you are not one of them. Stop calling.'

'Yep, okay,' I say. My voice crackles, just a little, because, y'know, I'm having a shitty time lately, and it only seems to be getting worse, and I just want to make sure this is sorted. Not just for myself, for Kelsey and Neil too, because this is their wedding, they're the main characters. I don't want to steal the stage, not even briefly, like I did at Al and Kira's wedding. They were lovely about it – I mean, come on, Al gave me the shirt from his back, but I really wish it hadn't happened.

'I'm sorry if I'm bothering you,' I tell her sincerely. 'This is really important to me. I just... I need a room of my own. Not one with Todd. It's not fair on either of us – or on Kelsey and Neil.'

There's a pause. A paper shuffle. The faint sound of Emma restraining a scream.

'It's equally important to Todd that he has a room with his new partner,' she says crisply.

'What? He's... bringing Nikki?' I blurt – not that Emma is going to engage with me about this.

Another pause. Another sigh. Emma sounds like she's aged five years just speaking to me.

'Leave it with me,' she says. 'Be patient. It'll get sorted.'

'Thanks, Emma, it mea—'

She hangs up on me. Unbelievable!

I chew my lip for a second. Has Kelsey told Todd that he can bring Nikki to the wedding? Adding her as his plus-one doesn't feel like something she would do but I'm too curious not to call.

'Hey, you,' she answers.

'Hey,' I reply.

'Oh, no, what's wrong?' she asks, clearly hearing something in my voice, something I hadn't intended to put in there.

'I'm just going to spit it out,' I tell her. 'Did you tell Todd he could bring Nikki to your wedding?'

Kelsey groans.

'Shit, Jessa, no, of course not,' she replies. 'But technically Nikki was already invited, she was one of Neil's guests. So I suppose they've just decided they're coming together.'

'I just spoke with Emma – she was a delight, as always – and she said they were sharing a room,' I tell her.

'Do you want me to ask them not to?' Kelsey replies like a shot. 'It's no big deal, I could talk to Emma—'

'No!' My voice comes out louder than intended. I take a deep breath. 'No. It's fine. It won't make a difference. It's all good.'

For a second or two there's just silence.

'Jessa, are you sure? Because if you're not okay with this, if it's too much – I would rather postpone the wedding. I mean it. You're my best friend. I want you to be there but I don't want you to be miserable.'

That's the thing about Kelsey. She means it. She'd do it. She'd cancel the whole thing with a polite smile. And that's exactly why I have to go through with it. For her. Because if our roles were reversed, she'd do it for me.

I squeeze my eyes shut, summon all my fake confidence, and lie straight through my teeth.

'I promise, it's okay,' I reassure her. 'I'm okay. If he's in a room with her then he's not in a room with me, he'll be distracted, and I can just focus on having a great time.'

She exhales, relieved.

'Well, that sounds great to me,' she tells me. 'I love you.'

'Love you too,' I reply. 'And I'm really, really looking forward to your super extra wedding, and watching you and Neil tying the knot. I really can't wait.'

'Oh, that means so much to me. Not long to go now!'

'I know! Anyway, lovely, I have to go, speak later, yeah?' I say, because if we end this call now, then it's perfect.

'Definitely, see you later,' she replies.

As I hang up, I catch sight of myself in the mirror.

Ugh. What are you looking at, huh?

It's going to be fine, it's going to be fine... and if I keep saying that, it might come true.

12

As I perch on the edge of my bar stool, I swing my feet anxiously. I'm in a trendy wine bar, in Leeds city centre, drinking a glass of champagne and trying my very best to feel something for Paul.

I met Paul through work – I'm selling his house in Alwoodley, a massive detached place with its own tennis court and, I don't know, a million bedrooms. It's a real dream of a place but, now that his divorce is through, he's moving to something smaller.

Why, yes, of course we bonded over being newly single. Isn't that tragic? The only thing more tragic, though, would be putting my life on hold while Todd lives it up with Kiki (I can't help but mock the sickly-sweet way he called her that). So I'm here, having a drink, with a man, seeing how it goes.

Paul is handsome, in a clean-cut, pinstripe-suit kind of way. I don't know what he does for work, we've not got to that bit yet, but it clearly pays better than my job.

He's really making an effort too. He's asking questions, laughing at my jokes – he even complimented my earrings, which had to be out of politeness, because he seems like a man with expensive taste, and I think these earrings were £4 from Primark.

'You really did such a great job with my house,' he says, reviving the conversation. 'I hardly recognised the place, when you had it all dolled up. My wi... my ex-wife was never really into that kind of thing. We had an interior designer come around, when we moved in, who told her what to put where. I can't remember her name, she was married to a footballer. Anyway, she told us what artwork to buy and where to put it, and which chairs spoke the same language as the trees outside and which paint colours gave off the right energy...'

His cheeks redden slightly, as his voice trails off.

'Sorry,' he says. 'I'm not making fun of your job. But what she did felt different.'

'Well, yeah, I suppose because what I do is to sell places, not for people to live with,' I explain. 'I couldn't come into your house and tell you what your taste should be – how can I know that? Artwork especially is such a personal thing, and it shouldn't "speak" to the trees, it should speak to you. You're the one who has to look at it every day. I don't make a home, I make a shopfront for a home. Interior designers do incredible work, but it has to be with you, not for you. Everyone's taste is their own, right?'

'You know what? That's an excellent way to put it,' he replies. 'It looked great – you saw the place – but it never felt like us. How do you fix that?'

'You can still use a designer, you just tell them what you want, rather than to do what they think or what's trendy,' I reply.

'Well, I know that for my new place,' he replies. 'When I find the right one. My rental is...'

His voice trails off again.

'Sorry, sorry, I can't believe I've got you talking about work, enough of that,' he says, pausing to take a big drink. 'Let's talk about something else.'

To be honest with you, I was at my most relaxed, talking shop, because it distracted me from the fact that this is sort of a date and yet all I can think about is bloody Todd. I just need to forget about him, lean into the conversation more, give Paul a real chance.

'What do you like to watch on TV?' he asks.

'Oh, everything,' I reply. 'I love a binge-watch. I think I set my record for most episodes watched in one sitting with *Breaking Bad* – seven episodes in a row.'

And yes, I am genuinely proud of that.

'Wow, seven? That's impressive,' he replies. 'Is that not... seven hours?'

'Near enough,' I say with a laugh. 'But sometimes you just need to get lost in someone else's life.'

'So, is that your comfort show, then?' he asks, one eyebrow raised.

As much as I love *Breaking Bad*, it would be a red flag if someone called it their comfort show on a first date, right?

'Oh, no, that's *It's Always Sunny in Philadelphia*,' I reply. 'That's one of those shows that I can just watch again and again, no matter what I'm doing, and it always makes me happy.'

'I've never seen it,' he replies. 'It sounds like a cure for all ills...'

'Oh, absolutely,' I reply. 'I remember when I... when... when I had...'

Shit. I was going to tell him a story – about bloody Todd – but it's not just that it's about him, it's a good story, about a time when he was great. A memory that makes me miss what we had – what he took from me.

'Ooh, go on, this sounds interesting,' he prompts me.

'Oh, no, I was just going to say, I had the flu, it was awful, I couldn't think straight, and my boyfriend at the time put it on for me, and I guess I just binge-watched it until I felt better. It got me through it.'

'Well, that was nice of him,' he replies.

'It was,' I say softly. 'Because he... he didn't really like watching TV. Only a couple of shows, and he hated *Sunny*, so... to put it on for me... for hours... yeah.'

The lump in my throat feels more like a hand wrapped around my neck.

Paul smiles politely, but I can tell the vibe has shifted. I've soured the air with something and now we're both struggling to keep smiling.

'But yeah, it was just... just one... just one of those things,' I say, trying to smooth it over, but the wobble in my voice grows more obvious with each word.

I stare upwards – because someone once told me that was a lifehack to stop yourself from crying – and try to get Todd out of my head. It's just that things were good between us, he was a great boyfriend, I thought we had a future together and now it's all over. Not just my dreams for the two of us, but my personal dreams too – they were tangled up with his and, if I take him out of the equation, there's just plot holes everywhere. I don't even know what my hopes are for the future now.

'So, music...' Paul says, trying to get the conversation back on track, but it's too late. I lean forward, still trying to keep my eyeballs fixed on the high ceiling above us, trying to blink away the feeling, the inevitable tell that I'm about to start crying. My eyes feel swollen with it, full of tears, and I don't know where else they can go but out. 'Erm... are you okay?' he asks, his body stiffening awkwardly.

'Yeah, I'm fine,' I squeak, subtly wiping away the first couple of tears to escape. 'Just... there's something in my eye.'

'Which one?' he asks.

'Both,' I reply.

Oh, boy, the tears are really flowing now. I mean, obviously I'm crying, and I'm doing my best to keep a lid on the sobs, but the tears wait for no man. They're really flowing now.

'Perhaps we should call it a night?' Paul suggests – trying to hide his discomfort, but failing even worse than I am at keeping his emotions in check.

'Yeah, good idea,' I say, sniffing hard.

He stands up so quickly he almost knocks over his empty glass. I grab my things and follow him outside.

'I'm really sorry,' I tell him, wrapping my arms around myself, giving myself the hug I need right now – not that I'm much comfort to myself.

'No worries,' he replies. 'I hope you get your eyes sorted.'

'Thanks.'

There's no way he believed that, and there's no way I'm ever going to hear from him again – not even if he wants to sell his next house, I'll bet, because as great as he thinks I was at my job, he's clearly not interested in an emotionally dodgy woman who cried on a first date.

I watch him walk away. He was nice and all that but, I don't know, it's not Paul specifically that feels like a loss, it's my ability to date, to move on, to be happy. I should feel bad for him, and embarrassed for myself, but I don't. What I do feel is the most jarring combination of hopeless, because I don't know where I go from here, and yet relief, because I don't want to move on. I just want my old life back.

I can't get it though, can I? I can't go back, I can't move forward, I'm just suspended in time – and what a shitty time to be trapped in.

I wipe my face with the napkin I brought out with me, which

is in tatters now – sort of like my love life – shove it in my bag, and pull myself together.

I don't know what I expected to get out of tonight. He was never going to be my boyfriend, or even my plus-one to Kelsey and Neil's wedding, but I think I just wanted to prove to myself that I was okay, that I could move on, that it was all going to be fine...

And the only thing I've proven to myself is the opposite. Fab.

13

Every now and then I'll just be going about my business and my disastrous date with Paul will pop into my head. Now that I'm a few steps away from it, fair enough, crying all over the man was incredibly embarrassing. Any time I have a minute to myself, I cringe about it.

I have a moment now, because dragging my suitcase through the packed train station isn't much brainwork, so I'm stuck with my thoughts, wondering how I got here. Not literally, I got an Uber, I mean here in this mess. I should be excited, getting a taxi to a train to a ship to a hot and sunny island. Getting dumped and then still having to take the trip with my ex – and his new girl-friend – doesn't exactly scream: nice, relaxing summer holiday. I kind of can't believe I'm using my time off for this.

What I thought would fly suddenly feels like it's going to drag. Multiple days at sea, a long weekend in Sicily, doing wedding-based activities that surely involve Todd and Nikki. Ugh. They've taken something I love and turned it into something shit – which I suppose applies to my life, as well as this holiday.

What sounded like a dream feels like an annoyance. Why do

Kelsey and Neil have to have such an elaborate wedding? It's the wedding equivalent of 'this call could have been an email'. Most people manage to get it done in a day.

I'm just being spiky, because the situation isn't ideal for me, but I do want Kelsey to have an amazing time, she deserves it. This cruise is a once-in-a-lifetime kind of thing, a dream – it's just my situation that's making it feel more like a nightmare for me. I just need to suck it up. It's a cruise – cruise ships are huge. I'm sure I can avoid Todd and Nikki.

I'm just going to get on the train, sit back, relax and try to clear my head. Well, try to clear it while drinking the cute little cans of Cosmopolitans I picked up in the station. I just need to relax, to take it a day at a time, and enjoy the peace and quiet while I can.

I drag my suitcase on to the train, find my seat, and practically collapse into it. Bliss. Nothing but the hum of the train, the sunlight pouring in through the window and – I take my first sip of my cocktail – ahh, glorious, you'd never know it came from a can instead of a mixologist. I'm going to chill, maybe read a book, and mentally prepare myself for what's to come.

I take my phone from my bag, to tap a message to Kelsey telling her I made the train the planner booked for me (I'm not usually the most punctual girlie) and I'm almost smiling to myself until a familiar voice wipes the vague happiness from my face.

It's two voices, actually. Talking, flirting, laughing. My heart drops – I think it's down on the tracks somewhere, waiting to be mullered by a train. It feels like it has been already.

Of course it's Todd and Nikki. Of course the wedding planner booked us on to the same train. Of fucking course we're sitting in the same carriage.

Yeah, I know, it makes sense, she probably booked the tickets all at once – but even so, this is just my luck, isn't it? My nice, peaceful, relaxing trip – my calm before the storm – being ruined by their presence.

I slump down further in my seat, hoping it makes me invisible. Maybe they won't see me. Maybe they're too wrapped up in themselves to even notice anyone else? They certainly weren't thinking about me when they got together.

They haven't noticed me thankfully, so I think I'll just stay slumped, carefully pour my drinks into my mouth, pop in my AirPods and mess around on my phone for a bit. Anything to block the sound of them being happy out.

There's an email from Emma, the wedding whatever, confirming that the cabin situation is sorted, so that's something at least. I'll have a space of my own to retreat to, so maybe that will be my new peaceful space, seeing as though my train carriage is now full of people I don't like.

Gosh, it's going to be a long trip, if I sit like this the whole time. What if they spot me and call me over to join them? What if I need a wee and they realise I've been hiding from them? Can I skulk off to a different seat? Probably not – not without them seeing me anyway.

Once we've set off, I rest my head against the window, allowing the train to gently rock me, hoping it shakes out some of my stress.

Oh, here we go again, alone with my thoughts I can only think about one thing: Paul.

Poor, sweet, terrified Paul. I still can't believe I cried on him. I'm not really one for crying in front of people, in a general way, but I've never broken down in a bar before, over a man, and over a man literally. This is just... a new low within a new low. And after one drink too, so I can't even blame being drunk. The cringe just keeps creeping up on me – can you give yourself the ick? Because that's what it feels like.

Paul won't want to go on another date with me, no way, and I don't blame him, but you know what? I don't want to go on another date with me either.

I suppose I'm just not ready – but why should I be? I think because Todd has moved on, I feel like I should be able to too, but every now and then I think about what Brody said to Nikki, when she called him out for not moving on. When she said it was embarrassing that he wasn't over her – what did he say? Something about it being more embarrassing that she was over him so quickly? I hate to say it, but he's right. I shouldn't be so hard on myself, this break-up is so fresh, and Todd obviously had more time to get used to it than I did, given that he was the dumper.

It isn't ideal, to cry on a random man, but it's okay to be sad about this. It's normal to be sad about this. It takes time to get over someone, if you really cared about them, and that's the bottom line. I cared, he didn't.

It also isn't ideal to be going on a cruise with the wanker, but we move... It's just a week or so, the wedding will be over, and then I can get back to getting my life back on track, and I won't have to see Todd or Nikki while I do it.

I just need to get through this week without accident or incident or hijacking a lifeboat to row myself back to the UK.

I can do this. I can survive this.

Probably.

Maybe.

I just can't imagine it being plain sailing...

14

It's almost impossible to compute the size of the ship. The closer I get to it, the bigger it gets, and as I cross the bridge to the doorway, it seems almost endlessly, impossibly huge. Like a Tardis or Mary Poppins's bag.

I know, cruise ships are big, but it's bigger than I was expecting it to be. It's like a hotel – no, a resort on the water. I suppose Kelsey did say it had everything, and everything takes up a lot of space, but damn. It's funny because when she was listing the things it had on board I started to wonder if she was joking or if it really had them. A gym didn't feel beyond the realms of possibility but an outdoor cinema and a laser tag arena – come on! Is that true?

After check-in, which is somehow both high-tech and extremely chaotic (passport control in a tent outside the terminal is not as glam as I was expecting – nor did I think I would have to have my photo taken for my ID card, and the photographer has done me so, so dirty), I'm finally on board, in and around the actual glam, and now it's delivering.

The first thing that hits me is the scale of it all. There's a huge open atrium – a multistorey bad boy – with glass lifts zipping up and down and a massive staircase that puts the *Titanic* to shame... not that the *Titanic* should be the benchmark for anything boaty ever. There's a chandelier too, because of course there is, one so big it looks like it could sink us – although I'm sure you're not allowed to joke about sinking when you're actually at sea, so enough of that.

Everything feels so shiny and new. I don't think it is, but it has definitely been polished ahead of its new guests. We're not going to need a bigger boat, put it that way. I am going to need a map though, because this definitely feels like somewhere you could get lost quite easily.

I'm directed toward the lifts, to head up to my room – yes, up, something I'm very pleased to learn because I hate the idea of being under the water. I feel a little ropey about being at sea generally, I'm not sure why. There's just something about the ocean that makes it feel so full and yet so empty at the same time. Like there's so, so much to be scared of, it's the closest thing to finding yourself in a void... ugh, somehow that feels even scarier, and there are plenty of things to be scared of already, so my imagination needs to take a day off.

Looking at the map on the wall, I can see things like the spa, the pool – oh, there it is, laser tag, so Kelsey wasn't making things up. I'm looking forward to exploring the place. The dark, deep, merciless ocean aside, I do like the idea of having so much stuff under one roof – including a cabin of my own. I'm a little worried, seeing as though Emma messaged me and said this was the last cabin available, but I've gone upstairs to it, so how bad can it be?

Of all the things I expected to find when I open my cabin door – and there are a lot of things, given everything Kelsey's been saying about this boat – I might be looking at not only the one thing I didn't expect to find but my worst fucking nightmare too.

A bath in the middle of the room – amazing. A tiny window – not great, but I could live with it. Poseidon himself – you know what, I'd take it, he might actually be quite nice if he wasn't dicking with the weather.

Instead, sitting on the sofa, there's Todd and Nikki.

Nikki screams when she sees me. Actually screams. Like I just popped out of a coffin instead of walking through the door – a door I opened with my key card.

I just freeze in the doorway for a moment, keeping the door open behind me just in case I need to dash. Todd – ever the hero – jumps to his feet and sort of half-steps in front of her.

I look down at the key card in my hand, then at them, then at my key card again. What the hell is going on?

'She's stalking us,' Nikki cries out, grabbing on to Todd's arm for dramatic effect. 'She's crazy. Didn't I tell you that she was crazy? She's out to get me!'

'I... what?' is all I manage to say.

Todd holds up his hands as he approaches me slowly. I really resent being treated like a crazy lady because all I have done is walk into my own cabin.

'What are you doing here?' he asks me.

'This is my cabin,' I tell him, slowly and clearly. 'What are you doing here?'

'We had a message from Emma,' Todd explains. 'She said she had sorted us a suite, the last one available that could accommodate our situation.'

Our situation. Ha.

'I had the same message,' I tell him, frowning.

'Oh, God,' Nikki cries. 'Oh, God, no. Is that why there are two bedrooms?'

'There are two bedrooms?' I repeat in disbelief. Surely not...

'That's what I just said!' Nikki snaps, gesturing wildly like I'm a pigeon she's trying to frighten away from her chips.

Todd sighs.

'I think... given that we were all making so many changes, the only thing Emma could do was move us into the same room. A two-bedroom suite,' he says.

This is information I will absolutely keep to myself, but I do wonder if Emma had to put us all in here together, or if she thought it might be a fun way to get back at me for – let me check my notes – asking her to do her job.

It is nice in here. There's a big open-plan living space with big, squishy-looking sofas, a little kitchenette, and a balcony with a few chairs out there. There are two doors leading off either side of the suite, so presumably they are the two bedrooms. Thank God they're on opposite sides. The idea of sharing a wall with those two? I'd rather jump overboard.

'I guess we're just going to have to make this work,' I say, sighing as I finally close the door behind me. 'For Kelsey and Neil. We're all adults.'

'Ha!' Nikki snaps, flopping back down onto the sofa like a stroppy toddler. 'We're adults. You tackled me the last time you saw me.'

'I didn't tackle you,' I say through gritted teeth. 'I fell.'

'Fell into me,' she says, folding her arms.

'Enough. Jessa's right,' Todd snaps, causing Nikki to visibly recoil with horror. 'We just have to learn to share the space. We're all here for the same reason, our friends.'

'That's easy for you to say,' Nikki huffs. 'It's your bloody ex who's here, not mine.'

Right on cue, the door swings open again... and in walks Brody.

And then there were four.

He's wearing one of his trademark tight t-shirts (or maybe they're just t-shirts, but his muscles stretch them out) and he's got what looks like a beer, something he's carrying like a prop, to show just how cool he is.

When he sees the three of us all together, staring back at him, he bursts into a fit of laughs.

'Oh, mate, what is going on here?' he asks through a grin.

'What are you doing here?' Todd snaps, puffing up his chest in a way that is frankly embarrassing.

'This is my room,' Brody says. 'What are you doing here?'

'This is our room,' I tell him – meaning mine, Todd's and Nikki's too, but Nikki misunderstands me and flies off the handle.

'Oh my God. Are you two sharing a room together?' she says, gesturing between me and Brody, her jaw briefly hanging in disbelief. 'Seriously? I know you spent the night together at the wedding but are you, like, a proper couple now?'

I glance at Brody. I know, I misled people into thinking we had slept together, and I probably shouldn't have done so without telling Brody, but this is different. This is a much bigger lie.

He glances at me and I can see the mischief in his eyes. Oh, God...

'Yes,' Brody says smoothly, without missing a beat.

I try not to react in any way but I feel like steam might be about to shoot out of my ears.

'So you're in that bedroom,' Nikki says, pointing. 'And we're in that one. And we all have to share this suite?'

'Erm, yeah, I guess so,' I reply as casually as I can.

'I can't believe you're together,' Todd mutters, clearly deeply unhappy about it.

'Well, you pushed us together,' I tell him sweetly. 'At the wedding. So thank you. Both of you.'

Brody glances at me again, one eyebrow raised like he's trying to decide whether he's impressed or bemused or what. I can't tell if I'm enjoying this or freaking out. Maybe it's a bit of both.

I jump as a voice booms through the room – presumably from a speaker somewhere – interrupting our epically awkward moment for us.

'Ladies and gentlemen, please report to your designated muster stations for the mandatory safety drill.'

'Come on, Nikki, let's go,' Todd says as he offers her his hand.

'This is literally horrendous,' she tells him – not at all in hushed tones.

Brody and I hang back a second, until it's just the two of us.

'Erm, right... so what exactly is happening?' Brody asks me, still oh-so cool about it.

'It would seem that, given our situation, the wedding planner has had to shove us all in here, to figure out sleeping arrangements for ourselves,' I inform him.

'How thoughtful of her,' he replies. 'I had to speak to her – she didn't seem like a happy person.'

'No, she didn't, did she?' I reply. 'I wasn't expecting to see you here. Not just in this suite – at the wedding. I didn't connect the dots.'

'I'm the best man,' he says, holding his hands out, ta-da style.

'Yeah, in hindsight, I remember Kelsey saying Neil's best man was one of his old friends,' I reply. 'Because I was surprised it wasn't...'

'Todd?' he replies. 'Not surprised now, are you? He's a tool, I'm a delight.'

I can't help but laugh, just a little.

'So we're sharing a room?' he checks.

'Unless we get off the ship,' I reply.

'There's no getting off now,' he replies. 'I was one of the last to board. They've shut the door or whatever. No turning back now.'

'Then yep, we're sharing a room,' I tell him.

'Unless we go boys in one, girls in another,' he suggests – presumably joking.

'I'd sooner swim back to shore,' I reply. 'So, you're just down for this? This whole weird situation, telling people we're a couple, sharing a room – and sharing a living space with our exes. You're the kind of guy who just puts his name down for shit like that?'

'Well, I didn't want to embarrass my girlfriend in front of her ex,' he jokes. 'And you didn't seem like you weren't up for it – for pretending, I mean.'

'Yeah, obviously, because I don't want to look like a loser in front of them,' I reply. 'Not because I'm so keen to share a room with you again.'

'You could have fooled me,' he replies.

God, he's infuriating. He strolls to the kitchenette like he owns the place, running his hand over the sleek worktops.

'You started this,' he tells me.

'Erm, how do you reckon?' I reply.

'Showing up for breakfast in my clothes was always going to get tongues wagging,' he says.

'You gave me the clothes,' I snap back.

'Because you didn't have any,' he replies. 'It's not my fault people think we slept together.'

I guess I didn't help put that rumour to bed.

'No one is going to believe I'd date someone like you,' I tell him, not meaning it to come out as offensively as it does.

'Ouch,' he replies with a chuckle. 'Why not? I'm a catch.'

'Crabs are a catch,' I reply. 'I just mean... you're very... I'm more... I don't know.'

Brody leans against the counter, his arms folded, looking way too entertained by all of this. At least he's decided not to take any offence.

'I mean, it would be sort of fun, right?' he says. 'Our exes are here, they're together, that sucks. Don't you want to mess with them? Us just being in that room is going to ruin their whole trip.'

I laugh.

'That does sound nice,' I reply.

'It sounds really nice,' he agrees. 'And I'm sure we can be believable. We can pretend to love each other. Nikki was really good at it, with me, so I'm just going to channel her.'

I laugh, just a little. It's interesting to see Brody's vulnerable side for a second. And I suppose we are in the same boat.

'So we're madly in love?' I check.

'Deeply,' he replies. 'And if they don't buy that, well, we'll just say it's a sex thing.'

'Will they really believe that?'

'They will if they see me,' he jokes – at least I think he's joking.

'How far are we willing to take this?' I ask.

'How far are you willing to go?' he replies as he approaches me.

The door beeps – a telltale sign that someone is about to open it – so Brody pushes me back on the sofa and throws himself on top of me.

'Oh my God,' Todd blurts. 'I forgot my ID card. If you're going to do that can you at least do it in your room? We all have to sit on those sofas.'

He grabs his card from the coffee table and leaves again.

'See, easy-peasy,' Brody says with a laugh.

He's still lying on top of me, his face inches from mine, the weight of his body pressing down on me like a seriously sexy weighted blanket.

And then he jumps to his feet, switching it off, just like that.

Wow, maybe we can do this.

'You are possibly enjoying this way too much,' I say, standing up, smoothing out the creases in my outfit.

'Maybe,' he replies. 'We'll see.'

'We're not seriously doing this, are we?' I say again, giving him one last out.

'We have to,' he says with a shrug. 'Just like we have to go do this safety bullshit.'

'Remind me not to rely on you in an emergency,' I tell him as we head for the door.

Okay, so this feels like going completely overboard – no pun intended, I promise – but what else can I do? We're just going to have to give it a go.

Sadly there's no safety drill for emergencies like this one though.

15

I know that the ship has multiple dining rooms but this one that we're walking through now is exactly what I think of when I imagine a cruise ship dining room. Elegant as hell, high ceilings, chandeliers, white tablecloths with polished cutlery. I thought it sounded silly, when I heard you had to dress for dinner here, but now that I'm in it I would feel so out of place in anything but my finery – well, my fine-ish-ery.

Brody has scrubbed up really well, in his black suit, his unruly hair slicked into something neat for the occasion. All of the men in here are wearing dinner jackets – even the waitstaff. There's a bloody string quartet in the corner, which is waaaay too *Titanic* for my liking, but oh-so fancy at the same time.

The air smells like wine and food and money – not literally like coins, just, like, expense. Expensive booze, expensive food, expensive perfumes and aftershaves. God, I hope the food is as nice as everything else is leading me to believe.

We're meeting Kelsey and Neil, Al and Kira, and Todd and Nikki. I suppose it was always going to be the eight of us at the table, before we went all wife-swap. Kira is a friend of mine and

Kelsey's – she's Kelsey's other bridesmaid – and Al and Neil are friends. Brody is friends with them both, and I guess Todd knows him, but Nikki has never been a part of our group. I guess she was in the mix, as Brody's girlfriend, and now as Todd's – otherwise she wouldn't even be here. I'm not even sure Todd would have a seat at the table, had he not been with me for the last year or so.

At least I have friends here, real friends, unlike Nikki. I might not have a boyfriend but I do feel secretly glad that I have Brody here by my side, my bodyguard – I'm literally wearing him like armour right now. I just feel like while we're pretending to be together he's like a shield for me, someone who – just by standing next to me – shows people that I'm over it, and I'm doing well, and I'm moving on. I'm unflappable – even if I am flapping on the inside.

It's just such a mess, and I suppose it's only going to get messier before it gets better – sort of like when you empty the contents of your wardrobe, to tidy it, only to make your room look like a bomb has hit it. Take tonight, for example. Not only do we have to navigate convincing our friends that we're the hot new couple on the scene (hopefully stealing Todd and Nikki's thunder) but we still need to have a conversation about sleeping arrangements. There's only one bed in our room, because of course there is, so I'm not sure what we're going to do about that one. A problem for future Jessa, let's leave it at that.

I glance at Brody as we walk arm in arm. He looks so chilled out, like he was born to be here, and super composed. Whereas I am bricking it about putting on a show for my best friends, because surely they can see right through me, especially Kelsey. You would think there was no way I could convince her I was in love when I wasn't.

'You look... smug,' I mutter as we approach the table.

He just laughs.

'You look... terrified,' he replies. 'And like you're punching.'

'That's because I am,' I tell him. 'Terrified, I mean. Not punching.'

I know he's just saying it to wind me up, because exchanging insults is apparently our thing now, but I will be punching if he doesn't knock it off.

'Just try to relax,' he says, giving my arm a bit of a squeeze. 'It'll be easy. We'll just ad-lib some bullshit, they'll lap it up.'

I whip my head around to face him.

'Oh my God, no, that's an awful plan,' I tell him. 'Some bullshit isn't going to cut it. just leave the talking to me, yeah?'

'But I'm so good at it,' he says with a playful pout.

'You're really not,' I reply. 'Quality, not quantity.'

Brody just shakes his head.

We're nearly at the table. Kelsey has spotted us, she's waving us over, and Neil is smiling beside her. Al's already got his jacket off, so no surprises there, and Kira's on the wine already. And then there's them. Todd and Nikki. Ugh. I still can't believe they're here, together, and I'm having to put up with them.

Nikki is wearing a red silky dress that is hugging her like it loves her. Her body is probably as close to perfect as a person can get, so it's no surprise she has men falling at her feet. Brody is perfectly chiselled too, they make sense together. Not me though. Nikki looks like she could model for Versace. I look like the lass from the logo.

We all exchange hellos as Brody and I reach our table. He steps forward to pull my chair out for me, tucking it in as I sit down. Okay, so maybe he's not so bad at this stuff after all.

'Look at you two!' Kelsey says, smiling widely. 'I can't believe it.'

'None of us can,' Nikki chimes in.

I ignore her.

Todd isn't saying much. He's staring down at his whisky, swirling it like the instructions for how to deal with this situation might be lurking in the bottom of the glass.

I notice Kelsey grinning at me from across the table. It makes me happy and sad to see that she looks so, so happy for me. I'll bet she has a lot of questions, like why didn't I tell her that Brody and I were a thing, and while the answer is quite obviously that the reason I didn't tell her is because it's not true, I need to make her believe it, just for now, just until the wedding of her dreams is over. Then Brody and I can break up, I'll say he cheated on me, or had super gonorrhoea, or got super gonorrhoea while he was cheating on me – bottom line, it will be his fault, because while he might look like more of a catch on paper, he also looks like the one more likely to cheat. As far as I'm concerned, he's got 'dump me' written all over him. I'm not surprised Nikki ditched him for Todd – I was going to say sweet, dependable Todd, but he wasn't fucking sweet or dependable for me in the end. Perhaps he'll do better with her.

'So... this is new,' Kira says, eyeing the two of us over the top of her wine glass.

'So is that,' Al adds, jerking his head towards Todd and Nikki as he smirks to himself.

Kira jabs him in the ribs with her elbow, hard. He doesn't look like he even feels it.

Brody smiles like he's enjoying this far too much.

'Well, we just hit it off,' he says casually. 'At your wedding, actually. We've been inseparable ever since, haven't we, princess?'

Ugh, I wish he wouldn't call me princess. I know, it sounds sweet, and it's probably good for the act, but I know it's him teasing me over the stupid valet parking thing. What can I call him that he'll hate just as much?

'Yep, inseparable,' I reply.

'In all ways,' he announces.

'Okay, boo, they don't need to hear about that,' I say, placing a hand on his arm, squeezing it just hard enough to tell him to cool it on that front for now.

'I find that hard to believe,' Nikki chimes in.

'Do you though?' Brody replies, his dimples deepening as he tries to stifle his smile.

'That you're so serious, so quickly,' she adds.

I tilt my head and smile.

'Well, it's only a week less than you and Todd have been together,' I point out, saying it like I really do believe that true love can take hold in a week or two.

Except I don't. Not at all. There is just no way that Todd and Nikki got together after they broke up with me and Brody. That would be wild, to figure it out in a couple of weeks, fresh out of their perfectly synchronised break-ups. Come on!

'Go on then, what could you two possibly have in common?' Todd asks, folding his arms as he leans back in his chair. 'You hate sport.'

'So what?' I reply, shrugging it off.

'So I didn't think you'd ever date a professional sportsman,' Todd says.

I can't help but turn to look at Brody because I obviously didn't know that about him. He gives me a wink.

'I mean, who wouldn't want to date a professional sportsman?' I say, turning back to Todd, keeping my game face on.

'I'm sure Brody won't mind me saying this,' Nikki pipes up, 'given how we've all moved on... but he's the self-proclaimed bad boy of cricket.'

'No, the press call me that,' Brody corrects her.

Can that even be a thing? I thought cricketers were sensible and posh. I definitely didn't think it had bad boys.

'The point is...' Nikki continues, looking me in the eye now. '... he'll never settle down. That's why we broke up.'

'Okay, come on,' Kelsey says quickly, nipping it in the bud. 'It doesn't matter, does it? We're all adults here. We can do what we want.'

I need to say something, to speak up for myself, to defend my man, to take control of the situation. And I know just the thing.

'Maybe he was just waiting for the right girl,' I suggest as I straighten up my cutlery.

I daren't even look at Nikki. I'll bet she's furious. Serves her right though – both of them – because supposedly they've moved on, so why is it me and Brody who are the main topic of conversation?

'And the right girl is right here,' Brody adds, reaching out to take my hand. 'And we have loads in common. Like, the fact that you come to the gym with me every morning without fail. The couple that trains together stays together, don't they?'

He smiles at me. I can see the mischief behind his eyes. We're in the thick of it, thinking on our feet, barely keeping it together and he's using it as an opportunity to mess with me. Well, two can play at that game.

'I love working up a sweat with you,' I reply to him. 'And I love how in touch with your feminine side you are with me. We love a spa treatment, don't we? We're pretty much going to live in the ship spa, aren't we? Getting all kinds of treatments together.'

'Brody... in a spa...' Nikki says in disbelief.

'All right, all right, their relationship is their business, let's just get back to dinner,' Neil says. 'Shouldn't we be talking about us, if we're talking about anyone?'

He laughs to let us know he's sort of joking. He's not wrong though.

'Well, just to let you all know, our plan while we're aboard is to split our time between our family and our friends,' Kelsey informs us. 'That way, when we get to Sicily, we don't feel guilty about not spending enough time with either group.'

There aren't many people who will be at the wedding actually on the cruise, this is just for their family, their close friends... and Todd and Nikki, I guess.

'Well, I know me and this little firecracker can keep ourselves entertained the rest of the time,' Brody says, leaning over to kiss me on the cheek.

'Oh, you bet, big boy,' I reply as I ruffle his hair.

Brody smiles as he straightens his hair up again. He won't have liked that.

It's a strange game we're playing: trying so desperately to pretend we're in love to everyone but each other. At the same time, desperately trying to make clear that we don't even like each other really.

And then there is everyone at the table, every last one of them sitting in silence, staring at us, like they can't quite figure us out. Perhaps we'll have to try harder, to lean more into to the love side of our love/hate relationship, but only for our audience, of course.

So long as people believe we're in love, I don't care if they think it's weird. We're doing it, the show is on the road, and it's working. Kelsey seems happy, which is what I care about more than anything, and Todd and Nikki seem miserable. I know, petty of me, but a little bit of bitterness keeps you young. And I would be lying if I said it wasn't fun, because it really is, even pretending with a himbo like Brody, it feels dangerous, kind of bonkers, but so, so much fun.

I just need to get through the next week, and I'll deal with the fallout later when I'm back on dry land.

I just need to keep up the act... and probably never call anyone 'big boy' again.

16

I'm standing here with Brody, at the foot of the bed, the two of us staring at it like we're waiting for some kind of divine intervention, or some act of God that either tells us what we need to do, or sinks the ship so that it no longer matters.

'So...' I say as I chew on my fingernail. 'This is... problematic.'

Brody is standing next to me with his hands on his hips, surveying the bed, not seeming as stressed about this as I am, to be honest with you.

'Is it really though?' he replies.

'Yes, Brody, it is. It absolutely is,' I reply. 'There is one bed. One. And two of us. Two.'

'As impressed as I am with your counting – very good for a big girl—'

'A big girl?' I snap back.

'No, no,' he insists. 'Give over. Not like that. I was implying you were acting like a child and...'

My face slips into a smile.

'Oh, okay, you're having me on, hilarious,' he replies. 'But let the record state that I have just been the mature one not once but twice.'

'Doubt,' I say with a snort.

'I'm suggesting we share the bed, like adults, because this isn't a romance movie,' he says slowly, patronisingly even.

'Yeah, and don't I know it,' I reply. 'Because if it were you would be way more charming and, to be honest with you, playing a much sexier sport like American football or hockey.'

'Well, when they shoot the American remake, I'm sure they'll do that,' he replies.

'All of this to say, I am not sharing a bed with you, mate,' I tell him. 'Not a chance. I'd sooner sleep on the balcony.'

'Well, that would solve the problem,' he jokes. 'Ah, come on, I don't snore... that much.'

'I don't care if you don't breathe,' I tell him. 'No way. I'm not joining what is clearly a long list of women who can say they've shared a bed with the "bad boy of cricket".'

Brody grins like I just gave him a present.

'You googled me,' he says.

'I did not,' I'm quick to reply.

'You did – was it when you went to the toilet for fifteen minutes?'

Oh, he's loving this.

'Ew, you were timing me?'

'Erm, I'm just being a supportive boyfriend,' he says with a shrug.

Okay, if I'm being honest with you, I did actually go to the toilet to google him. I was like Sherlock Holmes with an iPhone.

I didn't have much time – well, fifteen minutes, I guess – but I skim-read as much as I could. I had a peep at his Instagram and, oh boy, that thing is a thirst trap. I felt like I needed a cold shower and a cigarette after looking at all his muscle-flexing photos – and I don't even smoke.

I also looked over as many articles as I could and, as far as I could tell, there are far more about him being the 'bad boy of cricket' than about him actually playing the sport. Then again, the algo is probably more likely to serve me trashy tabloids than sports news. He looks like fun, I'll give him that. If you're a bottle of spirits or a hot blonde, you're in trouble when Brody Ryan is in town. I did learn that he doesn't only play for Yorkshire, he plays for England too, so he must be good, right?

Brody tips his head one way, then the other.

'You know what, I think it's one of those beds where it's two zipped together, to make one really big one,' he says.

'Really?' I reply, my voice full of hope and optimism.

'Yeah, the headboard looks like it separates, I reckon I can pull them apart,' he tells me.

He looks like he could pull the wall apart, so there's that.

'Wouldn't that be the answer to all of our problems,' I say with a sigh.

'Maybe one of them,' he says with a laugh as he starts unbuttoning his shirt.

'You're as bad as Al,' I tease him.

'It's hard to be flexible in a shirt,' he replies. 'Close your eyes if it offends you.'

My worry is that it doesn't offend me, quite the opposite.

Brody gets right to it, pulling at the beds, trying to separate them. He's right, it does look like the base should separate, but it's not giving up without a fight. He grunts and groans, the headboards banging against the wall as he tries to shake them apart, but still they don't budge.

'Harder,' I call out helpfully. 'You're almost there...'

'I'm... I'm...'

'Come on,' I say, just in case my encouragement is helping. 'Show it who's boss.'

Brody pulls on the headboard and it looks like it might be moving but then it snaps back to the wall, trapping Brody's finger in the process.

I can't help but scream, imagining it being much worse than it is.

'Ugh!' he shouts, shaking his hand, like he's trying to flick the pain off, as if it's water and the hand dryer isn't working. 'Baby,' he teases me for screaming.

'Oh, you're so hard,' I reply, rolling my eyes, because that must have hurt him, even if he's trying to style it out like it didn't.

He starts again, pushing, pulling, grunting, groaning – nothing. He's even breaking a sweat now.

'Come on, Ryan, put your back into it,' I call out. Okay, yeah, now I'm just trying to annoy him.

He flops backwards onto the bed, trying to catch his breath.

'You know what, I think it's bolted together,' he tells me, his voice quiet now. 'And to the floor or the wall or something – maybe it's a cruise ship safety thing.'

'Yeah, maybe,' I say, sitting down on the bed next to him. 'You tried.'

I give him a patronising pat on his sticky, sweaty abs. My God, they're rock solid.

'You know... there is a plan B,' I tell him, nodding towards the fancy free-standing bath in our room.

Brody lifts his head up just enough to look before flopping back down.

'Be my guest,' he tells me.

'Oh, no, no, no, dear boyfriend,' I reply. 'I already took the bath last time, remember? It's your turn tonight.'

'A princess, as always,' he replies. 'Tell you what. We'll take it in turns. I'll sleep in it tonight, you can take it tomorrow night – you'll be begging to get in bed with me.'

'It seems like no one has to beg to get in bed with you,' I tease.

'Yeah, you definitely googled me,' he says – to himself, I think.

I'm not even going to dignify that with a response.

'Right,' he says, pulling himself to his feet. 'I'm going to nab some cushions from the sofa, that might help. At least you were drunk when you slept in the bath...'

Again, I'm saying nothing. I just sit there and watch as he walks, shirtless, into the living room.

'Oh, hi,' he says, so I'm guessing Todd and/or Nikki is in there. 'I'm just grabbing some cushions – I'm doing a bit of overambitious exercising. I'll bring them back in the morning.'

Silence.

He comes back in, cushions in his arms, and closes the door behind him.

'Well, they look awkward as hell, so our little performance at dinner must have been convincing,' he says.

'I guess so,' I reply.

He starts chucking cushions into the bath, almost filling it, to the point where I'm not sure his muscular frame will fit in there too but he just about makes it work.

'Chuck me a pillow from the bed, will you,' he says.

I grab one and carry it to him.

'I'll give it a go tonight, seeing as though you asked so nicely,' he says sarcastically. 'But I guarantee you're not going to want to sleep in here. Not a chance. You'll be trying to seduce me, so that you can get in bed with me, I can see it now.'

'Oh, I highly, highly doubt it,' I tell him. 'I'd sooner get in with Todd and Nikki.'

'Ouch,' he says, laughing it off.

Nothing ever seems to really rattle him.

I head into the bathroom to get ready for bed, shutting the door behind me before looking at myself in the mirror.

What are you doing, Jessa, huh? What do you think is happening here? What do you think is going to happen?

Honestly? I have no idea. I flip back and forth between thinking this is the best idea anyone has ever had and this is a terrible, terrible plan. A plan where someone is going to get hurt, and I'm worried it's going to be me.

The thing is though, I already have been hurt, by Todd, and now I'm just here playing the hand I've been dealt, and my teammate is Brody Ryan. *The* Brody Ryan, it turns out. He's handsome, jacked, charming in his own way, he's got a good job and an even better sense of humour... but I know his type and I could never fall for someone like that. Still, all the better to have a fake relationship with him, to use him to make Todd regret breaking up with me – and to make Nikki wish she'd never let Brody go. Honestly, I really feel like those two deserve each other.

So long as I don't fall for 'the bad boy of cricket' (a concept that is still so hilarious to me) I'll be okay. And maybe after this wedding, I really won't ever have to see him again... I'm just going to have to see way, way more of him before that can happen.

17

I can't believe people actually get up early and go to the gym on purpose.

Brody woke me up at 7 a.m. – yes, 7 a.m. – to visit the ship's gym with him.

I told him to piss off, obviously, and rolled over to try to go back to sleep, but he reminded me that we're a couple who do everything together, including the gym – what if someone saw him there without me, they might think there was trouble in paradise already... I wasn't buying it but then he said that at some point I was probably going to ask him to do something he didn't want to do, and that he wouldn't say yes – not unless I made the same effort.

So here I am, in the gym, but as the saying goes: you can lead a girl to the gym, but you can't make her exercise. So I'm currently sitting on an exercise bike, next to Brody, not pedalling – just using it as a chair, occasionally taking my pulse, messing with the controls for no reason other than pure boredom...

It's strange because while it is super luxury in here – to me at least – it also looks like a torture chamber. Things with straps and weights and machines that look like they encase your body – like something nightmarish from a sci-fi movie. Or maybe I just have an unhealthy relationship with being healthy.

I find it absolutely fascinating that one of the walls is entirely covered with mirrors, so you can watch yourself working out presumably. Jesus Christ, I think if I saw myself huffing and puffing on a treadmill I would probably never want to leave the house again.

At least it's clean and nice, the music is chill, and it's not that busy. Obviously I would rather be in my bed, but it could always be worse.

Brody is on a mat, doing stretches which I don't think I could do if I tried. He makes them look easy, although he does breathe heavily now and then.

'What exactly do you get out of this?' I ask him.

His head lifts slightly.

'Well, my back is killing me, because someone made me sleep in a bath last night, so I'm trying to loosen it up,' he replies.

'No, I mean coming to the gym, generally, every day…'

He rolls onto his side, his head propped up on one hand.

'For my job, obviously,' he replies. 'And because I enjoy it.'

'But isn't cricket the one where you just stand around?' I check. 'And have a tea break?'

'Do you think we just smash packets of custard creams in the dressing rooms?' he asks.

'Now that sounds like fun,' I say.

Brody gives me a look. I don't know, I might be finally winding him up. Good, because I'm trying really hard. That'll teach him, bringing me to a gym in the early hours.

'You really think cricket is just standing still?' he asks me.

'That's what it looks like…'

'I'm a bowler,' he tells me, sitting up properly now. 'You have to be fit and strong.'

'To chuck a ball?' I narrow my eyes.

'Jessa, some fast bowlers exceed ninety miles an hour – can you even imagine?'

Oh, yeah, this is definitely working.

'Can you?' I ask.

'I'm medium-fast,' he tells me.

I'll be honest with you, I don't really know what that means, but I have the perfect reply.

'So, you're telling me there's room for improvement,' I reason. 'No wonder you're in the gym every day.'

Brody stares at me, his head cocked, a faint smirk on his lips like he can't decide if he's offended or entertained.

'All right then, princess, impress me,' he says. 'What do you do for work? Assuming you're a working royal...'

I fuss with the buttons on the exercise bike. One of them turns on the fan, blowing cool air in my face.

'I do high-end property staging,' I tell him.

'What's that when it's at home?' he asks.

'When people are selling their houses, I go in and stage them,' I explain. 'I dress them up to look their best. Set the scene. Help them to get the most out of the place to attract the right kind of buyer.'

'What does that even mean?' he asks, one eyebrow raised – almost sceptically.

'Sometimes I bring furniture, sometimes it's more like décor,' I tell him. 'It's all about telling a story, selling a lifestyle to potential buyers.'

'Do they get to keep the furniture?' he asks.

'No, it's just for staging,' I reply. 'Think of it like a set.'

He lets out a laugh and lies back down, arms stretched behind his head.

'That's not a real job,' he concludes.

'Erm, it is,' I correct him.

'It's literally playing house in other people's houses,' he points out.

'Says the man who does PE in other people's fields,' I clap back.

'Fair play,' he says, smiling to himself. 'As long as we're both happy, eh?'

I guess he's right.

And I am – happy with my job, at least. I love it. Transforming spaces, making them what people want them to be, telling a story. Perhaps that's why I'm getting a kick out of faking it with Brody, it's just a different sort of staging.

Sort of like me sitting here, in the gym, not working out. Sometimes how things look matters much more than how they are.

At least that's what I'm telling myself anyway.

18

Despite getting up early this morning for what turned out to be a sparring session in the gym, I actually feel great, and I think it might be all thanks to the bed in our suite. Even after Brody seemingly beat the hell out of it, I think it only made it comfier, like beating pillows or tenderising meat.

I'll never understand why people say they slept like a baby because I remember what my little brother was like when he was a baby and he screamed all night long. Really, going off what it was like in my family home, a more appropriate way of saying I had an amazing, uninterrupted night of sleep would be to say: I slept like a dad.

The bed was great, the pillows perfectly plump, the sheets felt so good on my skin. And, best of all, I didn't have to share it. I could stretch out, move to the cool side, starfish – the works. I could almost feel sorry for poor Brody, after his night in the bath, but I doubt he'd feel sorry for me, so screw him.

'My spine is ruined,' he groans for the – I don't know – eighth or ninth time, dragging his feet as we hit up the breakfast buffet.

'Completely destroyed. I'm an athlete, Jessa. I have to take care of my body.'

I glance down at his plate and notice that he's got four croissants on it.

'Then why are you eating four croissants?' I ask, deadpan.

'For energy,' he replies. 'And for morale.'

I've been there, I can't say anything about that. In fact, maybe I need more croissants.

You really can't beat a breakfast buffet, can you? Even the bad ones struggle to be truly terrible, because there's always something good to have for breakfast, even if it's just a tiny box of cereal in a hotel followed by toast that you get to feed through that fun little conveyor belt toaster yourself.

Here is a double win though because it's not just a breakfast buffet, it's an incredible breakfast buffet, with everything you could possibly want – and the best version of it at that.

They even have a chef, behind a serving hatch, who is constantly replenishing the hot items, making sure they stay warm, and cooking the eggs to order which is great, because I love to dip my toast in my egg – like a child.

I load up my plate with enough fruit and yogurt to justify the unhealthy items I have, whereas for Brody it's all protein – and his pile of mood-boosting pastries, of course.

Our plates piled suitably high, we look for somewhere to sit. We're supposed to be meeting Kelsey, Neil and the gang to make a plan for today. I wonder what they'll have in store for us. Not that I don't want to hang out with them, but I am looking forward to exploring more of the ship on my own – the fun stuff, not the gym.

'I don't think they're here yet,' Brody says. 'But Nikki and Todd are, and they've seen us.'

He nods towards their table and, yep, they've definitely spotted us.

'Ugh, do we have to join them?' I check. 'Can't we at least wait for Kelsey and Neil, or Al and Kira – anyone, just to not be alone with them.'

'Nah, we should sit with them, show them how unbothered we are,' he replies. 'If we retreat now, they'll realise.'

'Or they'll think that we just don't like them,' I reply.

'Which I would define as being bothered,' he says. 'Whereas joining them means we're too wrapped up in ourselves to even think of them.'

I follow his lead but, honestly, I think I'd probably sooner go back to the gym.

We make our way over, all smiles, and take our seats opposite them.

'Morning,' I say brightly.

'Good morning,' Brody adds, moaning theatrically as he sits down. I don't even think his back is that bad, I think he's trying to psych me out, because I'll be sleeping in there tonight.

Nikki scowls at him.

'Rough night,' he tells them, just in case they were wondering – I'm sure they weren't.

'Yeah, well, we're not surprised,' Nikki replies, clearly annoyed about something.

'Yep, we heard,' Todd replies. 'Loud and clear.'

'You heard what?' I ask, no idea what they're on about.

Todd clears his throat awkwardly.

'We heard you, last night, after dinner,' he says. 'In fact, I need to talk to you both about it, because you were being incredibly disrespectful.'

'What?' I reply. 'Why? What are you on about?'

I'm sure there is a more polite way to ask, but it's Todd, and I'm not up for his riddles today.

'We heard you. In your room,' he says, leaning in, lowering his voice.

'You... what?'

I turn to Brody and notice that he's sniggering. What am I missing here?

'Princess, they heard us, in our room, last night... our bed activities... y'know?' Brody prompts me.

Oh, God, okay, I'm there. He heard us moving the bed except, from the look on his face – on both his and Nikki's faces – they clearly think they heard us having sex, which... yeah, fair enough, the banging, the grunting, the things we were saying. I'm pretty sure I was saying 'harder' quite a lot – I even think I told Brody to 'destroy it' at some point.

My instinct is to set them straight, but this doesn't exactly hurt the story we're trying to tell, does it? I never would have had the guts to intentionally fake having sex with Brody but, well, if I've done it by accident, we'll call that a win. And it is a win, just looking at their faces, how horrified they are...

'So gross,' Nikki says. 'Honestly, you're just showing off at this point.'

Brody just shrugs it off with a grin.

'That was just the warm-up,' he says.

'Well, if you can save the main event until we're not sharing a suite,' Todd suggests. 'You two certainly wouldn't like it, if we were doing the same.'

Bold of Todd to think he could even put in a performance half as good (or half as long, to be honest with you) as Brody sounded last night.

Kelsey arrives just in time to save us from our awkward moment, setting her bowl of fruit and granola down on the table.

'I left Neil over by the pancakes,' she says, sitting down beside me. 'Frankly, it was embarrassing, the number of pancakes he was trying to fit on one plate. If he looked at me with as much love and adoration as he does pancakes, we might actually stay married forever.'

I laugh.

'A man after my own heart,' Brody says. 'Also, I didn't notice there were pancakes, so that's my breakfast dessert sorted.'

'How do you eat so much and stay in such good shape?' Kelsey asks him.

'Ah, I work up a sweat, don't I, Jessa?' he says, pulling the end off a croissant and popping it in his mouth.

Kelsey looks at me and smiles.

'We went to the gym this morning,' I tell her.

'Then, truly, marry the man,' Kelsey replies. 'I can't even get you to walk past a gym.'

'Because I'll probably sign up out of guilt and then never go,' I reply.

'That was always your problem, committing to things,' Todd chimes in.

'Yes, that was my problem, Todd, of course, I couldn't commit to things,' I say sarcastically.

'Did you all sleep well?' Kelsey asks.

'Not really,' Todd says.

'No, we have noisy neighbours,' Nikki adds.

Thankfully they don't tell Kelsey that their noisy neighbours are me and Brody.

'What about you, Brody, you look a little uncomfortable,' Kelsey says.

'Yeah, no, I'm okay, just... an awkward position, I think,' he tells her.

'Oh, aye, I've heard that one before,' Kelsey jokes. 'Jessa, you need to lay off the awkward positions, you'll wear him out.'

I practically choke on my orange juice.

'Or at the very least, don't break him until after the wedding,' she adds.

'I'll protect myself at all costs,' Brody tells her playfully. 'No harm will come to me.'

'Says the man on his third croissant,' I tease.

'It sounds like he's earned them,' Kelsey replies.

'Can we please stop talking about... such things at the breakfast table,' Nikki insists. 'You're putting me off my banana.'

There is such an easy joke to make there but thankfully I'm above it.

'So, what's on the agenda today?' Brody asks, changing the subject. 'Have you got loads of fun wedding party activities for us?'

'The wedding-related fun starts in a couple of days,' Kelsey replies. 'And it's a surprise but I'm pretty sure you'll all love it.'

God, I hope it's a good one, I can't take any more bad ones. The thing is, Kelsey is definitely a wedding person, she loves everything about them, all of the traditions and the formalities. If I get married – and yeah, it feels like something that will never happen now, thanks for reminding me – I can't imagine wanting all of these things. I'm not really into... the pomp, shall we say. The flowers, the detailed dress codes, the frankly archaic tradition of tossing the bouquet into a pile of single girls – although maybe I only hate that one after I was (a) the only single girl at Al and Kira's wedding and (b) that whole mess with Nikki, where she is adamant I rugby-tackled her. Ha, as if I could ever be so sporty.

I don't know, for me, when it comes to weddings I just like the idea of having a party, a celebration with the people I love the most. I'd probably wear trainers, because as much as I love a heel I would want to enjoy running around talking to everyone, dancing, not falling over or into fountains – and doing so without bright red, achy, blistered feet. For the food, do you know what, if I could get one of those pizza trucks – or five even, all churning out pizzas – and an ice cream van for dessert, how cool would that be? Of course, not only would I need a man who shared my vision for a party that sort of sounds like a kid's eleventh birthday party, but I would also need to find a man who would, y'know, marry me generally, and that sounds equally as hard.

For now I'll have to settle for attending my friends' weddings – and at least it will give me time to get more ideas of what I like, or what I really, really don't like. The day my wedding has a fruit cake will be a cold day in hell, that's for sure.

'What did you have in mind for today?' I ask, tearing myself away from my deluded daydreams.

'We thought a day by the pool might be nice,' she replies. 'They've got games, sports stuff – that kind of thing. But you can just sit and chill if you don't want to do anything sportsy.'

I open my mouth, to say she knows me so well, only for Brody to get in there first.

'We love sports, don't we, princess,' he says as he gives my shoulder a squeeze.

'Oh my God, can't get enough,' I reply.

'Wow, you really are a changed woman,' Kelsey replies.

'Hmm, are you?' Todd adds almost suspiciously.

'Well, it will be fun, no matter who does what,' Kelsey says. 'And there's no pressure.'

'I don't usually like games,' Nikki pipes up. 'But when I do play, I don't mess around. I'm actually really good at playing games.'

Maybe it's me, perhaps I'm paranoid, but that statement really felt like it was aimed at me, and I don't think she was talking about pool games.

Well, two can play at that game (or should that be four?). I'm pretty good at playing games too, and so is Brody, if the internet is anything to go by.

I just smile sweetly before carrying on with my breakfast.

Brody reaches under the table and gives my leg a reassuring squeeze. At first I assume he's doing it for our audience, but no one can actually see under the table, so I guess he really is just doing it to reassure me.

I tell you what, I'll feel a lot better playing games knowing he's on my team. How can we lose?

19

It isn't hard to understand how the cruise ship has so much going on inside – it's huge – but I still can't get my head around the vast outside spaces too.

Take this pool (and just this pool, because there are several!), for example. We're outside, by the large outdoor pool, and if you couldn't smell the sea air you could forget you were even on a boat, it's got more of a vibe of a luxury resort. To be honest, it just feels like being on the coast, at a stunning hotel – aside from the fact that it's quite a slow way to travel, I actually prefer it to flying, because it makes the journey part of the destination too. Not that I can afford these things, or have the time to take long trips, but you take my point.

I should focus on the here and now, rather than getting a head start on my holiday hangover.

The pool is big, surrounded by sunloungers and palm trees in planters that really make you feel like you have your feet on the ground, rather than having miles of ocean beneath you. The most impressive part is probably the waterslide, a sky-high spiral thing that comes down from one of the higher decks – not that you'll catch me whizzing down it any time soon. I'm here for the chill vibe. The cocktails with umbrellas, the sunbathing, breathing in the sea air. Oh, and playing games with my friends, my ex and my fake boyfriend, of course.

I'm sitting on the edge of Brody's sunlounger while he lies back, looking like an underwear model, soaking up the rays from behind his sunglasses. He's stroking my back, like the doting boyfriend he isn't, for the benefit of our audience. He trails the backs of his fingers along my spine, bridging the gap between my bikini top and bottoms, ever so slowly... almost like he's not even doing it. Every few seconds he presses a little firmer and it's just enough to send a weird tingle through my body. But it's just crossed wires, mixed messages, my body receiving signals without the bottom line: this isn't real.

Even if it is fake, there's no denying he's great at this. Playing the boyfriend of my dreams, making me feel like I'm the only woman on the ship – or the only one he has eyes for anyway. If he's the top shagger the tabloids make him out to be, well, it's not hard to imagine, given that he looks like a jacked Roman sculpture, has charm radiating from every buff bit of him, and does a really good job of passing himself off as perfect – even I could fall for this, if I didn't know we were pretending, obviously.

'Oi, Jessa,' Kelsey calls out from her sunlounger. 'Come here.'

'Back in a sec,' I tell Brody, blowing him a kiss.

The floor feels warm beneath my feet, and I feel mostly dry (apart from my hair) from my dip in the pool already.

'Hey,' I say, plonking myself down on her sunlounger.

As she takes a long drink from her bright pink straw, she gives me a look that says a thousand words.

'What?' I say with a chuckle.

'He's different with you,' she tells me, nodding over toward Brody.

I smile.

'Yeah, I don't know, I didn't know him before, but he's great,' I reply. 'Really great.'

'Let's play a game!' Neil says, clapping his hands together loudly, saving me from the rest of the conversation. 'They've got all these different boardgames. I went straight to the retro ones – they've got a Mr & Mrs kind of game. Perfect for us, right?'

I glance at Kelsey. Is this perfect? It sounds like a recipe for disaster.

'Sounds great,' she says.

Well, who am I to argue with the bride?

Brody stands up, stretching in a way that should probably be illegal. And then he beckons me over with a grin and... yeah... he's really good at this.

'Okay, how do we go about this?' he asks me in hushed tones.

'I guess, everyone knows we haven't been together long, so we'll lean into that,' I tell him. 'We're still enjoying getting to know each other, finding out new things – we can make a whole lovey-dovey thing of that.'

'Plus, Neil and I might be old friends, but we haven't spent much time together lately – just socially, at weddings and stuff, so I don't know when Nikki would have had the chance to spend time with Todd and get to know him. I've only met him a couple of times and I don't feel like I know much about him...'

Which, to me at least, only serves as further proof that something must have been going on between them earlier than they let on. Neil and Brody are old friends, and Al already knows Brody too – presumably from some kind of freakishly buff man club – Nikki was never part of our friendship circle, and I'd never noticed Brody before, even if we have crossed paths. Well, I suppose when you're happy with someone, you don't look at your friendship circle through that lens, you're not on the lookout for hot men – although I suppose I should have been, in hindsight.

'What are you thinking about? You're blushing,' Brody says, snapping me from my thoughts.

Shit. I was just thinking that he was hot, in a roundabout way, but there's no way he can know that, right? And no way I'm blushing, it must just be the sun. I guess some kind of psychic connection could be good for the purpose of the game – but not a thing else.

'Nothing,' I insist quickly. 'Just how to win.'

'Thinking about it, we don't need to win, we only need to do better than Todd and Nikki. If we have to cheat, so be it.'

Well, it doesn't seem like they were above that...

'How do we cheat?' I ask.

'No idea,' he replies. 'But if something comes up, we lean into it.'

'That's not very sportsmanlike of you,' I tease.

'This isn't a sport,' he replies with a smile. 'It's a war.'

'And I suppose they do say all is fair in love and war,' I reply. 'Let's do it.'

We all crowd around a low table at the side of the pool. Neil explains the game to us – it sounds pretty straightforward, and not at all like something Brody and I could be good at given that we hardly know each other.

'The pens are dry, so we'll have to play the honesty version,' Neil tells us. 'We're all adults. We can trust everyone will be truthful, right?'

Us lot? Ha.

First up it's Kelsey and Neil, the nearly-weds, and unsurprisingly, Neil nails Kelsey's favourite flowers – tulips.

Then Al and Kira – the newly-weds – and they kill it too. They're still in that phase of romance where they finish each other's sentences and food and everything. It's somewhere between cute and sickening – but only the latter because secretly I wish I had someone who was so in sync with me.

Next up, it's Todd and Nikki. This ought to be good.

'Okay, Todd, what is Nikki's favourite snack?' Neil asks.

'Easy,' Todd says confidently. 'It's crisps.'

'Crisps?' she claps back. 'Todd, it's white chocolate buttons – what are you talking about?'

'You like crisps,' Todd insists.

'I like lots of things, Todd, but white chocolate buttons are my favourite.'

Nikki throws back her hair on one side, clearly unable to hide her annoyance that they've fallen at the first hurdle.

Luckily my urge to smile is quickly quashed by my nervousness to be going next. I fear we're going to go the same way...

'All right, Brody,' Neil says as he takes another card, 'what strange food does Jessa love?'

'Well, that's easy,' Brody replies, with an impressive level of fake confidence, given the fact that he can't possibly know the answer. 'Pickles.'

My stomach turns just hearing the word, but as I look over at him I notice him widening his eyes at me, ever so subtly, silently urging me to play along.

I muster up a big, bright smile and then I say...

'Correct!'

'Bullshit,' Todd calls out. 'You hate pickles.'

'I love pickles,' I insist.

'You would always give me your pickles,' he reminds me – which is true.

Nikki looks furious, I suppose because Todd is talking about when we were together – it was just last month though, to be fair. Hardly ancient history.

'I love them now,' I lie. 'Brody introduced me to them and now I can't get enough.'

'Bullshit,' Todd says again, clearly more bothered by this than anyone ever should be. It's a board game, it's not that deep.

Brody wraps an arm around my shoulders and pulls me into him, grinning at everyone. 'I've introduced her to a lot of new things that she likes,' he says, giving me a wink.

There's an awkward beat where everyone looks uncomfortable (Todd and Nikki) or amused (everyone else), and it is glorious.

'I'm starting to feel suspicious about when exactly the two of you met, given how much you supposedly know about each other,' Nikki says, almost under her breath.

Oh, she's one to talk.

'We met at Al and Kira's wedding,' I remind her. 'I guess we're just more interested in each other than we ever have been with anyone else...'

'Come on, let's keep playing,' Neil insists, handing Al a card so that he can read it to him and Kelsey.

Of course, they smash it again, and so do Al and Kira, and then it's back to Nikki and Todd – and she's really on the edge of her seat, clearly determined to get this one right.

'Nikki, what is Todd's favourite TV show?' Neil asks her.

'One of the *Star Wars* ones – come on, I'm too cool to know the name,' she insists rather rudely. 'You've got to give me a point for that.'

'It's *Star Trek*,' Todd corrects her – offended by the wrong part of her answer.

'The really old ones,' I can't resist chiming in. 'It's the only thing he ever wanted to watch.'

'Like I always tell you – it's a masterpiece,' he reminds me, smiling just enough to infuriate Nikki.

'Anyway, let's move on,' Kelsey prompts, sensing trouble at sea.

'Yeah,' Neil says, clapping his hands together before grabbing another card. 'Jessa, what is Brody's favourite music?'

I mean... it could be anything. And if we're cheating, it can be anything.

'Early 2000s pop punk,' I say with faux confidence.

Brody's face doesn't crack, but I notice him swallow and it looks a little too hard for me to think I just so happened to get that one right.

'That is... correct!' Brody reveals.

Nikki's chair squeaks loudly on the ground as she pushes herself away from the table in temper.

'That's a lie,' she shrieks. 'They're cheating. There's no way. I mean, I mean... I've heard him listen to hip-hop and power ballads and just... inexplicably, a bunch of Bee Gees.'

'The Bee Gees are great, to be fair,' I chime in – and yes, I know I'm not helping.

'What's your favourite song?' Brody asks me with what looks like a genuine sparkle in his eyes... although we have established he's very good at this.

'Oh, "Love You Inside and Out" – no contest,' I reply. All of this is easy when you're telling the truth.

'Me too!' he replies. 'Wow, see, we're still learning so much about each other, finding out we have so much in common.'

His smile seems so genuine but, truly, I think he's getting off on this. If I'm being completely honest, so am I.

'Brody, you don't listen to pop punk,' Nikki insists.

'He does,' I reply. 'We listen to it together. He loves Sum 41, Blink 182...'

'All the number bands,' Brody jokes.

'So, what, you're just switching between moshing and jiving?' Todd asks, his brow furrowed with disbelief.

'You haven't lived until you've listened to "Still Waiting" with a "Stayin' Alive" chaser,' I add, trying to drop enough information, should Brody need to pick any up.

'It's like a HIIT workout in the bedroom,' Brody adds cheekily.

'Huh,' Al says thoughtfully. 'Good to know.'

'Okay, can we just... not? Thanks,' Nikki adds. 'I'm not playing unless it's fair. In fact, let's go, just us two versus Brody and Jessa, head to head, and the losers can't play.'

'What? Like penalties?' Todd asks, because of course he does.

'Sure,' Nikki says. 'But no cheating – we have to whisper the right answer to someone, who can verify if they match.'

'Right, okay, well, how about I ask the same question to both of you, that way you have an even chance... sort of,' Neil suggests, although he already looks like he regrets indulging Nikki in this.

'Do it,' Nikki says. 'Quick.'

We stand by the pool in our couples, Neil standing in front of us with his question card. Todd and Nikki have Al by their side and we've got Kira, the idea being that one person tells their answer to them first, so they can verify the match. There's no cheating this time.

'Okay, so Nikki and Jessa, step forwards, you'll be answering first,' Neil instructs us. 'The question is: if your partner had to live in another country, where would they choose?'

Oh, I mean, come on. It could be literally anywhere. How many countries are there? Pushing two hundred. I don't like those odds.

Todd and Nikki go first, which buys me some time. Todd whispers his answer to Al, who nods.

'China,' Nikki says confidently.

'China?' Todd blurts back.

'Because you love Chinese food,' she replies.

Al shakes his head, wincing slightly.

'Nope, sorry. He said Greece,' he tells her, breaking the news as gently as he can.

There's a few seconds of silence, no one quite knowing what to say. Nikki looks like she's chewing on a lemon. As much as I would love to get this right, as unlikely as it may be, I'm actually kind of scared about how she'll react. She's really not taking this well.

'Erm, Jessa,' Neil prompts me eventually. 'Your answer, please.'

I look at Brody, my heart pounding. I honestly have no idea. Not a clue. What country would he even pick? Well, I suppose it seems like he loves cricket more than anything, so where else do they love cricket? Australia? That sounds right. Plus, they have beaches, he can be all cool and chilled out there. I don't know, maybe there's something in it, maybe I'm reaching – but I have to say something.

I take a breath.

'Australia,' I say, without a hint of anything.

All eyes turn to Kira, to see if I'm right.

'Correct,' she says, looking delighted for us.

What? I got it right?

I let out a little squeal and leap into Brody's arms – and it's not part of the act, I am genuinely over the moon to have wiped the smirks off their faces. He catches me easily, spinning me around as I wrap my legs around his waist.

I can sort of hear Nikki, in the background, throwing a tantrum, but being twirled around by Brody, the background blurring around me, I feel like the moment is wrapping me up all warm and cosy.

'You cheated,' Nikki shrieks, approaching us. 'It's obvious! Kira, I don't know why you're lying for them.'

'Oi, I'm not lying,' Kira claps back. 'They got it right.'

'Come on, Nikki, stop being a sore loser,' Brody tells her, tightening his grip on me.

If looks could kill we'd be dead. Truly, it's like there's a fire raging behind her eyes, her cheeks flushing, nostrils flaring and then...

And then she shoves us, sending us crashing into the pool.

I cry out, for what it's worth, as we topple backwards into the pool with a huge splash, the cold water closing over my head – and it feels like forever, but it's probably only a second or two. I resurface, spluttering and laughing in disbelief, pushing my wet hair out of my face. Brody pops up beside me, slicking his hands through his hair and shaking his head like a golden retriever.

When I blink the water out of my eyes, I see Nikki, standing at the edge of the pool, laughing a little too hard.

'Okay, fine, you win!' she says, throwing her hands up like this is all just good-natured fun.

Behind her, Todd's face is frozen in this weird half-wince – like he's not sure if this is all just good fun – but then he forces a laugh too, and everyone sort of awkwardly chuckles along.

Brody shoots me a look and I can tell from his raised eyebrow and the way the corners of his mouth twitch that we're thinking the same thing. Nikki was not just messing around.

Sure, everyone was splashing around before, messing about in the pool, but this? Shoving us like that, in the middle of an argument, this wasn't harmless fun. This was Nikki losing her cool.

Well – good. I'm not the one floundering (although I suppose technically I am, at this particular moment), they're the ones who aren't handling it.

Brody swims closer, slipping an arm around my waist under the water.

'Are you okay?' he asks, his voice quiet and just for me.

'I've never been better,' I tell him – and I mean it. Because we're winning, and not just this stupid ancient Mr & Mrs game, we're winning at life, at moving on, and being the bigger, better people.

Well, we are as far as they're concerned, anyway.

20

I don't know if it makes it better or worse – the fact that Kelsey and Neil are having dinner with their parents tonight.

Better, I suppose, because it takes the pressure off a little. After all, this whole thing is mostly in aid of making sure their wedding goes smoothly, that they have the best day ever, that none of my drama causes trouble for them. On the other side of the coin, if Kelsey and Neil aren't here to see just how supposedly happy Brody and I are together, then what's the point in putting on a show?

The answer to that question, it turns out, is to continue to make Todd and Nikki jealous. I know, it's petty, but seeing the looks on their faces as they watch us – the ultimate plot twist in their relationship – is so, so sweet. Plus, Al and Kira are here, and it's always nice to spend time with them.

The restaurant we're in is more laid-back – it's not even like a restaurant really, more like a fast-food place, so we're tucking into burgers, fries and milkshakes. The only thing sweeter than revenge is the milkshake I'm drinking – chocolate, vanilla, peanut butter, Biscoff and cookie pieces. Incredible. Perfect for offsetting the saltiness of the fries and the cheeseburger. If we could eat here every night while we're on board, that would be great.

I'm sitting between Brody and Al, which, when you think about it, is the literal definition of being between a rock and a hard place. There is just a wall of muscle on either side of me. I must be living out someone's horny dream, being sandwiched between a bodybuilder and a professional sportsman, not that I would want to get my hands on either of them. Al is married. Brody is Brody. Of course, I'm doing a great job of pretending I want him tonight.

'Just trust me,' Brody tells me, every part of his face practically floodlit as he waggles a chip at me.

'I'm not sure about that one, baby,' I reply.

Baby. Ha. I would be embarrassed to even utter the word, were it not for the effect it's having on Todd. I can read him like a book and the heading of this chapter is so blatantly: *She never called me baby!* It's a side-splitter.

So far we've just been making small talk. Al and Kira are doing a lot of the heavy lifting, keeping things going, either chatting with me and Brody, or with Todd and Nikki, but never quite getting the four of us chatting with each other. Can you blame me, after what happened earlier? I keep sneaking glances at the two of them – especially Nikki. The thing I can't understand about her is that she wanted Todd, and she didn't just choose him, she stole him, so I can't understand why she has such a big problem seeing me and Brody together. No one wants to see their ex move on – take it from me – but she dumped him. She didn't want him any more. She would do well to remember that.

'Just trust me,' Brody says again. 'Have I ever steered you wrong before?'

'Hmm, I don't suppose you have,' I reply, my flirting game dialled up above and beyond what it would normally be. I'm not usually one for PDA – and Todd certainly never was – but it's all part of the act.

Brody dips another chip in his strawberry milkshake and holds it up to my face.

'Come on,' he says. 'If you don't like it, you can take it out on me later.'

'What, in the bedroom?' Al asks with a chuckle.

I mean, if I were to take something out on Brody in the bedroom, it would probably come in the form of me taking one of his nights in the bed, leaving him to sleep in the bath. Honestly, sleeping in a bath is savage, the things it does to your back... bondage fans could never.

I decide to go for it, leaning forward so that Brody can feed me a chip. I'm not convinced, about a chip dipped in a milkshake, but I'm just thinking about the optics. I'll take one for the team.

I don't just go for the chip, I take the tip of his finger in my mouth too, sucking it lightly. I see a cheeky little twinkle in Brody's eyes as I do, like he just knows we're putting on a great performance. And do you know what? He's right. The flavour pairing just works. Who knew?

'Okay, fine, you're right, that is actually really good,' I tell him.

'You know I'm always right,' he replies.

I know that he thinks he's always right.

'Nikki has something she wants to say, don't you, Nikki?' Todd pipes up, breaking up our little love fest.

'Erm, yeah, I suppose,' she replies, shooting him evils. Then she turns to face me and, honestly, she looks like she has a bee in her mouth. 'Jessa... I'm sorry for pushing you and Brody in the pool earlier, it was just banter.'

'Banter?' I reply simply.

'Yeah, it was just a joke, just for the laughs,' she continues. 'We were all having fun by the pool, I thought it would be funny, and that you guys would find it funny too, but Todd reckons you might have thought I meant it in a bad way so... yeah, I'm sorry.'

You know when teenagers apologise and it sounds almost sarcastic? You can tell she begrudges every word she's saying, so Todd must have told her she had to say it, but I know that if I were truly the bigger person, definitely over Todd, and genuinely head over heels for Brody, then the right thing to do would be to accept her apology. So I will.

'Don't worry about it,' I reassure her. 'It was funny. Brody and I had a right old laugh about it together, didn't we?'

'We did,' he replies, offering me another chip. 'When we were in the shower together, just after, we were saying it was kind of romantic.'

'Like our own little romcom moment,' I add. 'How many people even get those? So really, Nikki, we should be thanking you.'

I don't think steam actually comes out of a person's ears when they're mad in real life but, honestly, Nikki looks pretty close.

'My God, you two are cute,' Kira blurts, love hearts where her eyes should be. 'The way you've fallen so hard for each other, just when you needed one another – it's beautiful.'

'I know who I'm expecting to hear wedding bells from next,' Al adds. 'Is this because you caught the bouquet at our wedding?'

I open my mouth to speak but Nikki gets in first.

'We don't talk about that,' she snaps. 'And anyway, you're talking about wedding bells, for them? They hardly know each other. Surely Todd and I will be next!'

I mean, it's not a competition, but even if it were, and even with our relationship being fake, officially she and Todd have only been together, what, a week or so longer than us, tops. Do you know what, I should say that! Because I just know, in my gut, that there had to be some overlap, and I can't let it go.

'You guys have only been together a couple of weeks longer than we have,' I point out. 'So, really, our relationships are the same age.'

'How about we race you?' Brody suggests.

'The bad boy of cricket settling down,' Al says with a laugh. 'I can see the headlines now.'

'Perhaps you can get a magazine deal for the wedding,' Kira jokes. 'Like in *OK* or *Hello* or *Bacci* or something.'

'What? No!' Nikki practically explodes.

'Oh, no, I'm sure we could,' Brody replies, wilfully missing her point. 'You were always telling me I should get more sponsorship deals and do more press and stuff. I think a big wedding feature could be a good way to show the world the new me.'

'And I would be honoured to do it with you,' I tell him. 'I just want the world to see the incredible man I see too.'

'Aww, baby,' Brody replies, leaning in as though he's going to kiss me.

I think on my feet, dipping a chip in my chocolate milkshake, and placing it between our lips. As Brody takes it in his mouth, his lips ever so lightly brush mine before he pulls away again. I lick my lips, swiping away the salt and the chocolate.

'Almost as delicious as you,' he tells me with a wink.

'Well, I can't wait for the wedding now,' Al replies. 'So, Brody, if you could get a move on and pop the question. I've always fancied going to a celebrity wedding.'

'Me too,' Kira adds. 'I thought a cruise to a wedding was as fancy as it was ever going to get, but a celebrity wedding – wow.'

'He's not really a celebrity, though, is he?' Todd says.

We all turn to look at him.

'I'm just saying, he plays sport, it's not like he's Tom Cruise or Freddie Bianchi, is it?' he adds. Somehow, explaining himself only makes him look more pathetic.

'Mate, he plays for England,' Al reminds him. 'England!'

'Yeah, but – and I mean no offence by this – but at cricket, not football or something like that,' Todd replies.

I glance at Brody, and while it's a relief to see how unbothered he is by Todd's words, I do wonder why he doesn't speak up for himself.

'Erm, excuse me,' a waitress interrupts our conversation and it's probably for the best. 'A couple of gentlemen over there asked me to send over these shots, for the table. With their compliments for Mr Ryan.'

She gestures over at two men who are sitting by the bar. As soon as they realise Brody is looking at them, they come alive with excitement.

'There's only one Brody Ryan, one Brody Ryan, one Brody Ryan. Brody Brody Brody, oi oi oi...'

As they chant away, Brody just smiles to himself.

'Tell them thanks,' Brody says to the waitress. 'And tell them I'll come over to say hi, after we've eaten. I really appreciate it.'

'I'll tell them,' she says. 'And, while I'm here, if you could sign this... it's not a bill or anything, it's just an autograph, for my dad, he's such a big fan.'

'Of course,' he replies.

Okay, suddenly I get it, why Brody isn't defending himself to Todd – because he doesn't need to. Actions speak louder than words. Todd might be trying to make Brody feel like he isn't a big deal, but it's not true, Brody is a big deal, more than I realised, and he's comfortable enough with himself to not let Todd's words bother him. Oh, to be able to harness that sort of power. I swear, sometimes I feel like I form opinions of myself based on how other people see me, rather than how I actually feel.

I should take a leaf out of his book, and stop obsessing over when Todd and Nikki got together, whether they cheated on us, because what does it matter now? It doesn't matter when, just that they did, and the best thing I can do for myself is move on.

Problem is, with each day that passes, I'm not sure Todd and Nikki have moved on as well as they think they have.

We might have to test that theory...

'I'm so glad you find me so amusing,' I say sarcastically.

'I'm not laughing at you,' Brody insists. 'I'm in awe of you, if anything, because this is a stroke of genius.'

I smile – just enough not to give him the satisfaction.

I'm enjoying myself though, as twisted as it sounds, this is just so therapeutic. We get wronged by people all the time – probably every day – but how often do we get the sick satisfaction of actually getting revenge? I don't want to get Todd back, Nikki can have him, but I do want to get him back in the other way. I want to make him pay.

How? Well, tonight it's by putting my work skills to good use – or using them for bad, I suppose, depending on how you look at it.

We've rushed back to the cabin, ahead of Todd and Nikki, so that we can set the scene.

It feels a bit like staging a house – staging the cabin – although this is sort of like doing the opposite of what I usually do at work.

Instead of setting it up to look appealing and inviting, I'm staging it to look like Brody and I have destroyed the place, by getting it on, all over the suite. Making the place feel uninhabitable. Uncomfortable. A place you'd take one look at and immediately wish you could bleach everything – including your eyeballs. A UV light would have this place glowing purple from wall to wall. Well, that's the story I'm telling anyway. That Brody and I can't keep our hands off one another, that things in the bedroom – in every room – are so hot, driven by animalistic, unrelenting lust.

And say what you want about Brody – I know I do – but he's down for it. He's peeling off his shirt, tossing it nowhere in particular, like it came off in the throes of passion.

'Come on, Jessa,' he says, smiling like a madman. 'Commit to the bit.'

He's right. We were just with them – they know what we were wearing. This needs to look real.

I shrug off my dress and fling it. It lands on the coffee table, so messy and yet so perfectly staged. Then I run to the bedroom and grab underwear – mine and Brody's – and bring it back in, scattering it around like horny confetti.

He pulls a face at me.

'Well, obviously we're not going to take our actual underwear off, are we, perv?' I say.

He just laughs at me.

'Hey, I think you're doing a great job,' he says, knocking over a lamp, chill as you like, sort of like a cat would.

'Nice touch,' I tell him.

'Thanks,' he replies. 'Hey, by the way, are you sure you're okay?'

His question catches me off guard.

'What?'

'Are you sure you're okay, with all of this, with Todd, and—'

'Absolutely fine,' I insist, pausing for a second. 'I'm over him, it's all good.'

He stares at me for a beat longer than feels normal.

'I mean, all of this is fun, I'm down for it, so long as it's coming from a fun place, not a hurt one,' he replies.

I push over an artificial plant.

'Does this look like someone who isn't having fun?' I reply.

'You still seem pretty hung up on whether or not he and Nikki cheated on us,' he points out, swiping cushions from the sofa.

'Well, yeah,' I reply, throwing the faux lemons around. 'I don't want to look silly.'

He smirks at me. Okay, that's an arguably hilarious thing to say when you're lobbing plastic lemons around. I throw one at him.

'I don't like being made a fool of,' I say instead. 'It's not about wanting him back – I just want to make him feel as shit as I did.'

'All I'm saying is, energy spent on the right things is never wasted,' he tells me. 'But some people are just dicks. They don't deserve your energy or your effort, good or bad.'

I cock my head curiously.

'That's awfully profound, for a—'

I don't quite get to finish my compliment-insult because we can hear Todd and Nikki, behind the door, about to come in.

'Shit,' I whisper.

What do we do? I could throw myself at him, push him back onto the sofa, make them think they've walked in on the main event – but the two sets of underwear don't make sense. Why would it be on the floor and on us? It's perfect staging if we're not here. It's a plot hole if we are.

Brody's eyes widen. We're on the wrong side of the room – way too far from our bedroom door to make it before they walk in. They'll see us.

'Quick, this way,' Brody says, taking me by the hand.

He drags me out onto the balcony, sliding the door shut just in time. Well, almost shut, he leaves it open just enough for us to hear.

The balcony isn't that big and there isn't really anywhere to hide thanks to the patio doors. With just a small wall space on each side, Brody pushes me up against the wall, before pressing his body against mine.

Oof, now that's good staging.

I try to ignore the fact that my heart is beating faster – it's probably the fear of being caught. Nothing else.

Inside, we hear Todd and Nikki storm in.

They're chatting until they see the scene we've set for them. Then they fall silent for a moment.

'Oh my God – ew, ew, ew,' Nikki says. 'They're like animals.'

'What have they been doing in here?' Todd asks.

'Oh my God, that's a thong – ew, Todd, we know exactly what they've been doing in here,' she replies.

Mission: Accomplished.

'But Jessa was never—'

'Todd! Can we not,' Nikki snaps at him.

I blush a little. Was Todd about to say that I was never adventurous in the bedroom? I mean, we weren't exactly setting the bed on fire, but his match was one of those little ones you get in books, not those big bad boys that take longer to burn through. If y'know what I mean.

Not me blushing because I care that Brody heard him say that. I'm not boring. Would a boring girl be pinned to a wall, in her underwear, by a professional sportsman – the bad boy of cricket, no less? I don't think so.

Brody's face is so close to mine I can see all the little flecks of colour in his eyes, even in this dim light. I can feel his breath tickling my lips, almost like a preview of what his lips might feel like. I don't know, it's like there's this tension between us, this electricity – bloody hell, even I'm falling for it now. This is an act. I'm faking it, he's faking it, and we're doing such a good job that it feels real, even here on the inside.

Eventually, we hear Todd muttering something about 'sleeping in the bloody casino if they hear a peep from us' before their bedroom door slams shut.

Brody pulls back slightly, still grinning.

'Okay, Jessa, you're good,' he tells me.

I puff air from my cheeks, relieved to have pulled it off.

'Yeah, well, ever the professional,' I joke.

We stand with our arms on the railings for a moment, looking out to sea, admiring the view. There's something so captivating about all the stars.

I blow out a breath, feeling slightly dazed.

'Yeah. Total professionals, us.'

'It's gorgeous out here,' I say softly. 'I bet it would be lovely, to sleep out here, under the stars.'

'Well, maybe you should,' he says in a soft, breathy voice. 'Seeing as it's your turn in the bath tonight.'

Ugh, he's such a wind-up. Honestly, I deserve an Oscar, for successfully convincing even one person that I could ever feel anything real for him. Brody Ryan. Professional cricketer and semi-professional tosser.

He's good at this though, there's no denying that. I'll just have to put up with him a bit longer, I suppose...

22

I can't believe I'm a gym girlie now.

Well, I'm not technically, am I? Because I only come here to hang out with my fake boyfriend.

Brody is lifting weights – although that makes it sound far less impressive than it is, because to a layman like me, it looks more like he's lifting the machine than the weights. It's hard not to stare at his muscles – it's almost hypnotic, the way they contract, flex, twitch, ripple. It's like they have a mind of their own. In fact, I could swear his abs were flirting with me.

I'm almost exercising today, technically, because I'm using an exercise ball as a chair, lightly bouncing up and down on it.

Brody comes over to me, wiping his sweaty forehead with the back of his arm.

'I don't think you're allowed to do that in here,' he jokes, nodding towards the bar of chocolate I'm eating, the one I swiped from the minibar before we left our suite.

'We all have our morning routines,' I remind him, popping another square of chocolate into my mouth.

He just laughs as he lies down on the mat next to me. I

thought he was going to relax for a second then but, no, he's doing crunches.

'You never stop,' I tell him.

'You never start,' he claps back.

I keep bouncing, letting the momentum do most of the work.

'So what does a typical day in the life of a professional cricketer look like?' I ask curiously.

Brody stops for a second, rolling onto his side to look at me while we chat.

'Wake up, protein, gym, training most days – depends when we have a match,' he tells me.

'When even are cricket matches?' I ask, realising I have no idea when it's on TV, because I actively avoid sport.

'It depends,' he replies. 'I don't want to bore you, but sometimes they're in the day, through the week, sometimes they're on a Friday night – it varies.'

'Boring as it might be to watch, it's interesting to talk about,' I say with a smile. 'What does a free evening look like?'

'I live with one of my teammates, we share an apartment,' he explains. 'Something Nikki said was pathetic for a man in his early thirties, but we have a laugh. I go out to eat often, to bars with the lads, or we'll watch movies and play video games. What about you? What does your typical day look like?'

I swear, my brain has stopped working. What does a typical day for me look like? The more I think about it, the more I realise that it's not my mind that is blank, it's my day. Beyond work there's not much going on.

'It's not so much a routine, it's more like being on that treadmill,' I say.

'Would you know what that was even like?' he jokes.

'Har-har,' I reply. 'I guess I get up, get ready, rush off to various appointments, different houses, different clients. Sometimes I'm shopping for furniture or smelling 500 candles until I find the exact right one for a particular en suite. I've started dressing holiday rentals, and I'm about to do some stuff with a boutique hotel. They want their guests to have the best time and you would be amazed how the right colours, the right pillows, the right accessories can make a difference.'

'Sounds more exhausting than my job,' he replies.

That almost sounds like a compliment.

'I'm not sure about that,' I say with a laugh. 'I love it though. I love that no two days are the same. It keeps things interesting. And it's not always plain sailing, sometimes people need convincing that they need to take down all of their family photos.'

'Why do you do that?' he asks curiously. 'Surely it's nice, to see it as a family home?'

'Well, that's the thing, not everyone wants to see it as a family home,' I reply. 'If people think it's a family home, not a swanky bachelor pad, it can put them off. Even the people who do want a family home, they want to imagine their own family in it, not someone else's. You want people feeling like it's their house from the second they walk through the door.'

'Okay, I'll admit it, I thought your job sounded kind of silly the first time you told me about it but, now that you've explained it, I get it, it makes sense,' he says. 'So, what about after work? How do you relax?'

How do I relax? Do I even relax?

'It's interesting, since Todd…' My voice trails off.

'You don't have to talk about it,' Brody insists.

'No, it's okay,' I reply. 'Since we split, the days kind of… drop off after work. We used to go out with our friends together some-times, but most nights we would just hang out together. Watch Netflix, get a takeaway, cuddle on the sofa. So I don't do that any more, obviously, I do a version of it on my own, I guess. I'm hoping that once wedding season calms down, I'll get my friends back, figure out a new version of normal. One that doesn't include him.'

Brody watches me quietly for a second, not teasing me or laughing at me.

'Were you really happy with Todd?' he asks curiously. 'And, again, you don't have to answer if you don't want to.'

'No, I'm happy to talk about it,' I tell him. 'And, yeah, I was happy. Really happy.'

'You just... talk about your life like it was a bit... boring with him?'

I pick at the empty wrapper in my hand.

'Do I?' I reply. 'No. It wasn't boring... I don't think. It was... comfortable. The kind of love where you're best friends first, you know? That's what makes it last. Friendship. That's the foundation of a long-lasting relationship. Would you say you and Nikki were friends?'

'No, no way,' Brody replies. 'She was my girlfriend. My friends were my friends.'

And that's exactly why I could never entertain anything happening between me and Brody – not that he's entertaining it either. Because there's no world in which he and I would ever be friends. I'm attracted to him physically, sure, I think anyone who is attracted to men would be. And his charm, when it's not pointed at me like a loaded gun full of jokes and sarcasm. But his personality? No, thanks. He drives me absolutely mad. Constantly. Consistently. Unrelentingly.

'Maybe that's one of those things lads and lasses see differently,' he replies, 'or maybe I just don't know Todd that well but... he seems boring. It's hard to imagine him being anyone's type.'

It sounds to me like Brody can't quite get his head around

why on earth Nikki would leave someone like him for someone like Todd.

I hate to say it, but I've asked myself the same question.

'Unlike Nikki, who's everyone's type?' I reply.

Brody laughs again.

'She was all right at first,' he replies. 'Beautiful, sharp, intense in a kind of exciting way. But then she started pushing me about work, trying to get me to do things I didn't want to do. She wanted to turn me into an influencer, have brand deals. She even talked about me going on *Celebrity Welcome to Singledom* once. I told her that even if I did fancy a TV dating show – which I don't – I'm hardly a celebrity. She said I needed a brand, something to fall back on when I retire. I know, it's closer than I think, but that's not what I want to do. I want to step out of the light, not have it shining on me even brighter. I just wanted to play the sport, not have the *Daily Scoop* print my face on beer mats and send them to almost every pub in the country the week before the Ashes.'

Okay, that does sound awful. I don't suppose, when he was a kid growing up, starting to get excited about sport, that he thought about getting papped when he grew up.

'So what do you want to do?' I ask, genuinely curious.

'Coaching, maybe,' he replies. 'Not pros though. I think I'd rather work with kids. Help them fall in love with the game, the way I did.'

That... is surprisingly sweet. And unexpectedly normal.

'Plus, I get to be the cool guy they can look up to, they won't know about the bad press or anything like that,' he adds. 'I'll just be, like, this rock star.'

'Well, as long are you're impressing kids,' I tease him.

Right on cue, a man in a sweaty tank top walks over and claps Brody hard on the back.

'Mate. Legend. Seriously. That five-for you took against India last year? Man, me and my mates drank all night after that,' he tells him. 'That last delivery – pure filth. Top of off. Beautiful.'

At least I think that's what he said. Is he even speaking English right now? What does any of that mean? It's like they're speaking in code.

Brody grins, looking almost bashful even.

'Cheers, mate,' Brody replies.

They chat for a second, cricket-language flying over my head like, well, a cricket ball. I have nothing to contribute, beyond puns, like this guy seems pretty bowled over by Brody. He's knocked him for six. Even I know those ones – not that I think they would be appreciated right now.

'See what I mean – most people think I'm great,' he tells me when we're alone again.

'And so modest,' I reply.

I know, he's playing it cocky with me, but I could see how much that meant to him, to be acknowledged for how great he is at what he does. That guy didn't care how much he allegedly drinks, or if he was the *Daily Scoop*'s 'top shagger' two years in a row.

'Well, you deserve it,' I tell him. 'No one ever congratulates me on... a really well placed chair.'

Brody laughs.

'I suppose what you do isn't supposed to be obvious, it's supposed to feel natural,' he replies. 'When people start noticing that you're putting chairs there to get a sale, maybe that's when it stops working.'

'You know what, that's a really good point,' I say with a laugh. He's right, but it's still kind of funny.

'However, that bra you left on the floor in our suite, for Todd and Nikki to see – next level,' he says, getting up to pat me on the back. 'Expertly done. They had no idea it was a plant.'

'Aww, you're just trying to be nice,' I reply.

'Nope, honestly, best bra placement I've ever seen,' he insists. 'I've always said the best place for a bra is the floor...'

I get off my ball and kick it at him. He just chuckles.

Sometimes I think I'm seeing a slightly different side to him, sometimes he's exactly as I expect him to be. I'm not sure how much I hate it any more though.

23

If there's one thing no one talks about enough, when it comes to weddings, it's just how wild it is that the happy couple expect you to do so much stuff, just because they're getting married.

Has it always been like this? I swear, when my parents got married, it was just one day, people turned up, ate food, gave them some kitchenware, ate cake and then went home. A wedding day.

Now though, it's so different – weddings shouldn't require annual leave, surely? And, destination weddings, come on. It's not a day, it's a whole thing.

I remember going to a wedding where the groom had roped all of his friends into dressing up like famous singers and doing a surprise choreographed dance – probably just some cringe attempt to go viral, which I think it did. But that's not about the wedding, is it? Although I don't suppose they'll ever forget it (and they are divorced now, so take from that what you will). There was another girl we know, a friend of Kelsey's, who made all of her bridesmaids do juice cleanses in the run-up to the big day –

and they did it! Can we normalise telling people to fuck off, please?

Then again, I say that, but I am here, about to do something for Kelsey and Neil. I like to think I'd say no to her forcing me to go on a diet (not that she ever would, that's why I love her) but this... as much as I hate it, I want to make her happy.

I cringe as I catch sight of myself in the mirrored wall. I'm in – wait for it – the ship's dance studio. Yep, dance studio. Generally I think it's reserved for the cruise performers to practise their routines but, when Kelsey said she was looking for somewhere for a group dance class, they said she could use this space. Joy.

'This was definitely Kelsey's idea,' I whisper to Brody. 'I saw Neil do the Cha Cha Slide once – the song literally has the instructions as lyrics – and he still fluffed it.'

'I heard that,' Neil calls out – amused, thankfully.

'We both thought it would be so cute if all our favourite people joined in on the first dance,' Kelsey says, sounding like a woman who has just discovered coffee and had six. 'We thought it might make Neil feel a bit more relaxed.'

'Like a flash mob, but classy?' Nikki asks. 'I'm in. I used to be a dancer, you know...'

She stretches like she's about to perform *Swan Lake*.

'No offence to my husband, but dancing isn't really his strong suit,' Kira says. 'Nor mine...'

Al throws an arm around Kira.

'I lift fridges for a living, Kira. I can lift you,' he tells her.

Kira raises her brows.

'Where to begin with that?' she replies with a laugh.

'Neil and I have already been practising and we're basically experts now,' Kelsey tells us. 'So you can all just follow our lead.'

Easy as that, eh? Somehow I doubt it, because I have two left feet, and while Brody might be a professional athlete, he's a sportsman, and they aren't exactly known for their ballroom dancing, are they?

'Have you ever danced before?' I ask Brody.

He purses his lips. Yeah, okay, this is going to go terribly.

Kelsey and Neil show us their routine. I don't know nearly enough about dancing to tell you what kind it is – the music is sort of salsa style and the dancing has a lot of stepping and hip wiggling. Kelsey and Neil are killing it, honestly, they don't need us up there as a buffer (unless the plan is for us to look bad to make them look good) but what are friends for?

They start by showing us the basic steps, very slowly, on our own. Without the music, doing it bit by bit, it's not so bad, but when it's time to do it all at once, to the music, I panic. It's going to be a disaster, so embarrassing, because whether Nikki really did used to be a dancer or not, she's clearly better at this than I am.

At least I'm braced for it being awful, I'm at one with it, and no matter how I'm feeling on the inside, on the outside I will act like I don't care.

I'm practically wincing, as the music starts, but the second Brody places his hands on my waist I feel better and not only that but... I don't know, it's like we're good? Well, no, I'm not good, I stepped on my own foot twice while I was practising, but Brody is great. He moves so confidently, not only nailing the steps, but guiding me too. I feel like I'm dancing, although I don't feel like it's me who is doing it.

'Brody, what the hell?' I say, delighted but low-key suspicious. 'You're, like, really good at this. How are you so good at this? Are you secretly training for *Strictly Come Dancing*?'

'Not exactly,' he says with a smile as he walks me through the steps. 'My grandma's always loved dancing. When my grandad passed away, I promised I'd go with her. So I've been doing it ever since. She'll be pleased to hear you think I'm good – she doesn't think I'm up to scratch.'

I can't help but laugh because that's as funny as it is adorable. The bad boy of cricket has a soft side, huh? I didn't read about any of that when I was Google-stalking him.

'She's in her nineties now,' he says. 'Not as mobile as she used to be, but still much better on her feet than me – obviously. She doesn't go out much, so I go to her house, put a record on, have a bit of a dance in the living room with her.'

Amazing really, that he's still finding dancing with me so effortless, when I'm in a puddle on the floor.

'That's so nice,' I tell him. 'She's so lucky to have you.'

'I'm lucky to have her,' he replies. 'I've lost my grandad, my other grandparents, my dad... Hopefully I have my grandma's genes.'

His usually sunny outlook dips behind a cloud, just for a moment, before that optimistic smile returns.

'Hopefully,' I reply.

I'm only just realising it but we're getting closer, our bodies moving in perfect sync. It's the first time I've ever danced and not felt like a six-year-old in a school play. It's just so easy to lean into him and let him take the lead.

'Oh, wow,' I hear Kira say.

Looking around, I can see that we've got an audience. Everyone has stopped to watch us – even Nikki, not that she'll be giving us a round of applause.

'Shall we give them something to look at?' he asks me.

'Are we not doing that right now?' I reply.

'Ready?' he asks.

'For wha—'

Brody locks his hands around my waist and lifts me high into the air, *Dirty Dancing* style, and all I have to do is keep my body straight, and my gosh, he makes it seem easy, holding me up like I'm nothing – who knew bowlers were so strong?

I can see myself in the mirrored wall. The smile on my face is something else, one that I've not seen for some time – I swear, the muscles in my face are aching from using ones I don't usually (which is why, when I go to the gym with Brody, I just chill out – no one wants or needs achy muscles on a cruise). I dare to throw my arms out, squealing with glee, because I know I'm not actually flying, but this might be as close as I can get.

'All right, all right, we get it, you're perfect,' Kelsey jokes. 'Do not do that at my wedding – you'll make us look rubbish.'

'We won't, we promise,' Brody says as he lowers me down. He keeps his hand on my waist and pulls me close.

As he slow dances me on the spot I can look over his shoulder and see that both Todd and Nikki are furious. Honestly, had I not sworn off crying on men, I could weep with joy.

'That was amazing,' I whisper into Brody's ear.

'Not so bad yourself,' he replies.

'Have you seen their faces?'

'What?'

'Have you seen Todd and Nikki's faces?' I say again.

'Oh, right, yeah, they look pretty jealous,' he replies.

'This plan is working so, so much better than I thought it was going to,' I tell him.

He just laughs.

This, right here, ladies and gents, is how you handle a break-up. Not like an adult, like a boss.

24

There is definitely a vibe in the suite tonight, and it's not a good one.

Well, after our little performance at the dance lesson, both Todd and Nikki seem really put out, but they're not just taking it out on me and Brody, they're taking it out on each other too.

Sort of in their defence – not that I would ever tell them this, or defend them in any way generally – they are trying to compete with my and Brody's relationship when in reality they can't, because ours isn't real, it's made-up. It seems like a perfect dream, because it is just that, a dream, a work of fiction – sort of like I do at work, I'm telling a story, presenting a version of reality that looks great. Everything I do is supposed to make the people on the outside look in and want it, have to have it, that's how you get the sale.

I'm selling something to Todd and Nikki that they can't actually buy and, do you know what, it couldn't really happen to a nicer couple, could it?

Still, it's awkward in here, sort of like when your parents argue in front of you and you don't know where to look.

Maybe it's karma, maybe it's because I had two desserts or maybe it's both, but the ocean is being especially rough this evening and I'm feeling kind of sick.

'I'm just going to get some air,' I tell Brody, who is currently making himself a cup of tea – he's making Nikki one too, because she asked, and Todd didn't look happy about that one bit. In fact, he's sitting in an armchair, staring at them, keeping a close eye just in case – I don't know – Brody leaves a hidden message in the tea leaves for Nikki.

'No worries,' he replies.

I've looked it up and, as far as I can tell, the best cure for seasickness is to get some fresh air, so I'm heading out onto the balcony for a breather.

You know what, I feel better already, just for taking a big gulp of sea air – or perhaps the air is thicker in there, harder to breathe, from all the tension.

You just can't beat that smell, can you? If I were born 100 years earlier, I'd be the kinda woman they called hysterical and threw in the ocean to try and cure me. Or to see if I floated.

Yeah, it's much nicer out here, alone, chilling with my thoughts – so long as I don't look at the chop below, that is. It's all well and good on board the ship until you think about it too much and you start questioning how it works, how it stays afloat, how it moves, how deep the water is, if there's a storm coming – I can do this all day.

Instead I focus on the beauty. The stars in the sky – more than I've ever seen in my life – the brightness of the moon, the way it reflects on the water, and the cool feeling of the metal railing underneath my bare arms.

Just as I'm starting to feel more grounded – ironically – I hear the door open and close behind me. I'm expecting Brody, obviously, but it's Todd who leans on the railing next to me, resting his arms next to mine.

For a moment he looks out to sea, not saying a word. Then...

'Hi,' he says simply, gently even, like he doesn't quite remember how to talk to me now.

He sounds deflated. Not that he's usually a happy-go-lucky-sounding kind of guy but he's never had any trouble being moody. When his heart is heavy it somehow tugs on his vocal cords, apparently, because his voice changes.

'Hi,' I reply, matching his tone.

He seems like he's fidgeting a little, like he's trying to say something, but it's not coming out.

We never used to have any trouble talking to each other, he's always been the kind of guy to say exactly what he thinks, but I guess we're not the same people we used to be – not together anyway.

'You doing all right?' he asks after a moment or two, a weird mix of casual and concerned.

I let his question hang in the sea air for a moment because, honestly, what the fuck does he want me to say?

'Fine,' I tell him. We'll leave it at that.

'Are you sure about that?' he asks, turning to face me.

I match his pose, looking him in the eye. God, it's like I don't even recognise him. How is it possible that a person's face changes when you stop loving them (or start hating them, anyway)? The features that once warmed your heart suddenly give you the ick. The deep blue eyes I used to love looking in suddenly seem so empty and pathetic. The way his mouth turns downwards like he's always frowning, like he permanently looks sorry for himself.

'Todd, I'm fine,' I say again.

'Okay, but are you happy?' he asks, catching me off guard.

I puff air from my cheeks. Am I happy? A month ago I thought I had my life all figured out. Now I'm untethered, with no idea where I'm headed. Sort of like if this ship didn't have a captain, steering it towards our destination. I'm an unmanned vessel on the path to fucking nowhere. Not that I literally need a man, to know where I'm headed, but you take my point.

'I think so,' I say.

Why did I say that? Why didn't I just lie?

'You think so?' he repeats back to me, his eyebrows knitting together for a second or two.

'Well, you know, my boyfriend did break up with me fairly recently, on the dance floor at a wedding if you can believe anyone could be so cruel, and it took me by surprise.'

He winces. Good. It was a horrible thing to do, he deserves to feel guilty about it. It's sort of vindicating, to see even a flicker of remorse, because up until now he's been all about himself, about his happiness, whether I was collateral damage or not.

'You made your decision and I'm just living with it,' I tell him. 'Just like you are.'

'What if...' he starts, looking back inside through the glass. Brody and Nikki are on the sofa, facing each other, talking – not that we can hear them. I watch as Nikki reaches out, her hand finding Brody's, their fingers entwining. He doesn't pull away. In fact, it looks like he's smiling, a genuine curve of his lips that feels like a knife twisting in my chest for some reason.

Todd must see it too because he puffs air from his cheeks. Then he turns back to me.

'I know it's complicated, that we've let things get a bit... messy,' he says. 'But we had a plan, Jessa. A real one. We were going to build our dream house, the one we've always talked about. Get married. Start a family. It wasn't just talk, it was our future. What happened?'

'I mean, not to be a cow about it, but you fucking dumped me, Todd,' I say plainly. 'I didn't abandon the plan, you did.'

'Then perhaps I shouldn't have,' he replies, his tone much more confident now. 'Perhaps I made a mistake. People panic, don't they, when they think they're going to spend the rest of their lives with one person?'

'I mean, look at our friends, Kelsey and Neil, Al and Kira – they're tying the knot, willingly, without so much as a panic attack to make them rethink their life choices,' I tell him.

'Perhaps it takes a mistake to realise you've made one,' he says.

I pull a face, as if to say: give over.

'I just mean that, if everything happens for a reason, maybe I need this... this blip, to get into a good place, to be able to go for what I really want,' he says. 'You.'

The silence that follows is almost suffocating, like we're in a vacuum all of a sudden.

I mean, come on, what does he want me to say? Does he think Celine Dion's 'It's All Coming Back to Me Now' is going to start playing and I'm going to throw myself at him? Because I'd sooner chuck him overboard, 'My Heart Will Go On' style, like there's only enough room on this balcony for one of us to survive.

Because that's how I feel, right? I don't want him back...

It's hard not to compare him to Brody, to his good points anyway, but that's dumb, because Brody and I are not a real couple, and even if we were, it's starting to look like Nikki might be trying to get him back too.

Are they allowed to do that? To make a mistake, to blow everything up, have their cake and eat it and then get their old life back? Only if we let them, I guess.

'Just... think about it,' he says, clearing his throat. 'Please. Just promise me you'll think about it, because we can get it back, we can get the dream back on track. Seeing you here, with Brody, it's given me a clarity I didn't have before.'

I chew my lip, unsure how to reply to that.

'I think I need to go to bed,' I say. 'Get some sleep. I can't think straight with this seasickness.'

'Right, okay, good thinking,' he replies. 'Sleep on it, see how you feel tomorrow.'

As I head back inside, I notice that Nikki and Brody are still chatting, his hand still in hers. As I walk through the door, he quickly snatches it back – whatever that means.

'I'm going to bed,' I say, my voice steady, cold even, as I head for the bedroom.

I don't give either of them the chance to reply, and it's my turn in the bed tonight so my plan is to get in it as quickly as possible and go straight to sleep – or pretend to be at least, because I don't think I want to speak to anyone else tonight.

I've got a lot of thinking to do.

25

Another morning. Another ungodly early start in the gym.

Although, if I'm being honest with you, I don't hate it, not like I used to. It's amazing how quickly your body adapts to a new routine – mine genuinely believes I'm an early riser now.

Granted, I might feel differently about it if I were actually working out, but coming here to spectate is actually kind of fun.

Brody is currently on one of the treadmills, running like he's being chased by something terrifying. He's all hot and sweaty but I'd be worried if he wasn't, the way he's pounding the conveyor belt below him – if that's what you even call it.

In contrast, I'm lying on a yoga mat, with a couple of the pillows propped underneath my head. Unsurprisingly, I didn't sleep all that well, which is a real shame because it feels like a waste of a night in the bed.

You know I'm not usually one to shower Brody with praise but, credit where it's due, he does work really bloody hard in the gym. It's exhausting to watch. Even I need a shower afterwards – I don't mean that as dodgy as it sounds, I promise.

He starts to slow down, transitioning to a walk, then stopping altogether.

He wipes the sweat from his brow with the back of his forearm as he walks over to me.

'Come on then,' he says, plonking himself down on the mat next to me. 'What's on your mind?'

'Nothing,' I say, shrugging my shoulders as much as I can when I'm flat on my back.

'Except I know you better than you think,' he says. 'Part of my job is to get in the head of my opponent.'

'I'm your opponent, eh?' I ask with a smile.

'Or my teammates,' he adds. 'You learn to read people. I can see your brain going at 100 miles an hour – you overtook me on the treadmill.'

I laugh.

'Come on, what's up?' he says. 'You can talk to me.'

Should I tell him? Should I ask him?

Screw it.

'Do you want Nikki back?' I ask, cutting to the chase.

Okay, I definitely have his attention now. I don't think he was expecting me to say that. He turns his head toward me, one eyebrow raised.

'What?' he replies.

'You heard me,' I say. 'And that wasn't an answer.'

He shifts slightly, propping himself up on one elbow, his chiselled body like a work of art and it's bloody distracting.

'Why are you asking?' he replies.

That's not an answer either.

'I saw her holding your hand last night, when the two of you were talking,' I say, trying to keep my tone all easy-breezy, even if it's more nosey-wosey and jealousy-wealousy.

'Ahh,' he says simply. 'While you were outside having your secret intense chat with Todd?'

I smile slightly. Perhaps this is on his mind too.

He lies back again, folding his hands behind his head, almost like he's sunbathing.

'She did take me by the hand,' he says – although I know that, and he knows that I know. 'She started talking about this holiday we were meant to go on next month. She said she was sad we weren't going any more and asked if we could still go "as friends"...'

'And what did you say?' I ask – do I even have any right to ask that? I don't suppose he has to tell me.

'Well, I didn't say I fancied it, let's put it that way,' he replies. 'I don't know if she misses what we had and genuinely wants me back, or if she's just seeing me with you and getting jealous.'

'Either way, it sounds like you could get her back, if you wanted to... do you want to?'

Again, I shouldn't ask, but I really want to know.

'No,' he says – it's one word, but he couldn't be clearer. 'We ended for a reason. It might have been her who pulled the trigger but she did that because she could tell I wasn't serious about us, and I didn't fight her on it. Looking back, I think I might have had one foot out of the door – so to speak – and she probably picked up on that.'

'I see,' is all I can think of to say.

Brody glances sideways at me, only with his eyes, only for a second.

'Do you think Todd wants you back?' he asks.

'Maybe,' I reply. 'I'm not sure. Same kind of deal really. I think he sees me with someone like you and thinks he's let something valuable go.'

'Well, he does love to steal my girlfriends,' Brody jokes.

'Yeah, there is that,' I reply.

'Are you entertaining the idea?' he asks.

Now he's the one cutting to the chase.

'No!' I say quickly – perhaps a little too quickly.

'Really?' he replies.

'Really, I mean, look at me, I'm flying through the stages of grief,' I half-joke.

Brody nods thoughtfully.

'Do you want him back though?' he says, giving me one last chance to convince him.

'I don't want to get him back, I want to *get* him back,' I reply. 'I want revenge. That's why we're doing all of this, right? Why we're faking it, sleeping in the bath – why I'm in a gym in the a.m. If they're thinking they've made a mistake then, good, it's working.'

'I guess,' he replies. 'And you know I'm happy to help with that. But at some point we're just going to have to accept it, right? And move on for real.'

'Yeah, absolutely,' I reply. 'And I will let it go...'

Just not yet.

26

Okay, either the sea air is getting to me, sleeping in a bath causes me to sleepwalk, or… someone is messing with me.

I suppose it's to be expected, you play stupid games, you win stupid prizes – but I'm not doing anything to sabotage the wedding plans. If what I think has happened is correct then Nikki is messing with the wedding, and that's not cool at all.

Kelsey and Neil decided pretty early on that they were going to have a joint stag and hen party and, do you know what? I'm here for it. Call me old-fashioned – or the opposite, I suppose – but I hate the idea of a couple starting married life after he gets a lap dance while chained naked to a lamp post, and she gets hit in the face with a stripper's monster dong.

They knew we would be here with them so they thought it might be swanky for us all to spend an evening in the ship's casino. We were all instructed to bring evening wear, with a James Bond kind of vibe, so I bought myself a floor-length gold dress for the occasion. I took it out of my bag, and it was a little creased, so I left it hung up in the living room.

Well, would you believe it, it's gone. Vanished into thin air. Or found a life of its own and waltzed out. Or... Nikki stole it.

I'll tell you why I'm suspicious of her (other than her just being a generally shady man-stealing chick), because I asked the boys if they had seen it and they said no. I asked Nikki and she said: maybe the cleaner stole it, then again, maybe she thought it was rubbish and threw it away. To say something so mean, come on, it had to be her.

I could've kicked off, accused her, thrown all of her clothes off the balcony – instead I have decided to show her that she can't get to me (even if she actually can, quite easily). I'm looking at the glass and it's half full. I get to go dress shopping for something even nicer – and, to add insult to injury for her, I'm going shopping with her ex-boyfriend. Then again, she is sleeping with mine, so maybe she still wins that one.

I'm just trying to focus on the positives: like I said, I get to buy a new dress, and Brody is here and he's got big strong arms for carrying loads of things.

'Thanks for coming with me,' I tell my emotional support sportsman.

'It's something to do,' he says with a shrug. 'I like exploring the ship, seeing what it has to offer.'

'And yet we still haven't been to the spa...'

'Now, now, darling, we'll get to it,' he teases.

'I am going to the gym every morning...'

'I know, I know...'

As we arrive at the ship shop, it stops us both in our tracks.

'Wow,' I blurt.

Calling it a shop seems sort of silly now – I was imagining a gift shop but what I'm standing in is pretty much a department store. There are so many spaces on this ship where you could easily forget you were at sea. I overheard someone saying these waters were pretty calm, compared to others, so I'm counting my blessings that I can't feel the water beneath my feet.

I'm like a kid in a sweet shop – there are rails and rails of clothes, shoes, cosmetics, perfume, jewellery... I'd be in so, so much trouble if I was rich. I could do the kind of spending in here that would make my credit card company call me and check if I'm okay.

'It's so easy, being a man,' Brody announces.

'I mean, I already knew that,' I reply. 'But why specifically today?'

'Well, it's easy for us to find a James Bond-style outfit – it's just a suit,' he replies. 'I can see a billion dresses right now.'

'And you get to help me pick one, you lucky man!'

He yawns theatrically.

'I'm tired just thinking about it,' he jokes.

'I'm doing this for Kelsey,' I point out. 'And because your crazy ex clearly stole my dress.'

'We're all someone's crazy ex,' he reminds me. 'Let's not be judgemental.'

I just roll my eyes. He's only saying that because his crazy ex is crazier than mine.

I grab a few things to try on – well, I might as well find the perfect dress, seeing as though I'm having to buy one. Brody picks up a few bits too, saying there's nothing else to do while he's waiting for me.

The fitting rooms are unisex, so we pop in ones that are side by side, so we can keep chatting.

'Of all the travelling I've done, I have to say, I kind of like having all of this stuff on my doorstep,' he tells me through the thin wall.

'Do you travel a lot for work?' I ask curiously.

'Yeah, quite a bit,' he replies. 'All around England, obviously, because we play the other counties, but we play abroad too.'

'God, I bet you break hearts wherever you go,' I reply. 'I bet you have girls eating out of the palm of your hand.'

'You're not wrong,' he replies – and it takes me aback, because I know it's true, but he doesn't usually say as much. 'Wait a sec, I'll show you.'

Ew. No thank you.

'That's okay...'

'Trust me, you want to see this girl,' he replies. 'Look...'

I notice his hand appear at the top of the cubicle – he's handing me his phone and, unsure what else to do, I take it.

'Flick through those,' he says.

I reluctantly do as I'm told and the second I see the first picture I just laugh.

'What's her name?' I ask him.

'Kaya,' he replies. 'She lived at this sanctuary we visited. Gave me love bites, followed me around all day. Totally obsessed with me – but it was love at first bite for me too.'

Safe in the knowledge Brody can't see me, I smile widely at the photos of him and the adorable lion cub. Photos of them playing together, cuddling, him feeding her – okay, now I get why the 'palm of your hand' comment was so funny.

'She's beautiful,' I tell him.

'Yeah, but I wouldn't fancy play-fighting her in a few years,' he replies. 'So it never would have worked out.'

I laugh, handing him his phone back over the wall.

I'm still smiling when I try on the final dress I brought through. It's ruby-red silk, backless, with a thigh slit that makes me feel like I need some kind of tit tape for my downstairs. It clings in the right places, floats casually in the others, and it's perfect for the casino.

I step out of the fitting room, mostly just to prove to myself that I can walk in it, and admire myself in one of the big mirrors.

Brody steps out too and I wouldn't go as far as to say his jaw drops, but it looks like it bounces maybe, just a little...

'Wow... Jessa...' he says.

'Is it okay?' I check.

'It's more than okay,' he replies. 'You look unreal.'

I blush, making my cheeks match my dress.

'I feel a bit self-conscious in it, if I'm being honest, it's not me, it's—'

'Nah, don't do that,' he interrupts me. 'Don't look for reasons not to wear it. Don't think it's not you. It's just a dress and you look hot in it.'

My jaw does drop.

I look in the mirror, trying to see what he sees, or what he says he sees anyway. Do I look good? I feel good, and it's a really nice dress...

'Screw it,' I say firmly. 'I'm going to get it.'

'Yeah, you are,' he replies. 'Come on, let's go...'

'Wait a second,' I say, eyeballing him suspiciously. 'Are you just saying all of this, to hurry me up, so that I don't try on more dresses?'

'Maybe I am, maybe I'm not,' he replies cryptically. 'But maybe you should just buy it, and see what happens.'

Again, I have no idea what he means by that, but I can't resist giving it a go. I'll buy it, I'll see what happens – who knows? I might even like it...

27

The ship has a karaoke bar – of course it does. It has everything. What doesn't it have? I just made the mistake of asking a bartender this question and I didn't like the answer.

'Did you know there's a prison and morgue on board?' I ask the gang as I plonk myself back down with my bay breeze cocktail – my third, or is it my fourth?

'What?' Kelsey shrieks.

'Yep,' I reply. 'I asked him, half joking, if the ship had everything on board, and he confirmed it. I suppose it makes sense but it's not really something you want to think about on your holidays.'

'You asked him,' Nikki points out, scowling, which is crazy because it's not that deep.

'Well, it's like my granny used to say: fuck around, find out,' I joke – my favourite joke.

Brody laughs.

'Okay, well, maybe you don't talk to people without me,' he suggests playfully.

'Haven't you heard of women's rights?' I reply.

'It's women's wrongs I'm worried about,' he teases.

'You don't usually complain,' I reply.

Almost everyone finds our flirtatious bickering adorable. The only ones who don't? Todd and Nikki, obviously.

I know why the ship needs a morgue, of course I do, but a karaoke area seems less important. Maybe. It is a lot of fun, I suppose.

There are a few rooms, with private booths, so I'm in one with the usual suspects: Brody, Kelsey and Neil, Al and Kira, and Todd and Nikki.

It's a cool space, with disco lights, and a big screen that shows the lyrics. Everything is so colourful and sparkly and it really is hard not to have a good time when everyone is singing.

Todd and Nikki are tucked into a corner, not quite having as much fun as the rest of us, but I guess that's because Brody and my presence is just ruining the trip for them. Boo-bloody-hoo. They didn't want this? Neither did we. They would do well to remember that they chose this, in a roundabout way. It really is like my granny didn't actually say: fuck around, find out. Play stupid games, win stupid prizes. Dump your ex, don't be upset when they move on.

'Put me down for basically every Elvis song they have,' Al announces.

'If you think you can do Elvis, sure, I'll put you down for that,' Kira says, sounding unconvinced, and she's the one who hears him sing in the shower.

'Thank you very much,' he says – in the way you'd expect.

'I'm thinking I might do a Lady Gaga track,' Kelsey replies. 'Not that I can sing.'

'I was going to say, is that a promise or a threat,' Neil teases her.

'Oi!' she replies. 'Perhaps we could pick some songs for each other too. That could be fun?'

My mind goes into overdrive, wondering what songs I would choose for everyone. Al, I don't know why, but 'YMCA' by the Village People just feels right. For Brody, I do know why, 'I'm Too Sexy' by Right Said Fred. Perhaps I shouldn't be allowed to pick for anyone, I'm not exactly reaching for modern masterpieces.

Neil returns from the bar with a tray full of drinks, saying that way no one has an excuse to dip out. The drinks have names like Sex on the Deck and Ship Happens. Hilarious. I don't think I've eaten or drunk anything on board that wasn't totally delicious, so I'll try anything.

Al has a tray too, full of snacks. Popcorn, pretzels, crackers, olives and... pickles. Shit.

I look up, from glaring at them, to realise Nikki was doing the same, except she has the biggest smile on her face.

'Jessa... pickles... your favourite,' she points out.

'Yay,' I say, trying to muster up some fake enthusiasm.

'Fill your boots,' she prompts me.

'I don't like to eat, before I sing,' I tell her, hoping that's the end of it, but I can tell by the look in her eyes that she's not going to let this one go.

'I'm starving,' Brody says. 'I could eat them all, to be honest. I'll get Jessa some more.'

He picks up the little bowl and starts popping mini pickles into his mouth.

'Okay, but it kind of seems to me like Jessa doesn't want to eat one,' Nikki says. 'And I think that's because she doesn't really like them. Because you guys cheated at Mr & Mrs.'

'Not this again,' Neil says, laughing, but I think his patience is wearing thin.

'It's fine,' I tell Neil, not wanting him to feel anything negative in the run-up to his wedding – especially not caused by me. 'Brody – can I have one?'

'This is the last one,' he says, holding one between his thumb and finger.

It's only small – how bad can it be?

'Please?' I say, pouting at him.

'Okay, sure,' he replies. 'Just so long as you don't love them more than you love me. Taking a man's last pickle isn't cool...'

'Ah, but if you love me more than you love them, you'll give me it,' I reply.

He smiles. We both know I don't want it, we both know I have no choice.

I lean forward, my mouth open, taking his hand in mine, and eat it straight from his fingertips.

Oh, God, it's so nasty. So salty and sharp and... and what does it even taste like? It's vile. But I keep my game face on, I eat it like a champ, and then – partly to upset Nikki, because she's backed me into this corner, and partly to take the taste away with literally anything – seeing as though I'm still holding Brody's hand in front of my face, I take his index finger in my mouth and suck it. I notice his eyes widen for a split second, but his game face is as good as mine.

'You really can't get enough, can you,' he says.

'I really can't,' I reply with a wink.

'Ew,' Nikki blurts.

'Okay, well, now we all know Jessa likes pickles, can we have fun?' Kelsey asks. 'Jessa, come look at the music catalogue with me.'

I do as I'm told, following her to the screen where you choose the songs, just away from everyone else's ears – and drowned out by Al, who has just started singing 'Suspicious Minds'.

'This is actually so much fun,' Kelsey says, swiping on the screen. 'I'm going to pick a song for Brody.'

'What song?' I ask.

'You'll see,' she replies. 'It's mad, I've never seen you so flirty, so into PDA, so loved-up...'

I freeze for a second. Kelsey is my best friend. Did I really think I could pull the wool over her eyes? She must know it's all an act.

'You must really like him,' she says with a smile.

'Yeah, I do,' I reply.

'And watching Todd and Nikki watching you both so happy, and seeming so bothered, well, that's a lovely bonus,' she adds.

'Are they bothered? I hadn't noticed,' I reply, feigning ignorance.

One by one, people start taking the mic. Neil and Kelsey do 'I Got You Babe', which is more adorable than it is on-key. Kira chickens out of doing her song, not wanting to sing one on her own, so Al does one with her – but of course it's an Elvis song. 'Viva Las Vegas' is always a crowd-pleaser though.

Even Todd gets up and sings a Coldplay song, an old one, not a fun new one. There's nothing wrong with Coldplay, but 'Yellow' doesn't really get anyone lit, and I could swear he was spitting a few of the bars in my direction.

Then it's Brody's turn. Now this I'm excited to hear.

He grabs the mic and takes to the front of the crowd – facing us, instead of the screen, so he must know the lyrics. He's got all the performance of a rock star. I guess he's used to standing in front of large groups of people and performing, although singing and bowling are really different skills.

As the opening bars of the Bee Gees' 'Love You Inside and Out' start playing, I can't help but smile.

It's our dumb little in-joke. The song we bonded over in front of the others. And it really is my favourite Bee Gees song, that wasn't part of the act.

There may not be any crossover between being good at bowling and being good at singing but a performer is a performer and he's killing it, every note. He's strutting around, shaking his hips, leaving everyone a mixture of amused and impressed.

And then he turns his attention to me, extends a hand, pulling me up next to him, serenading me.

I cackle as he pulls me up. He places his free hand on my waist, my palm finds his shoulder, and suddenly we're swaying under the disco lights and it's so cheesy but so perfect.

He dips me. He twirls me. And then he finishes by doing a seriously extra – but absolutely spectacular – slide across the floor on his knees, finishing the song at my feet.

Everyone goes nuts – well, almost everyone. The usual two refuse to enjoy the moment.

'Jessa, it says you're next,' Kelsey announces.

'I haven't chosen a song,' I reply.

'Someone has chosen a song for you then, I guess,' Kelsey replies with a shrug. 'You got this.'

I feel empowered and emboldened by Brody's performance, like his confidence is contagious. There's no way I can be as good as him but his happy vibes make me not care all that much. I just want to have fun.

I grab the mic and take a deep breath.

The screen lights up, the music starts, and a song starts that I'm not all that familiar with. It's a country song – not my favourite genre. I look out at the crowd, to see if anyone can shed any light.

'I don't know this one,' I say as the intro plays.

'It's Carrie Underwood,' Kira announces. 'Country is my guilty pleasure.'

Did Kira choose this for me? Just because she wanted to hear it? Surely not.

I try my best to follow the lyrics, singing along, but as I do I realise what I'm saying. It's a woman singing very uncomplimentary things about a blonde woman who – I'm assuming – is with her man.

I only need to glance at Nikki for a second to realise that she's chosen this song for me, because she's actually smiling, clearly enjoying how uncomfortable I look. Presumably I'm the blonde tramp in the song and Brody is the cheater. Rich, so rich. And as subtle as a nuclear bomb.

'What song is this?' Kelsey asks.

'It's "Before He Cheats",' Nikki says. 'I'll sing it, if you can't...'

Do you know what? She can have it. I hand her the mic just in time for her to belt the chorus.

I'm about to sit down when my emotions get the better of me. I know, Brody and I are rubbing it in their faces a bit, but only in retaliation. But the two of them are supposed to be happy. And yet Nikki just seems to get off on embarrassing me.

'I'm feeling pretty tired, I think I might go to bed,' I tell the others, raising my voice over Nikki's warbling.

'Are you sure?' Kelsey replies, sensing something is up.

'Do you want me to come with you?' Brody asks.

'No, no, I'm all good, you guys have a good time, I'm just shattered – I think it's the sea air, or the early mornings in the gym, or both,' I insist. 'I'll see you guys later.'

I leave and I don't look back – and I pick up the pace, because Nikki's voice is like nails on a chalkboard.

What is wrong with her? Why does she have to be so mean? She took my boyfriend from me – and with him, as corny as it sounds, my hopes and dreams, because I factored Todd into the rest of my life, and I just can't picture what it looks like without him, as much as I want to. It's just going to take time to figure that out, I guess. Perhaps that's why I'm so happy here, in the delusion, having fun, playing make-believe.

I step outside briefly, on to one of the decks, to get some fresh air. I suck it in and puff it out, trying to clear my mind, and flush out my emotions, because the urge to cry is creeping up on me.

'Hey,' a voice calls out from behind me.

Speaking of creeping up…

I jump but it's just Brody. I'm glad it's him.

'Are you okay?' he asks me.

'Probably not,' I reply. 'But I will be. Has Nikki always been so mean?'

'I didn't notice it at first but, yeah, it was coming through thick and fast in the end,' he replies. 'I know it's not nice, or fair, and it's hard, but try to ignore her. She wants to get a rise out of you.'

'I know, I shouldn't have stormed out, but I was getting emotional,' I confess.

'Well, don't worry, because I made them all think we had a plan to sneak off early, to get an early night,' he replies with a smile. 'Come on, let me walk you back.'

'My hero – again,' I tell him. 'Thanks.'

'We're in the same boat,' he says, laughing at his own joke. 'I've got my iPad with me, I've got Netflix – want to watch something together?' he asks.

'I'd love that,' I reply. 'My kind of early night.'

'Anything you fancy watching?'

'I love *It's Always Sunny in Philadelphia*,' I reply. 'Have you seen it?'

'Only all the way through maybe ten times,' he says. 'Maybe we could pick our favourite episodes for each other?'

'I'd really, really love that,' I reply.

Back in the suite, we both climb into bed like it's the most normal thing in the world to watch TV together and it's so nice. We laugh together, quote lines together – and even more amazingly, we have the same favourite episode.

After a few episodes and a lot of laughter, he yawns and stretches.

'It's your turn in the bath,' he says, giving me a faux-pitying look.

'Ugh, I had somehow forgotten about that,' I reply. 'It's not nice, is it?'

'Nope,' he replies. 'Tell you what, you've had a bad night – how about we trade, and I take the bath tonight?'

'I've had a great night,' I correct him. 'And, thanks for the offer, but that's not fair on you. I'll be fine.'

'I don't mind,' he insists.

'I'm not stealing the bed from you...'

'Then don't steal it from me, share it with me,' he suggests. 'We're in it together, right now, and it's not awkward. Plus, it can't be weird when we're sleeping, can it? How would we know, we'll be asleep...'

I laugh.

'Really? Are you sure?' I check.

'We're boyfriend and girlfriend,' he jokes. 'It's only natural.'

'Well, if it's for appearances,' I reply. 'Then it would be weird not to.'

After I get ready for bed, the sheets are cool when I slide under them, and they smell of Brody's delicious aftershave – or maybe that's him, the man in bed next to me.

He stretches out, so naturally, like he's where he belongs – and I guess like I belong here too, because he seems so comfortable with me. I'm comfortable too, for the most part, but it's hard to ignore how weirdly hot this is.

He's shirtless, because of course he is. And I'm in the vest and pants that I sleep in – that cover more than my bikini does, and yet I feel so... naked.

'Night night,' he says softly, his voice almost tickling my ears, almost like I can feel the vibration through the bed.

'Goodnight,' I reply.

I want to say more, but I can't get the words out. I'm nervous, not because I don't want to be in here with him, but because I do.

He reaches over and flicks off the light. Darkness fills the room, only leaving room for silence.

I swear, the air changes. There's a shift, it's subtle, but I can feel it...

I lie still, on my back, staring up at the ceiling, wondering if he's as wide awake as I am, if his mind is racing too... Wondering if he can feel the heat radiating between us.

He didn't have to serenade me to make me laugh. He didn't have to come find me when I left, upset. And he definitely didn't have to let me sleep in the bed with him. And yet, here I am. Here we are.

I glance toward him in the dark. He's facing me, I think. Or maybe just turned that way in his sleep.

It's too dark to tell and I'm too nervous to ask.

I lie there for a little longer, letting the rhythm of his breath steady my own breathing, wondering what would happen if I just... reached out.

'Thanks for being perfect tonight,' I whisper.

I don't know if he hears it. I don't know if he's already asleep or if I didn't say it loud enough, but he shifts slightly closer, just enough for our bodies to brush.

It's going to be a long night...

28

Life is full of surprises – Lord knows I've had my share of them this month – but in a twist that absolutely no one saw coming: I'm a gym girl. I know, I've said that before, but it's really true now. I'm not just here to fake it for everyone else, or just to hang out with Brody, I'm actually working out.

I don't know why I've always shied away from exercise – it's probably a little light PTSD thanks to an especially vile PE teacher – but today I decided to give it a go, not because Brody told me to, just because seeing how great it made him feel made me curious.

Honestly? It's been great. I feel like I've had a proper workout. No fake stretching that's actually napping, no using the exercise bike as a chair or messing around on the yoga ball.

'Who are you and what have you done with Jessa?' Brody asks, watching me bouncing up and down on an elliptical machine – it's sort of like stepping crossed with running, both things I usually shy away from, but this is fun.

'She's in here, behind the sweaty mess,' I reply, huffing and puffing.

'You're not sweaty, you're glowing,' he corrects me.

'That's an incredibly generous interpretation of the truth, so thank you,' I say. 'I can't believe I'm saying it either but... I think I'm enjoying myself.'

'What?' he says with a theatrical gasp.

'I'm just as shocked as you are,' I say, hopping off the machine, my legs a little wobbly.

He's sitting at one of the weight machines – the one where you pull a bar down behind your head (no idea what it's called, this is my first workout, after all) and it's captivating, the way his muscles ripple through his arms and across his back. I feel like I can see each one individually – it's almost like his muscles have muscles.

He catches me staring at him and smiles.

'I want to try that thing,' I say, trying to make out like I was admiring the machine, not the muscular man sitting at it.

'Really?' he replies. 'Because I kind of miss watching you pretend to stretch.'

'Really,' I reply. 'In fact, I want to try to lift the weight you're lifting.'

'I don't think that's a good idea,' he tells me.

'Why not?'

'Because it probably weighs as much as you,' he replies.

'Okay, wow, are you saying I'm too heavy?' I tease. 'Way to mansplain.'

'My looking out for you is not mansplaining,' he insists.

'Woooow, and now you're mansplaining mansplaining to me,' I clap back, trying not to smile. 'It just gets worse.'

Brody laughs.

'Okay then, princess, be my guest,' he says, making way for me to probably embarrass myself.

I straddle the seat and take the bar in my hands. It doesn't budge an inch.

'Okay, unlock it or whatever,' I tell him. 'I'm ready to try.'

I notice him purse his lips, trying to stifle a chuckle.

'What?' I ask.

'It doesn't need unlocking,' he tells me. 'It's ready when you are.'

'Honestly?' I check.

He nods.

'Oh, okay, then yeah, you're right, this isn't a good idea,' I admit. 'And you must be freakishly strong.'

'I try,' he says through a grin. 'We'll start you small, build you up if you want. You could be Al-sized before you know it.'

'Oh, no, thank you,' I reply. 'I can't be trusted to wield that level of strength. I have too many old scores to settle.'

Brody chuckles.

'You laugh, but I'm in awe of you, having the physical ability to throw Todd overboard, but resisting the urge to do it. That's impressive,' I tell him.

'Well, maybe if you get jacked, it will be a deterrent for the next guy who thinks about messing with you. Do you think anyone messes with Al in the first place?' he points out. 'We all know he's a big friendly giant, but everyone else thinks he's terrifying.'

'That's a great point,' I reply. 'Would I scare you?'

'You already scare me,' he tells me. 'Because I've seen your psychological and emotional warfare strategies.'

I hop off the machine to do a playful little curtsey. Oof, my arse muscles hurt – I wasn't under the impression I had any in there.

'You've been a great sport, you know,' he says. 'Considering I only told people you came to the gym with me to wind you up.'

'Yeah, and yet when I said you came to the spa with me, some-how, you've still yet to visit it with me,' I point out. 'People might start to get suspicious...'

'Okay, fine, come on, let's go to the spa, you've earned it,' he says. 'We've got some time to kill.'

'Honestly?' I reply.

'Yeah, why not?' he says.

I could never get Todd to go to a spa with me, but I don't want to ruin my own day by saying his name a second before I have to.

'You told people I love it,' he reminds me. 'So I'd better go and I'd better love it. I don't want people thinking I'm a bad boyfriend, that's not going to look good on my CV.'

'Then let's get washed up and go,' I reply.

'You know...' Brody starts, as we finally wander towards the spa. 'It's going to be weird when we go back to our real lives.'

'It really is,' I reply. 'I feel like I was just getting used to the fact I didn't have a boyfriend any more, being alone, and then you turn up and – I know, we're faking it – but for all intents and purposes, it's like being with someone, being with you. We share a bedroom, we spend all of our time together, we share our problems...'

'That's an excellent point,' he says with a laugh. 'I'd question whether it was healthy but... we're in too deep now.'

'I guess we are,' I reply. 'But know that, as far as boyfriends go, real or fake, you've set the bar pretty high.'

Brody smiles.

'You too,' he tells me. 'You'll be a tough act to follow.'

'It's going to be a shock to the system, isn't it?' I say, my smile falling from my face. 'Going back to being on my own.'

'Yeah, I get that,' he replies. 'But even when it feels like we're alone, we're not. We've got great friends.'

'You've got a whole team of friends,' I point out. 'I've got

Kelsey, who is getting married, and Kira, who just got married. They're moving into the next phase of life, and I'm happy for them, but... I don't know, I guess I just feel like I'm standing on the train platform, waving them off, being left on my own.'

He doesn't say anything right away. Instead, as we turn the corner, he gently wraps his arm around my shoulders.

'They're not leaving you behind,' he reassures me. 'It's great that you're happy for them. But it won't be long before Neil is abandoning Kelsey for golf and Al's busy with bodybuilding and meal prep. Your friends are going to be begging you to rescue them from their new phase.'

I smile and lean slightly into him.

'Yeah, I guess you're right,' I reply. 'I guess it's just hard not to look on the dark side of life at the moment.'

'Well, if you ever get desperate, my team could always use a new mascot,' he jokes, instantly lifting my mood.

'I'm probably not that desperate,' I reply with a laugh.

'Probably?' he replies. 'So, you are considering it...'

'I'd never rule it out,' I joke.

I love the way Brody takes the heaviness away from me, making me feel lighter. His big strong arms have multiple uses, it turns out.

The spa appears like a mirage at the end of what felt like an endless hallway. Double frosted doors with the creative name 'The Spa' plastered across them, the frame of the door edged with flowers, greeting the most beautiful floral arch. I feel more relaxed just looking at it.

Inside, the first things you notice are the dreamy scents being diffused into the room, and the sound of trickling water – which usually I find peaceful, but on a cruise it's sort of disconcerting.

The staff are on it, getting us into white fluffy robes and plying us with glasses of cucumber water and before either of us can think of a reason to say no, we're on our way to a treatment room for a couple's facial.

'I've never had a couple's facial,' I whisper to Brody.

'I've never had a facial,' he replies.

We're led into a private treatment room and I don't know if it feels more or less awkward for us not being a real couple.

There are two massage beds, soft towels, and two therapists in matching linen uniforms who greet us with unnervingly zen smiles. So serene they almost seem dead behind the eyes.

I lie back and exhale as my therapist starts working her magic on my face. It's so relaxing until I hear a strange noise, coming from Brody. A snort – no, a snigger.

'Try to keep still,' his therapist tells him.

'Sorry, sorry,' he replies.

The room is only silent for a second or two before he starts giggling again and, honestly, it's contagious. Hearing his adorable chuckle sets me off smiling too.

I'm able to glance sideways at him, and he's trying to tough it out, bless him, but his whole body is shaking as he tries to contain his laughter. The therapist gives him a gentle, disapproving shhh, which only makes things worse.

And then I lose it too. Well, that's how it goes, isn't it? If one person starts laughing when you know you shouldn't, it's impossible not to join in.

It's almost a relief when it's over, and our patient therapists leave us to have a moment of quiet – I do wonder if they said that sarcastically.

'That's supposed to be relaxing?' Brody says as he catches his breath.

'It usually is,' I reply. 'When there isn't a hyena in the room...'

'I'm so sorry,' he says sincerely. 'I tried to hold it in but, I don't know, she started flicking water at my face and I just kept thinking about how funny it must look...'

'It's fine,' I tell him. 'I don't remember the last time I laughed so much.'

'They do say laughter is the best medicine,' he points out. 'Maybe it's good for skin too?'

'You'd better hope so, because I don't think they'll let us back in here,' I reply.

We decide to leave, before we're kicked out, but do you know what? I feel like I've been here for hours. I feel relaxed, I feel happy – in a way that no spa treatment can achieve.

I can't help but laugh, as we walk back towards our cabin.

'What?' Brody asks. 'You're not still laughing at me laughing?'

'No, no,' I say, the corners of my mouth twitching upward. 'Okay, maybe, just a bit, but it was hilarious.'

'Tell people we came, but not what happened,' he says firmly, but jokily.

'Listen, there's not a doubt in my mind that you're officially the best boyfriend I've had this year,' I tell him.

'Well, given the competition, I won't get too excited,' he replies. 'But thanks.'

I love his smile – it's as contagious as his laugh.

'How is it possible that we've never met?' I ask him.

'The phrase is: where have you been all my life?' he jokes. 'We have met though.'

'What do you mean?' I ask.

'You and I, we've met, before all of this,' he tells me.

'At a wedding or a party or something?'

'You really don't remember, do you?' he replies with grin. 'You were sitting at a table, alone, in a beer garden in Headingly. You were being harassed by... I think it was a Mario Brother. I told him—'

'You told him you were my boyfriend,' I interrupt him. 'Oh my gosh, that was you. You swooped in, saved the day, then disappeared.'

'I did pop back, to see if you were okay, but I could see you had a man sitting with you, and you looked happy so... yeah.'

I'm gobsmacked. And suddenly it makes so much sense, why Mario was fawning over him, it wasn't because he was dressed as someone famous, it's because he *was* someone famous – Brody Ryan, the bad boy of cricket, a Headingly celebrity.

'You're a regular hero, aren't you?' I say.

'I promise you, I don't go around making a habit of it,' he insists. 'I've only done it the two times you know about. Only with you.'

'Well, thanks, for both times,' I tell him. 'I've only ever needed someone to pretend to be my boyfriend twice – I'm glad it was you.'

Convincing people I went to the spa won't be an issue, I can feel the happiness beaming out of me like sunshine. Convincing myself that it's not because of Brody is a different matter...

29

You know what? I know this is a pre-wedding cruise, and I'm part of the wedding party, but does there really need to be so much stuff? I love Kelsey, and Neil, and spending time with Al and Kira, and even Brody, it turns out, is a delight to hang out with. But do we really need to spend so much time together and, if we do, do we always have to be competing?

What fresh hell today, I hear you ask? Basketball. Yep, sport. And on the day I decided to have a workout, so my body is knackered. I could blame my inevitable poor performance on that, I guess, but it just feels like PE all over again. Adult me really couldn't care less how good or bad anyone is at bleep tests, but twelve-year-old me was always mortified to be out at, like, level 3 (and it was a long time ago, so I'm probably remembering that more favourably than it actually was).

Anyway, I'm here, I'm on Brody's team, he seems to be good at actually everything, and I'm told that having Al on the other team is also an advantage, because his arms are only good for throwing fridges over HGVs and looking great with a tan.

Personally, if this were my wedding, I would be keeping well away from literally anything that could see me getting hurt – I once gave myself a black eye pulling up my tights in a public toilet, so truly, nothing feels safe.

But sure, why not, let's have a game of four-a-side. Let's throw hard balls at each other. See what happens.

'Right,' Al says with a clap of his hands, because the man cannot turn off his competitive nature for a moment. 'Let's do this. I may be hungover, and I may not have played this before, but I came to win.'

He's on a team with Kira, Todd and Nikki, leaving me, Brody, Kelsey and Neil on the other side. I'm happy with that. Kelsey was on the school netball team, so those skills must translate, Neil is sportsy, and Brody is Brody. Todd likes watching sport, Al is made of marble, Kira hates physical activity, and Nikki screamed during the warm-up when Todd threw a ball to her. I like my odds. The only thing wrong with our team is me, I'm the weak link, but I've advised everyone to refrain from passing me the ball unless it's absolutely necessary. I'm happy to be on the winning team, of course I am, I just don't believe I'm capable of doing anything to help us get there. My help would hurt, without a doubt, but apparently this is supposed to be fun...? So I'll try not to over-think it.

'A relaxing day of trying not to get hit in the face by balls,' I say with a sigh. 'Although I suppose you're used to it.'

'A day of trying not to get hit in the face by balls?' Brody repeats my words back to me and, fair enough, they were a poor choice.

'You know what I mean,' I say with a roll of my eyes.

'I've got your back, don't worry,' he reassures me. 'If there's one thing I'm good at, it's throwing and catching. I'll be fine with bigger balls.'

I purse my lips. Now it's his turn to phrase things terribly –

then again, knowing Brody, he probably did that just to make me laugh.

'I'll body-check Al, if I have to,' he adds. Yep, he has to be kidding.

'Body-checking Al would be like body-checking a Boeing 747,' I reply.

'And I'd do it – for you,' he continues.

I snort.

'Let's hope it never comes to that,' I reply. 'But how very gentlemanly of you.'

'I try,' he says with a wink.

It's an outdoor court – of course it is, the ship is endless – surrounded by a safety net that presumably stops balls going overboard, or hitting the other guests. Knowing myself, I'll find a way to breach that, if not with a ball then with myself.

'Todd and Nikki are staring at us again,' I tell Brody quietly, through gritted teeth.

'Shall we give them something to stare at?' he replies.

'Yeah, do that really horny thing you see in the movies, where men teach women sport and basically hump them,' I reply.

'You want me to... hump you?' he replies, smirking, one eyebrow raised.

'I want them to see you humping me,' I reply – phrasing! 'I mean, I want them to see us humping... to see you and me, you flirting with me, or whatever. Honestly, men are usually much quicker to accept general invitations to do stuff like this.'

'My reputation is bad enough,' he replies. 'And I don't want to get put on a list. But, go on then, seeing as though it's you. I'm sure it works better for golf, snooker – even cricket, if you're batting. But basketball...'

'You're a big boy, you'll figure it out,' I reply.

Our laughing and joking always seems to edge into flirtatious and it's like I'm getting so into character, my brain starts to think it's real, which isn't ideal for me, but it's great for the performance we're putting in.

As I try out my grip on one of the balls (everything sounds dirty now), Brody sidles up behind me, his hands finding my waist with ease as he presses his body up against mine. His chin rests on my shoulder, his warm breath tickles my neck.

I knew he'd be good at it – just not this good.

He adjusts my arms, gently guiding the ball into position.

'Try to relax your wrists – and everything else,' he tells me. 'Bend your knees a little. Yeah, just like that.'

I do as I'm told, which only makes me back up into him even closer. I know, I know, it's an act, I asked him to do this, but it's very confusing for basically every sense I have.

It's a game. It's all pretend. This is for show – for them, not for me, I'm not getting anything out of this except smug satisfaction. I remind myself of that on a loop as I feel every inch of him pressed against me.

If this weren't for show, if he really was flirting with me, this would be so, so hot.

'Oh, for God's sake, get a room!' Al teases us, shielding his eyes dramatically. 'This is a basketball court, there's no fourth base here.'

'We've got a room,' Brody calls back. 'This is just the warm-up.'

'Yeah, except you're sharing a room with us,' Nikki snaps. 'And I think we've both had enough of your little... sexploits, thanks.'

Sexploits.

I'm not even looking at her but I can feel her glare burning holes in me. If looks could kill, I'd certainly be dead.

'Ignore them, focus on me, my body guiding yours, and make the shot,' Brody tells me.

I focus on his body a little too hard because I miss the basket so spectacularly, it was probably technically closer to going through the hoop at the other end of the court.

'It wouldn't be fair, if you were hot and good at sport,' he tells me, very much for our audience's benefit.

'But you are,' I reply.

'Lucky you,' he says with a smile.

I don't even care that I missed – and that I'll probably miss every shot – because this isn't about scoring points on the court, it's about scoring points off it. Whether we win at basketball makes no difference, we're winning the ex wars, and that's the only battle I care about. Todd looks so miserable and Nikki looks so angry – if it's just a taste of how they made me and Brody feel, it's a fraction of what they deserve.

'Okay, let's play, before this turns into an orgy,' Kira jokes.

We start playing and I'm surprised how fast-paced and chaotic it is. Everyone is moving like they're fighting for their lives, and yet it's so unserious, and so much fun. Well, it is until it isn't. Todd is getting more into it, playing like a man who has something to prove, and while playing the game might be child's play for Brody, most of his effort is going into thwarting Todd's. They're using Al like a sort of goalie, having him stand by the net, ready to reach up and bat the balls away, so it takes speed to get around him, but between Brody and Kelsey, they're running rings around him.

I've touched the ball a couple of times, never for long before I offload it, but even I'm having fun. Perhaps I should have paid more attention, when Brody was showing me how to throw, but I think he was giving me a fake horny lesson, rather than a real one.

The ball comes to me and I panic, flinging it towards Brody, but making it almost impossible for him to catch.

'We're aiming for the basket, not the sea,' Brody teases me.

'Sorry, I was just so distracted by your big... arms,' I reply with a grin.

'Makes sense, that's why I'm so good at cricket, I distract my competitors,' he replies jokily. 'But my eyes are up here. Focus.'

I snort with laughter.

'I'll do my best,' I reply.

He runs past me, fingers grazing my waist as he goes, and it sends a silly little shiver down my spine.

We're winning – not by a landslide, and not that it has anything to do with me, but enough to get under their skin (well, Todd and Nikki's).

I catch Todd staring again. Not glancing. Staring.

He's got that look on his face, like he's trying to do a cryptic crossword. It's like he just can't make sense of what's happening. Like all of the pieces of the puzzle are here, but he can't quite fit them together.

Al calls his name and passes him the ball, but Todd doesn't react in time, he's too busy looking my way. The ball bounces off his shoulder with a loud boing, ricocheting straight into Nikki's face.

It happens so fast I almost don't register it. One second she's flipping her hair and shouting at Kira to at least make an effort, the next she's clutching her nose and making that noise. And it's so familiar. A high-pitched, almost yodel-like cry. I've heard that cry before and... oh my gosh... it's her... Nikki is the crying girl from the toilets at the wedding where Todd dumped me... the crying girl from the wedding where Todd dumped me is Nikki.

'Shit,' I blurt to myself.

'Are you okay?' Brody asks me as everyone crowds around Nikki to make sure she's okay.

But it's like I can't really hear him. I'm right back in that cubicle, replaying my conversation with Nikki, trying to remember what she said, what I said. How could I have known it was her? I didn't know her, she didn't introduce herself, I didn't even see her face. But she was talking about Brody and I... I told her to dump him. I said that if she wasn't happy, that wasn't enough, she should find someone who made her happy.

Ha, and then she found Todd, so that serves me right for getting involved in someone else's business, but I was just trying to be nice and supportive and a girl's girl and... shit.

I can't believe I told her to leave him. That was the night that changed everything. It can't be a coincidence that she dumped Brody and Todd dumped me. I wonder if they were talking about getting together, or already together – I wonder if I gave her the push that made her give Todd the ultimatum that made him dump me.

The fallout zone just feels so huge, and it feels like me who dropped the bomb, who got us dumped, who got Brody bad press. Even if I didn't technically drop the bomb, I helped build it, or detonate it, or something.

I drag my mind back to the present. Kira is checking Nikki over – Nikki who looks fine, but is definitely milking it.

What am I supposed to do? I could say something, I guess. I could connect the dots out loud, for everyone to hear. I could confess. Explain. Apologise... if I need to? I sort of feel like I do need to, for indirectly messing up Brody's public image, with one poorly timed pep talk.

Or... I could stay quiet. Let it go, pretend I haven't pieced the puzzle together. Well, Nikki didn't see me either, she doesn't know it was me who encouraged her to pull the trigger. Everyone's getting along well enough. Brody and me, whatever we are, it's working. It's fun. It's helping us get the closure we need. And I'm not crying over Todd any more – I know for sure that I don't want him back, Brody doesn't want Nikki, the plan is working. It has worked.

Perhaps this is what moving on really looks like – choosing to leave the past where it is. Not because you're running from it, but because it's no longer chasing you.

Brody jogs back over, wiping sweat from his brow, his eyes scanning mine as he tries to work out where I went.

'Are you sure you're okay?' he asks. 'Nikki is fine, don't worry.'

I look at him. Really look. And then I smile.

'Yeah, I'm good,' I tell him. 'Great, actually.'

His smile matches mine.

'Don't look quite so pleased she got hit in the face,' he whispers.

I laugh.

'That's not why I'm smiling,' I insist.

'I'll believe you,' he replies. 'Let's get back to it then.'

The game picks back up – Nikki still sulking, Todd glaring harder, Kelsey yelling strategy like I'm even listening, Al being huge and Brody being Brody.

He looks so happy, like he's having a blast, and he really doesn't seem all that bothered about Nikki.

Telling him the truth might hurt him, and allowing myself to wonder about the details will only upset me. I just need to let it go – and let go of any guilt I might have too.

For the first time in ages, I feel happy, and that's nothing to feel guilty about… right?

Let's not rock the boat now…

30

It never ceases to amaze me how big and impressive this ship is. Just when I think I've seen it all, something else dazzles me. The thing I can never quite get over is how many whole things it has in it. I know, that sounds silly but, like, I'm in a casino right now. A whole casino right here on the ship, along with all the cabins, the restaurants, the gym, the spa, the cinema, the pools, the gaming rooms. All here.

You could think you were in Las Vegas right now, because this place is big, nice, flashy and full of people. Everyone is dressed in their best to play cards, roulette, slot machines – and of course to drink cocktails and just be genuinely fabulous.

I'm wearing my red dress, the one I picked out from the ship shop, and I actually feel great in it. Say what you like about Brody – Lord knows I have – but that man gives one hell of a confidence-boosting pep talk. No wonder he makes such a great teammate. Even I could probably score runs or wickets or whatever – I'm still not 100 per cent on how you score points in cricket.

Brody looks amazing in his suit. Effortlessly stylish, super dapper – to liken him to James Bond would be to make him sound corny or old-fashioned, but no, he just looks snappy and super cool.

I'm sitting on a high stool at the blackjack table, sipping my drink while I watch Brody play. He's doing a good job – I actually think he's up, unlike Todd. Every time I glance over at the craps table I can see him despairing. I guess, even with Nikki blowing on the dice for luck, he's on a bit of a losing streak.

Neil and Kelsey are doing rounds, seeing how people are doing. I think Neil played a few hands of poker but Kelsey looked bored, and Al and Kira are too wrapped up in their drinks, and each other of course, to roll the dice on... well, rolling the dice.

It's all very fancy. Very elegant. But very, very, very boring, if I'm being honest with you.

'This sucks, doesn't it?' Kelsey says, appearing from nowhere, seemingly reading my mind.

'It's lovely,' Kira chimes in.

'We're having a great time,' Al adds, doing his best to sound convincing.

'Really?' Kelsey replies. 'Because five minutes ago I thought I saw you sleeping.'

'I told you,' Kira says, giving him a playful shove.

'I think it's exactly what you wanted to do,' I tell her. 'It's fancy. Classy. Mature.'

I'm pretty sure that's what we were going for.

'Look at us. We're having a great time,' I add.

'Everyone but Todd,' Brody mutters under his breath, because he and Nikki are heading over to join us.

'I can win it all back,' Todd practically snaps at her, like a shit version of a character from a Scorsese movie.

'No, you won't,' Nikki replies. 'You need an intervention.'

Kelsey sighs and turns to Neil.

'I just... I really thought you would love this,' she tells him. 'It's a bit of you.'

'Okay, but tonight is supposed to be a bit of us,' he replies. 'I want you to be happy too. We can do whatever you want.'

'Ugh. I wish I'd planned something actually fun,' Kelsey says with a pout.

'I've planned something fun,' Brody pipes up.

'Have you?' Kelsey replies.

'Yeah. I was thinking about what to do with Neil after this, just the lads, and I got chatting to one of the crew...'

Here we go.

'...and it turns out, there's a kids' zone on board,' he says excitedly. 'With a pool and a big soft play area. Disco lights. Slides. Ball pits. The works.'

'So what?' Nikki says, unimpressed. 'We're not six.'

'So,' Brody continues, 'it's closed right now, because this voyage is adults-only. But the guy I spoke to, he said he was a big fan of mine, and that I could hire it out – just for us.'

'Sorry,' Nikki replies in disbelief. 'Have you been hit in the head with too many cricket balls? You want us to go to a kids' play area?'

I wonder if she's being even harder on him, now it's starting to seem like she can't get him back.

'It's not a kids' play area tonight,' he corrects her. 'I'm turning it into a club.'

There's a pause. Then Kelsey gasps.

'Oh my God, Brody Ryan, I love you,' she tells him. 'That's amazing. It sounds like so much fun.'

'It really does,' I add – well, after ten minutes of one of the dealers trying to explain what Kalooki is to me anything sounds preferable.

'Can we go now?' Kelsey practically begs him.

Brody jumps to his feet, straightens his jacket, and smiles like a man who knows he's just saved the night.

'Yes! Catch me up,' he says, already walking off. 'I'll go tell him we're ready.'

I watch him go, half-laughing, half-sighing.

Honestly, I can never quite work out if he's a dream or a nightmare.

I love that Brody runs off like an excitable child – hilarious, considering where he's headed.

'Well, you heard the man, let's follow him,' Neil says, rallying the troops.

As everyone else heads off, Kelsey takes hold of my arm, holding me back just a little so we can chat.

'Okay,' Kelsey says, her smile stretching from ear to ear. 'You've got a great one there, with Brody.'

I feel myself smiling before I can stop it. I know, I know, he's not really mine, but it's nice to pretend that this is my life.

'I know,' I say, trying to play it cool. The interesting thing about my smile is that it's genuine though. It's not a part of the act.

'Come on, you two, keep up,' Al calls back to us.

He seems genuinely excited – I really hope for his sake that he can actually fit in wherever it is we're going. I know the ship has its own morgue, police, things like that – but I'd be surprised if it had a fire brigade with the kit to cut a bodybuilder out of an enclosed slide.

'I knew it, you know,' Kelsey says, linking her arm with mine. 'You and Brody, being the perfect couple, ending up together.'

'No, you didn't.' I laugh. 'You're just saying that because he's got you a ball pool.'

'It's true,' she insists, shaking my arm. 'I knew the moment I saw you at Al and Kira's wedding. When you came down for breakfast in his clothes.'

I feel my smile widening again.

'You came down in his clothes – smiling just like you are now. Glowing, actually,' she tells me. 'And not just the morning-after kind of glow either. The kind where you realise you're head over heels for someone and you don't know what you're supposed to do about it.'

'Is that so?' I say. 'You're psychic now, eh?'

She ignores me.

'He is amazing though, right?' she says, like she's trying to coerce a confession out of me. Surely I have the right to remain silent?

'Yeah. He kind of is,' I admit.

'Told you,' she says.

Well, when he's not infuriating me, that is.

'And I'm not pretending I have psychic powers or anything,' she adds. 'But there's a reason we're not seeing each other much this trip, I'm leaving you two alone for a reason, so you can spend time together, enjoy that first flush of romance. It's just so obvious you've been into each other since day one.'

She really does seem pleased with herself and it's so cute.

'Oh, you don't have to do that,' I insist. 'We love you guys, we want to spend time with you.'

'We've got plenty of time to all hang out together later. I'm just so happy. Because it's you and it's Brody – my childhood best friend and Neil's childhood best friend. With Todd it just wasn't the same, none of it was. I know, I never really said anything before, and I never would have if you'd stayed together, but with Todd... I don't know. You just always seemed like you were trying so hard. Like you were convincing yourself that it was okay to settle.'

'Really?' I reply.

'Oh my God, yes,' she says, relieved to have finally got it off her chest. 'There were nights where I would lie awake, worrying. Wondering if you were settling. And I hated the idea of you doing that because you deserve to be with someone exciting, someone who adores you – someone like Brody.'

Okay, so Brody and I may not be an actual couple, but the rest of it is eye-opening. I had no idea she felt that way and suddenly I feel like I've had a really lucky escape.

'Hey, don't be upset,' she says, clocking the look on my face. 'I don't worry any more. Not since you've been with Brody. He's such a sweetie. I know the press give him a hard time, and say all of this bad stuff about him but, honestly, I think they're just trying to make cricket exciting. But you know the real him, you know he's not like that. Yeah, he's had some trouble settling down but that's just because he hasn't found the right girl. But look at him with you, he's so different. I'm just so happy you've both found what you were looking for, and that it's each other, and that I maybe get to take some credit... maybe.'

She laughs.

I don't know whether to smile or cry, because I want to believe it. I want to take every word she just said and run with it. But why would I delude myself like that, telling myself it's real when I know for a fact that it's fake because we planned it that way? This was only ever an act, I need to keep reminding myself that. And maybe I'll come clean to Kelsey, once her wedding is over, or maybe we will just have our fake break-up. I'll have a think and see which one will make her the least sad.

My bloody brain won't shut up now, it's running away from me. I need to rein it in.

But are we kind of perfect for each other though? Do we complement each other? Kelsey seems to think so but Brody doesn't even fancy me, does he? No, surely not. I think he's just doing a really good job of pretending, for the act, for me... And he doesn't have to do this, does he? He seems pretty okay about stuff, happy to move on, and yet he's still faking it with me. Is he faking it? Am I? I'm not even sure what's real or pretend any more.

So much of what Kelsey's saying is built on gut feelings and the things she's noticed, and most of those things have been carefully staged by me to tell the story I wanted people to believe so... can she even be right about this? I have no clue.

Well, we're here, so all of that needs to go back in the box for now.

I don't know what I was expecting from the kids' area but... not this. Nothing this cool. It's like I said before, I don't know how they're fitting whole places in this one ship. If this was in a city, it would be in a big building of its own.

The moment we step through the doors, Dua Lipa's voice blasts through the speakers, thudding along with the beat as multicoloured disco lights flash and dance across every available surface. The pool water glows under the lights, causing rainbow-ripple patterns on the walls which only adds to the vibe.

There's a huge soft play space in the corner, with monkey bars and slides and a ball pool. The place really has been transformed into a nightclub – oh, and now waitstaff are carrying in trays of cocktails that wouldn't look out of place at a beach bar in Ibiza. Now the party can get started.

Kelsey runs over to Brody and kisses him on the cheek.

'This is amazing,' she tells him.

'Best wedding present ever,' Neil adds. 'Other than getting to marry the love of my life, of course.'

We all watch as Al peels off his shirt (because of course he does, he's Al) before running towards the dance floor and sliding across it on his knees – so the same energy as a six-year-old at a wedding then.

Then he jumps to his feet and starts grooving to the music like someone's drunk relative at a wedding who's had just the right (or just the wrong) number of shots.

The man moves well for a big fella. I never expected it.

Kira rushes out to join him, declaring the dance floor officially open.

Brody, of course, is next. He takes Kelsey by both hands and pulls her toward the makeshift dance floor, twirling her around before the two of them dance together.

Neil turns to me and smiles.

'Come on, Jessa. I guess you're stuck with me,' he says.

'Better you than Todd,' I murmur under my breath.

I glance over at Todd and Nikki, who are choosing to drink instead of dance. They don't look like they're having fun – they don't even look happy – and you might think I'd be happy to see it, but I guess I'm not. They just did so much to be together, they caused so much trouble, hurt people, and for what? If they don't even stay together then what was the point?

Neil dances me off to the side, over by the pool, away from the others, just enough for us to talk.

'You're really bringing out the best in him, you know,' he says into my ear. 'I know he's been really stressed.'

'Brody? Stressed?' I reply.

'Yeah, don't worry, he confided in me, I know all about it,' he replies – obviously assuming I'm covering for him.

'Oh,' I say – well, what else can I say? I didn't know he was stressed.

'It's okay, you don't have to pretend with me,' he reassures me. 'He told me. I know it's the press stuff getting to him. The constant stories. All the stuff that went down when he and Nikki split. I mean, I'm not surprised he wonders if she tipped them off. How else would the papers know it ended because he wouldn't settle down?'

Wow, I didn't know he was going through all that. I knew that the press gave him a hard time, and that he didn't like the publicity, but I didn't know they knew about his break-up. I suppose I should count myself lucky that the goss on my break-up didn't reach far beyond the wedding where it went down.

'Front pages. Comment sections. Everyone calling him a bad boy, a lad, man-child who can't commit,' he continues. 'I know it gets under his skin. I tell him not to read any of it. I imagine you do the same?'

'Erm, yeah,' I reply.

I don't know what else to say. Wow, poor Brody, carrying all of that around with him without letting on. I know, he's got big shoulders to carry it, but it must weigh heavy on him sometimes.

He seems so big, so impossible to knock down. Like nothing could actually hurt him – but I suppose that's only physically. There's no gym for your emotions, is there? If there were I might actually entertain that one. I often tell myself I'd be invincible, if I didn't cry at videos of dogs doing absolutely anything or feel annoyed over... well, again, absolutely anything.

I'm not surprised though. I've seen his softer side while we've been pretending to be together. Yes, he's got the charm, the bravado – everything you'd expect of a sportsman who spends his days surrounded by bros, but I see his softer side in the things he says to me, the way he cares – the fact he still dances with his gran. He's Brody Ryan... although to his gran I guess he's just cute little Brody. That's what he is to me too, kind of, because I had no idea who he was, or what he was, and even now I do know it doesn't really mean much to me. Obviously I think it's amazing, that that's his job, that he got to where he is, but I could never be drawn to him just because he has a good job. He's so much more than his job, than what the press writes about him.

'Mind if I cut in?' Brody asks, interrupting our conversation. 'I think your wife-to-be is getting jealous.'

'She's getting jealous, huh?' Neil says with a wink. 'Sure thing.'

'Hello, Mr Ryan, children's party planner extraordinaire,' I tease him.

'Hello, princess,' he replies. 'Fancy a roll around in the ball pool?'

'The words every girl wants to hear,' I reply.

'So what were you two talking about?' he asks curiously.

'Oh, this, that, the other,' I say vaguely.

'Me then?' he replies.

I laugh.

'Neil and Kelsey clearly think really highly of you,' I tell him.

'You sound surprised...'

'I am,' I confess. 'I know we met under... unusual circumstances.'

'Like you thinking I was the valet and making me park your car?' he replies.

I pull a fake pouty face.

'I thought you just really wanted to drive a Fiat 500!' I reply.

'If anything, it drove me,' he tells me. 'Or did you mean me pulling you out of a dirty fountain, after you kneecapped someone for a bouquet of flowers?'

'Pretty sure her kneecaps were unscathed,' I add. 'But yeah, that.'

'And don't forget you snoring the night away in my bath before stealing my tracksuit,' he continues.

My God, he's unrelenting – and impossibly charming.

'I didn't steal it!'

'You didn't give it back,' he reminds me.

'Didn't I?' I say as innocently as I can, although I think my smirk gives me away.

'No, you didn't,' he replies, his hands shifting closer to the small of my back as we dance together.

'Okay, yeah, fine, I know I didn't,' I admit. 'I actually have it here with me – it's just so comfortable. But when I realised you were here I thought it best I didn't get it out, just in case you asked for it back.'

'Don't worry, I've got loads,' he replies with a smile. 'Would you rather have a fresh one?'

I shake my head.

'There's just something about stealing a man's clothes,' I confess. 'They're so much comfier when they feel a little worn in, when they still smell of aftershave.'

He narrows his eyes and cocks his head.

'Jessa, have you been sniffing my drawers?' he asks.

'Mostly the top,' I insist. 'Whatever it is you wear... it smells really good.'

'I didn't think I'd worn any aftershave with those,' he says.

'Hmm,' I reply. 'Maybe they just smell like you.'

'Come on then, give me a sniff, see what you think,' he demands. 'Because now you've got me thinking that I might actually be intoxicating, which I could get on board with. Imagine the power.'

'Okay, I'll give it a go, but don't be disappointed if your powers don't work on me,' I reply. 'It could just be your washing powder.'

'There's only one way to find out,' he says, practically goading me.

We're still over by the pool, away from the others, like we're in our own little world. Brody's invitation to get even closer to him is one I can't turn down.

My nose brushes the skin just under his ear, and, yeah, he really does smell good. I don't know if it's just his smell or his aftershave or both but it sends my senses into overdrive.

My face lingers there longer than it should, my nose nuzzling into his neck like it has a mind of its own. His skin is warm and smooth, and I feel him shift, like he's leaning in to me too, like we're magnetised.

His arm tightens slightly around my waist so I press my body closer to his. I feel like his heartbeat just got much stronger, and faster, or maybe it's my own beating out of my chest but the moment is dragging me in, refusing to let go, and I've never felt so alive.

I pull back ever so slightly, just enough to look at him. We catch each other's eyes, and there's something undeniable between us, something unspoken but loud and clear, it's that perfect moment, the one where you both know you should kiss. We lean in so slowly it's like an especially delicious kind of torture and...

I don't know if we do actually kiss or if I just imagine it, but suddenly I'm gasping for air. Not because it was that good (although I'm certain it would have been), because I'm in the pool, fully clothed, flapping around like a fish out of water (ironically) as I struggle to my feet. Luckily it's not deep, it's the kids' pool, but I'm even more relieved that it's not too shallow because we could have been seriously hurt.

Brody is in the water next to me. He wipes it from his eyes and runs his hands through his hair to stop it dripping in his face.

I only have to wonder what the hell just happened for a second when I spot her, Nikki, standing at the edge of the pool, staring angrily down at us.

'Oh my God,' Kelsey says, rushing over. 'Nikki, that's not okay at all.'

Al, ever the hero, gets into the pool to make sure we're okay. It's not deep, we're clearly fine, but that's Al – a well-meaning hero.

After checking us over, he looks back at Nikki.

'Nikki, that was really dangerous,' he tells her.

'Yeah, what was that?' Neil asks. 'We thought it was light-hearted, the other day, when they were in their swimwear. But this? This isn't funny.'

'It's totally unacceptable,' Kelsey says. She isn't normally one to get angry and she hates to say or do anything that could be considered impolite, but Nikki has clearly crossed a line. I like to think I would do the same, if someone pushed my best friend into a pool at a party. No, I know I would, because honestly, what the hell was Nikki thinking? It's not my problem if she has buyer's remorse, if Todd isn't turning out to be the man she thought he was – tough luck, I went through the same thing. And maybe she does want Brody back, maybe she's jealous, maybe she blames me for everything but even so... don't bloody push people into bloody swimming pools.

I try to rub the water from my eyes without rubbing eye make-up into my eyeballs, because that's never fun.

'It's okay. It's fine. Let's just leave it.' I force a smile.

I just want Kelsey and Neil's wedding to be okay, I don't want Nikki ruining it by making it all about her.

Al takes me by the hand and helps me out of the pool in my waterlogged dress.

Brody hauls himself out, water cascading off him, as he marches over to Nikki who is still just standing there, her arms crossed, her face like thunder.

Her cheeks are beetroot red, but whether it's from embarrass-ment or rage, I can't tell. I'm assuming it's both, but I'm not sure she's capable of feeling shame.

'Jessa didn't deserve that,' Brody says, cool and calm but clearly really pissed off. 'You owe her an apology.'

Nikki shrugs. I don't think she thinks she's done anything wrong, which is absolutely wild.

'Jessa, I'm so sorry,' Kelsey says.

'No, no, I'm sorry,' I insist. 'This is your party and your wedding and this shouldn't be happening.'

Poor Kelsey looks like she might cry. Kira stands nearby, wide-eyed and stunned into silence. And then there is Todd, who is still across the room, a drink in his hand, watching us all, completely expressionless. Erm, this is his partner, should he not say something? He's always been a coward now that I think about it.

'I'd better go get changed,' I say, lifting the edge of my dripping dress, as though I'm examining it to see if it's that bad – it's really bad. I'm pretty sure it said dry-clean only so that's fun!

'Yeah,' Brody says with a heavy sigh. 'Me too.'

We walk out together, and I hold my head as high as I can (which is tricky when it's waterlogged) and try to keep my cool.

Inside though... inside I'm screaming. Nikki has gone too far this time. She can't get away with this.

31

'So, we're just not going to talk about it?' Brody says as he dries his hair with a towel.

'Nope,' I reply, not even looking at him. I'm busy rifling through drawers, looking for something. I'm a woman on a mission.

'Okay... what about this then?' he tries again. 'Are we going to talk about this?'

I look at him and realise that he's referring to me still in my wet dress (but wrapped in a towel) running around Todd and Nikki's room, rifling through their things.

'No,' I say again.

'Remind me why we're doing it at least?'

I can't help but smile at his use of the word 'we're' because while he clearly is not down for this at all, he's taking his role as my fake boyfriend very seriously. Nothing says 'ride or die' like turning over someone's room together.

'Because Nikki is clearly crazy,' I remind him – as if there's a chance he might not know, he did date her. 'And out to get me.

And she obviously stole my dress. We both know that she did. It's got to be in here somewhere – check that wardrobe.'

'Okay but...' Brody starts slowly, walking towards me. 'Why are we doing it?'

'To prove that she did!'

Brody takes my face in his hands and looks deep into my eyes.

'Jessa, we know she did it,' he says softly. 'Everyone knows she did it. She took your dress, she pushed you into the pool – you could probably accuse her of anything right now, whether she did it or not, and everyone would believe you because she showed the world who she really was tonight.'

I sigh, letting my shoulders sink, letting go of some of my tension.

'She just went full villain,' he continues. 'You don't have anything to prove to anyone, everyone loves you, everyone is mad at her. But if she comes here and finds us going through her things it's only going to make her worse and give her ammunition to say you're giving as good as you're getting. Don't give her oxygen, suffocate her.'

I open my mouth to speak, a cheeky smile taking control of my face.

'Not literally,' he says with a laugh. 'Come on, let's go get changed, let's go back to the pa—'

We hear the door beep from where we are, letting us know that Todd and Nikki are back, and you just know they're going to come in here. It sounds like they're arguing.

'Shit,' I whisper. 'They're going to find us in here. She's going to go mad.'

Brody's eyes scan the room.

'Quick, the balcony,' he says, nodding towards the door. 'It connects to the living room one.'

We rush to the glass door and slip outside, closing the door behind us. There's a privacy screen between the two balconies, which you can open from this side, so we head through it, closing it behind us. I swear we do it just in time.

'I think we might actually have got away with that one,' Brody says, puffing air from his cheeks.

'Thanks to you,' I tell him.

The cool night air clings to our wet clothes. I'm chilly, even with a towel wrapped around me.

Brody peeks in through the glass door into the living room.

'No one's in the living area,' he says. 'We're good. Let's go.'

He tries the door handle but nothing happens.

'Very funny,' I tell him – he's such a wind-up merchant, even when the timing isn't ideal.

He jiggles it again, then turns to me, sheepish.

'It is actually locked,' he says. 'From the inside.'

I stare at him.

'And the privacy gates only open from the other side, don't they?' I say, already knowing the answer. 'So we can't get back to their room, or to ours.'

'I could try and climb over?' he suggests, eyeing it up.

'Oh my God, Brody Ryan, don't you dare,' I say firmly. 'I'm not jazzed about being trapped out here, but it's definitely preferable to you falling overboard.'

'I'm an athlete, I'd be fine,' he says. 'Climbing, I mean.'

'I suppose, on the plus side, if you did fall to your death I could probably tell people that Nikki pushed you,' I joke. 'You did say they would believe me.'

'Well, just for you, I won't attempt the climb, even though I'm absolutely certain I can do it,' he says, potentially a little tongue in cheek. 'But if I meet a watery demise any other way, you have my blessing to pin it on Nikki.'

'Thanks,' I say, reaching out, squeezing his shoulder. 'Wow, how are you still warm?'

'I took my wet clothes off faster,' he says. 'While you were rifling through Todd's underpants drawer.'

'Fond memories of that,' I say sarcastically. 'Can you help me take my wet dress off, please?'

'Of course,' he replies.

I take off my towel and turn around so that Brody can unzip my dress. My breath catches as his hands graze my bare back, his touch so warm against my cold skin. He lets the dress fall to the floor around my feet – well, there's no point being precious about it now, is there?

I start to shiver, just a little.

'Does this stuff happen to you all the time too?' I ask him.

Brody laughs.

'This is the third time I've seen you take a spill into the drink,' he tells me. 'I can't say I wasn't expecting it generally – I'm just surprised you haven't ended up in the sea. Pleasantly though. I think I'd miss you now.'

As I turn around to face him, Brody notices how cold I am.

'Come here,' he says. 'Let's warm you up.'

He starts rubbing the side of my arms with his hands, then my shoulders, then down the arms again, then his hands find their way to my waist and he pulls me close.

'Steal my body heat,' he insists. 'I don't mind.'

'I bet you don't,' I say with a smirk. 'You know, for a second, before Nikki pushed us into the pool, I thought you were going to kiss me.'

'That's interesting,' he replies. 'I thought you were going to try to kiss me too.'

'Try?' I echo. 'You don't think I would have succeeded?'

'I mean… you didn't succeed,' he reminds me, reaching up to push my damp hair from my eyes.

'Hmm, that's true, I guess I didn't,' I reply. 'No sense in trying again then, right?'

'Absolutely not,' he says firmly. 'Unless it's for, like, survival.'

I chew my lip thoughtfully.

'Hmm, I do in fact want to survive, so…'

'So I guess it's on me, to keep you warm, until someone comes to let us back in, right?' he suggests.

I playfully glance around the empty balcony, then out to sea, the dark sky and the even darker waters revealing that, sadly, there is no one else here who can help.

As he holds me close, he looks at me like there's something he wants to say, or something he wants to do. I feel the same way, I'm just not sure what to do first.

No, wait, yes, I am.

His hands find my waist again. Mine find the back of his neck. This time when we lean in our lips get to meet. No games, no pretending, no one to push us into the water. It's actually happening.

Brody scoops me up into his strong arms and sits me down on the wooden table that stands between the two chairs. He crouches down on his knees in front of me, takes one of my feet in his hands, and starts kissing my ankle. Slowly but surely, he makes his way up the inside of my leg, stopping as he approaches my upper thigh.

'Just making sure I warm up every inch of your body,' he tells me with faux seriousness.

'Oh, of course,' I reply.

'Because these legs are freezing,' he says as he hooks them over his shoulders, one after another.

As I look down at him, I can't help but laugh.

'Well, aren't you just a regular hero,' I tell him.

'You ain't seen nothing yet,' he replies.

32

I'm woken up ever so gently by the sound of the ocean crashing against the shore, the golden sunlight beaming down over me, warming my bones, and Brody's body underneath my head, supporting me – in more ways than one.

Last night was pure magic. It was a long time coming because, honestly, we both went crazy. I don't know if it was the sea air, being locked outside, or the sexual tension that has been building between us but it was like we couldn't get enough of each other, I've never felt passion like that with anyone, I've never felt so wanted – needed, even. I needed him too. Not just for warmth – although that did work a treat – but because he makes me feel like I matter. Like I'm someone worth touching, kissing, spending time with. And okay, sure, where is he going to go if we're locked outside together, but he didn't have to cuddle me all night, we're not an actual couple, are we?

It's nice lying here, my head on his chest, listening to his heartbeat. It feels almost a shame to wake him up, I could lie here all day now that the sun is shining, but we're here. We're in Sicily. We've got a wedding to get ready for.

'Good morning,' I say to him, gently rubbing his stomach to wake him up.

Christ, his abs feel like marble.

'Morning,' he replies. He drapes one arm lazily over his eyes in an attempt to block out the morning light, while the other remains securely wrapped around me, holding me close. It's almost like now that we've actually got together, we're too scared to let go. Well, that's how I feel anyway.

For once, his usual cocky smile is absent, replaced by something far more peaceful. Even his dimples look like they're still snoozing.

We slept on the balcony under the stars. Honestly, it was bloody freezing, but I wouldn't change it for the world. It was magical – not just the sex, after that, lying there, talking, falling asleep in each other's arms. I've never had an experience like that before and I still can't quite believe it happened.

Blinking away the sunshine, I sit up slowly, taking a moment to stretch out my back, which isn't happy about sleeping on a hard floor. But to be honest, I don't care, because last night was amazing and now we're here, looking out at a postcard-perfect Palermo, with its beautiful buildings and rolling hills in the background. The sun is shining, the sea is sparkling, I'm going to say the birds are singing too because, when you're this happy, it's like the world has a filter on it. I defy anyone to upset me today.

He arches his back with a relaxed groan, blinking slowly as he squints at me through one sleepy eye.

'Are we still locked out?' he asks, his voice deep and low, like he's half asleep.

I glance over at the door and see that it's not only unlocked but it's open too, meaning someone had to have done it for us, meaning they saw us snuggled up asleep and didn't go mad.

'Erm, no, the door is open,' I tell him. 'And we're here – we're in Sicily.'

That simple statement seems to do the trick. He's awake now, sitting up with a stretch that flexes his biceps in a way that makes me want to lay him straight back down.

'Wow, it's beautiful,' he says.

'I can't wait to explore the place,' I reply. 'Maybe when the wedding is done, we...'

'I would love to,' he says, putting me out of my misery.

He turns to me, his hair a dreamy mess, tousled and sleep-rumpled, and a lazy smile spreading across his face.

'It's almost as beautiful as you,' he tells me, his tone playful yet sincere.

I roll my eyes, but I can't help the smile that creeps onto my face. I can't stop smiling, honestly. Something has shifted between us – changed for the better. We're not pretending any more, not doing anything to impress anyone, or for anyone's benefit but our own, not trying to put on an act.

And honestly? I'm not sure I ever was putting on an act, not really.

I kept telling myself that he was annoying and infuriating and I didn't like him at all. A walking tabloid headline, a certified top shagger, the bad boy of cricket. I convinced myself I didn't like him, I really did. In hindsight, I think it was almost like a reflex, some common sense from somewhere, trying to bully me into not falling for the first bad boy to flex his muscles at me while I was on the rebound.

Now though, he doesn't seem all that bad to me.

'Did you open the door?' he asks me.

I shake my head slowly.

'Nope,' I reply.

'Todd? Nikki? Maybe?' he says, rubbing his chin thoughtfully. 'We're alive, so my money would be on Todd.'

I laugh.

'That's exactly what I thought,' I tell him. 'Well, if he's done it, perhaps we have his blessing, even if we don't have Nuclear Nikki's.'

'Yeah, maybe,' he says with a smile. 'Perhaps they've both calmed down now. We do all have a wedding to go to, and even Nikki wouldn't make someone else's wedding about herself... would she?'

He looks like he isn't so sure.

'I don't know but if we could all have a fresh start, that would be great,' I reply. 'Or if we could all pretend to have a fresh start, until Kelsey and Neil are married and safely off on their honeymoon, that would do too.'

'It has to be,' he replies, and we exchange a look of intrigue and maybe just a touch of apprehension. But for the first time in a while, it doesn't feel like we're bracing ourselves for a fight, a confrontation, or any kind of dramatic scene. There's an unspoken understanding lingering in the air around us, a sense of possibility. Maybe this is the fresh start we both desperately needed – a clean slate. A strange kind of peace.

Brody stands up, extending his hand toward me, and without a second thought, I take it, intertwining my fingers with his.

'Sicily seems like a great place for a fresh start,' he says, inhaling the sea air, exhaling slowly as he looks down at me.

He takes my face in his hands and kisses me, only lightly, only for a few seconds, but it's heaven.

'Let's get dressed, find the others, and get this wedding back on the road,' I say, suddenly feeling like I could do anything, like nothing could possibly rattle me.

'It's nice to see you looking so happy,' he tells me as he tucks my hair behind my ear.

'It's nice to be so happy,' I reply.

And I am, for the first time in what seems like ages, truly happy. I'm not out to prove anything, to get back at anyone, I'm just happy.

And it feels amazing.

33

It's a beach resort, where Kelsey and Neil are tying the knot and, honestly, if I'm ever lucky enough to get married to someone I love, I'm thinking it's going to have to be by the sea because this place is like a dream.

The resort sits right on the edge of the beach, all perfectly white walls and terracotta tiles. Everything smells so good too, like the air is just cleaner here, like there's always this faint citrusy smell but you know it's not a diffuser or a scented candle, it's real.

Emma, the wedding planner (and I know this now, because the wedding coordinator is here, and she is lovely), unsurprisingly did not do her job, and I would say I was more convinced than ever now that she was acting maliciously because I annoyed her, but to be honest she's done me the biggest favour, giving me and Brody our own little bubble to fall for each other in. Well, she's struck again, because she hasn't altered our hotel booking, meaning there are still only two rooms for the four of us, but Brody and I said we would be happy to share, leaving Todd and Nikki to have the other one – not that any of us have seen them since the ship docked.

Our room has these huge shuttered doors that open straight onto a little terrace, where two loungers are tucked under a canopy – not that I'm planning on sleeping out here, but it looks much more equipped than the ship balcony did. It's good to know we have options, because you never know with us.

Inside, the bed is massive and draped in white linens that look so, so comfortable. After a night partly on the floor (partly on Brody) I could happily get in right now, curl up in a little ball, and fall asleep. There's a large free-standing bath at the foot of the bed, meaning there's an obvious joke to make. I'm keen to crack it before Brody does.

I drop my suitcase and turn to face him.

'Okay, so who's taking the dreamy-looking bed and who is sleeping in the bath?' I ask, completely straight-faced.

He stretches, arms up, shirt rising just enough to distract me completely.

'I mean, I'd offer you the bed... but I was the last one to sleep in the bath so... I guess it's your turn,' he tells me. 'Officially, we take turns, and we don't want to break tradition, do we?'

'Oh, so it's tradition now, is it?' I check. 'Are we going to do this forever?'

'For as long as you'll have me,' he replies with a smile.

'The gentlemanly thing would be to take the bath first, right?' I say as I sit down on the bed, claiming my spot.

'Well, there's where you're wrong, because the gentlemanly thing is: ladies first,' he corrects me.

'Ladies first in the bed,' I reply.

'Okay, then I'll flip you for it,' he says.

'What, like tossing a coin?'

'No, like this...'

Brody launches himself at me, grabbing me as the two of us

fall back onto the bed together. He flips me onto my back, pinning me down.

'If this were wrestling, I would have just won,' he points out.

'Well, I can't argue with that, can I?' I reply. 'Are we going to resolve all of our issues like this?'

'It's like I said before... for as long as you'll have me,' he jokes.

'Well, I suppose we could share it,' I suggest. 'We are already both in it, so...'

'...so I suppose we could,' he says. 'But can you keep your hands off me, that's the issue.'

'Says the man who is currently on top of me,' I reply.

'Want me to move?' he asks, although from his smirk I can tell he already knows the answer.

'No,' I reply.

He leans forward and kisses me, holding my wrists above my head with one hand while the other takes his weight.

'Is this a wrestling move?' I ask between kisses.

'Yes,' he replies. 'Perfectly platonic, no funny business, just sports.'

'Ah, and I do love sports,' I say sarcastically.

'Just wait until I take you to your first cricket match,' he says.

'Oh, boy, can't wait,' I reply.

I'm teasing him but I actually can't wait. I know, I don't like sport, and I definitely don't understand cricket, but I can't wait to see him in action, doing his thing. I don't care if it's on the field, on TV or just him coaching kids.

Being here together, sharing this room, it feels so different to sharing a room on the ship. Obviously we don't have our room-mates – not sad about that at all – but this time it feels like ours, like something has shifted between us.

'You want to be careful,' he warns me. 'Because this is starting to feel pretty real.'

'I think it might be real,' I joke.

Brody fakes a gasp as he strokes my cheek.

'No more pretending?' he replies.

'No more gym, no more spa...'

'Oh, but I did love the spa,' he replies. 'I don't remember the last time I laughed so much.'

'And I'll miss the gym,' I tell him. 'Even if I did mostly go just to perv over you.'

'It's comments like that, princess, that make me think that you might struggle to keep things platonic later,' he jokes.

'Only if you play your cards right,' I reply.

I really could stay here all day, in his arms, but we've got a dinner to get dressed up for.

This is it. No more secrets, no more pretending. Just us.

Tomorrow we'll watch our best friends tie the knot and then after that... who knows? But I'll bet it's going to be good.

34

The hotel coffee bar looks like something you would see on Instagram and instantly wish you could go there – the kind of thing you see and forward to the person you love or your bestie. Well, I don't need to, because Kelsey is here with me.

It's all marble counters and rustic furniture that give the place a good mix of luxury and charm. Everything is so ornate. Fresh-cut flowers sit in miniature vases on every table which is a really nice touch. Over in the corner, there's a man playing piano – a quick takeaway coffee back home is never going to hit the spot again.

I spot Kelsey at a table near the piano, legs crossed, looking really relaxed, sipping away at a massive cappuccino. She's got one for me too – I assume.

I sit in the seat across from her.

'Please tell me that's your first cappuccino and not, like, your third,' I tell her. 'And that the other one is for me.'

'Of course it is,' she replies, raising her cup to me. 'The pastries are to share too. They're called sfogliatella – I may have already tried one.'

'It's your wedding weekend, I'll let you off,' I reply with a smile. 'This place is gorgeous.'

'This whole place is unreal,' she replies. 'I don't know if I want to marry Neil, or basically everything I eat and drink.'

'I'd marry this,' I say through a mouthful. 'Perhaps Neil will share you.'

'Perhaps,' she replies.

I feel like she's watching me – observing me, studying me... The kind of look only a best friend can get away with. The prying kind, that sees too much.

'You seem happier today,' she says, her voice hinting at a deeper meaning. 'You seemed happy yesterday, but you seem really happy today.'

I shrug, trying to play it cool.

'I guess I just am,' I reply. 'Really happy. I'm so excited for your wedding.'

'Hmm.' Her brows lift slightly – suspiciously I'd say.

'Really. I'm excited for you,' I say, meaning every word. 'It's going to be a beautiful day.'

'I'll accept that answer – for now,' she says. 'But I still think there's something you're not telling me.'

I take a long sip of cappuccino as I try to find the right words.

'I'm really happy with Brody too,' I tell her.

That makes her smile.

'He seems like he makes you... lighter,' she tells me.

'He does,' I reply. 'He's made all my silly problems seem, well, silly, like they don't matter.'

It's true too. And I thought I was going to stumble, being honest with Kelsey, but the words come out so easily. As easy as it feels to be with him.

Kelsey glances down at her coffee for a second, then back up at me. It's time for me to read her mind now.

'You're nervous?' I check.

She nods her head.

'Is it that obvious?' she replies.

'Isn't it always obvious, between the two of us?' I point out.

'True,' she confirms. 'It's not that I'm worried about marrying Neil. That bit is the only thing I'm not nervous about. I just want the day to go well, you know? No disasters. No wardrobe malfunctions. No fallings-out...'

'Well, we have Al, and he's basically like having the world's scariest doorman, so he'll make sure no one scraps,' I tell her. 'And, you know, if anyone needs a car moving, and can't find their keys, he's on hand to do that too – by hand.'

'I'd pay to see that,' she replies. 'That would make the day memorable.'

'Remind yourself you said that when he's shirtless, doing press-ups with Neil's mum on his back,' I joke – but that's one of his party tricks, so I wouldn't be surprised.

'I should be careful what I wish for,' she replies.

Kelsey gives me a grateful kind of laugh, but I can tell she's still worrying so I reach across the table and take her hands in mine.

'Listen,' I say gently. 'No matter what happens tomorrow – rain, bad food, trousers splitting, shirtless bodybuilders – none of it matters as much as what comes after. The wedding's just a day. The marriage is the rest of your life. And it's going to be perfect.'

'Thanks, Jessa,' she says, squeezing my hands. 'You always know exactly what to say, to make me feel better.'

'And you aways know what snacks to buy me,' I reply. 'Sfogliatella, you say?'

She nods.

'I'm going to sneak a thousand home in my suitcase,' I half-joke.

Kelsey lifts her cappuccino, clearly feeling more like herself again. 'Just promise me something,' she says.

'Anything,' I reply. 'What can I do?'

'No falling in the fountain,' she jokes. 'Just get through the wedding dry, like normal people, please?'

I laugh. I wasn't expecting her to say that.

'Kelsey, just for you, I will refrain from getting in the fountain – and even if I've got form for it, it's okay, Brody will have my back,' I promise her. 'Do they even have one?'

'I don't know, but I do know you, and if there's something to fall in, you'll find it...'

'I mean, yeah, you're talking to the girl who tore a ligament while spectating PE,' I remind her.

'You loved that though – you got a note for weeks,' she points out.

'Yeah, it was almost worth spending the summer on crutches,' I say. 'At least I got to miss sports day.'

'We're so different sometimes,' she says with a laugh. 'But so similar too. You're like the sister I never had.'

'I never wanted a sister,' I tell her. 'I don't know anyone with a sister who makes me feel like that is something I would want. Having you is so much better. We're not close because we're related, we opt in, every day, to love and care for each other. The best relationships are the ones we're in because we want to be.'

'If they ever invent a wedding or a marriage kind of thing for best friends, I'm popping the question,' she jokes.

'Not if I ask you first,' I reply.

'I wouldn't be surprised if Brody asks you something, before I get the chance to,' she half teases. 'He really likes you, you know. I know, I know, I've said it before, but I've never seen him like this before.'

'Really?' I reply, all doe-eyed, because now that we're sort of together, it really matters to me.

'Yep,' she replies. 'I told you, that bad boy rep, it's all just the press. He's a sweetheart and he's just been looking for the right girl. Nikki was never right for him. But you… you're perfect. The two of you are perfect together. It makes me so happy, to see you both, and it's just going to make my wedding even better. It's the only present I want.'

'Oh, shall I return the expensive thing I bought from the list you sent around then, because…'

'Don't you dare,' she replies with a grin.

'I'm only teasing,' I reply. 'You can have both – seeing as though you're my bestie.'

'Maybe I'll return the favour one day.'

'You'll be my bridesmaid and get with the best man?' I say. 'Neil might have something to say about that…'

'Neil won't mind at all,' she replies. 'Because my bet is that it will be Brody you're marrying, and Neil will be the best man – and everything is coming together so well.'

'Don't get ahead of yourself,' I tell her.

Obviously, she's way, way in the future but, do you know what, I don't hate the idea of it. Let her have her daydreams – I don't think I'll be far behind her with ones of my own.

35

Brody and I walk arm in arm down the candlelit path that winds through the hotel's gardens. This time, it's not a show, we're not talking strategy, not trying to convince anyone we're in love. It's not for anyone else's benefit. This time it's all real.

The resort is unreal. A grand old villa right by the sea with a series of smaller villas dotted around in the grounds. It's a dream place to get married, that's for sure, like something out of a movie.

As we step through the arched entrance of the restaurant, I hover for a moment, taking it all in. Tables are dressed with green, white and red tablecloths, glass lanterns on each table, and then there is the old olive tree that is growing around the place, almost like it's hugging the room and everyone in it.

Brody pulls out my chair for me when we reach the table, joining our friends – well, the ones we're actually friends with. It's a small gesture, but my chest flutters all the same.

'You two all good?' Kelsey asks, watching us with a smile that stretches from one ear to the other.

I think I have a grin to match.

'We really are,' I say, and I mean it.

Neil glances around.

'It might just be the six of us tonight,' he says. 'We haven't heard from Todd or Nikki.'

'Good,' Kelsey replies. 'The way she behaved? Disgusting. I don't want that around my wedding.'

Al shrugs.

'I'm a lover, not a fighter, but... yeah. Maybe best they stay away,' he says.

It's a good job he's a lover, not a fighter, because he's the strongest man I've ever met, he could kill you just by staring at you too hard. To be honest, I'd be scared to let him love me, he's that much of a giant.

'No one is fighting you, babe,' Kira tells him.

'I could take you,' Brody jokes.

'You could, pal, because I love you too much to hit you,' Al replies.

'Whereas I would put you on your back,' Neil says, scowling playfully.

'It's not actually so bad when he does that,' Kelsey jokes.

We're all laughing until a voice interrupts us.

'Sorry we're late,' I hear Nikki's voice from behind me.

We all turn and... wow.

'Oh my, Nikki. You look...' Kelsey's voice trails off.

Nikki is dressed like she's about to walk the red carpet at the Oscars, not eat dinner with her friends. A glitzy low-cut dress. Sky-high heels. Hair curled to perfection. Make-up bold and bright. She's definitely trying to send a message, I'm just not sure what it is. Maybe she's trying to show Brody what he's missing, not that he's looking at her.

Todd is just behind her, looking sheepish and awkward in his linen shirt. But he's here. I was hoping they wouldn't come – I think we all were.

'Evening,' Todd mutters.

Kira's the first to break the ice. 'So, are you two excited? Big day tomorrow,' she says to Kelsey and Neil.

Neil smiles. 'Very,' he replies. 'Except this one is insisting we spend tonight apart. She says it's tradition.'

'It's a bit late to be old-fashioned now, isn't it?' Nikki chimes in.

Kelsey pulls a face but doesn't rise to it.

'I think people will love the food,' she tells us. 'It's authentically Italian.'

Nikki scoffs. Honestly, what is her problem?

Kelsey turns to her. 'What now?' she asks.

Brody slides his hand into mine under the table. He doesn't say anything, just squeezes gently. Reassuring. I appreciate it, but I'm not too worried – mostly because there's no pool here, so Nikki can't hurt me.

'Authenticity matters,' Nikki says. 'Not everyone around here is authentic though.'

Kelsey keeps her smile firmly in place.

'I love everyone here, and that's what matters to me,' she tells her.

Nikki sits forward in her seat, like she's gearing up to say something else.

'Whatever you're getting at, Nikki, just let it go,' Brody tells her.

Presumably she's talking about him.

'Actually,' Nikki says, leaning in, looking far too pleased with herself, 'this is information you'll want to hear – you especially, Brody.'

'I doubt that,' he replies.

'But it's about Jessa,' she says. 'She's wanted you longer than she's let on.'

Brody and I exchange a look and a smile. She couldn't be more right, could she? It's like our own little in-joke.

'You're smiling now, but wait until you hear this,' Nikki continues. 'She – Jessa – told me to dump you.'

Okay, she's got everyone's attention now.

'She told me to break up with you, Brody. She said you were supposed to be my partner, I wasn't supposed to be your therapist, and that your commitment issues were your problem,' she says. 'And then she said, like her granny used to say: fuck around, find out. Meaning if you're going to mess me around, then I should show you the consequences. Dump you.'

'That is your line, Jessa,' Todd points out. 'That's your joke.'

'Okay, but we all heard her say it the other day,' Kelsey reminds everyone.

'Yeah, but look at her face,' Nikki replies. 'It's got guilt written all over it. And someone is clearly tipping the press off...'

I do feel flushed. Well, it's true, isn't it? I did say that. I didn't know I was talking about Brody at the time – I didn't even know who Brody was – because we were in the toilets. She's spinning it to try to make me look bad. And it certainly isn't me tipping the press off.

I don't want to lie, obviously, because that would only make me look worse. But if I'm going down, she's coming with me. Todd too.

'You were the one saying you wanted to dump him, and now I have all the facts, I know that you were saying it because you'd met someone else,' I reply. 'And I know it was Todd because right after we spoke you went to find him, and you told him to dump me, so that you could have him.'

There's a voice in the back of my mind that says this sounds a little bit like we're fighting over Todd and that seriously gives me the ick, because Todd is really not worth fighting over.

It seems like we're attracting a bit of a crowd, our raised voices catching people's attention. Typical loud English people abroad, ruining the ambience for everyone.

'The two of you were so, so obviously cheating on us,' I say. 'It's so bloody obvious.'

Brody pulls his hand away from mine, and maybe it isn't, but it feels fast and tense. It isn't violent, but it stings all the same. It feels like rejection. Like I've gone too far.

'I need to get some air,' he says. 'You guys have dinner without me.'

I'm about to go after him, because I need to explain, to tell him that I didn't know the random girl crying over her boyfriend in the toilet cubicle next to me was his girlfriend, when I notice Nikki smirking, delighted to have scared him away from me.

'Why are you so determined to take every man I like?' I ask her.

'Erm, you took him from me,' she snaps back.

'I didn't even know it was you, for fuck's sake,' I reply. 'Not until I heard your stupid yodel cry again the other day.'

'I don't have a stupid yodel cry, do I?' she asks the table.

The silence speaks volumes.

'I need to go after him,' I say, standing up, my voice catching in my throat because I know that I should have done so right away, I just had to stay and get the last word, didn't I?

'Do you want me to come with you?' Kelsey asks, gently.

'No, no, I'm fine,' I insist. 'You guys enjoy your dinner. We'll catch up later.'

I walk away before my tears can betray me, before I say something that makes this bad situation even worse. I head back toward the room, hoping maybe Brody's there, but the door is locked and he has the only key card. I try knocking but there's no reply, so either he's not in there, or he knows it's me.

My chest aches. I can't believe Nikki has done this, bringing it up in a last-ditch attempt to throw a grenade into my and Brody's budding relationship. I'm worried it's dead in the water now. Maybe I have gone about this all wrong, maybe I should have come clean when I realised it was Nikki I spoke to in the toilets back then, or when I realised she was bringing it up today, or maybe I should have kept a dignified silence. I don't know what I should have done, I just know that it's not this. I shouldn't have let Brody out of my sight because without him being here I can't explain, and the version of events in his head will be pieced together from bits of information from all of us. It needs to come from me, but for that I need to find him first.

I'll go for a walk around the grounds, have a look for him, he's got to be around here somewhere.

Plus, he's the best man at the wedding tomorrow, and I know he won't miss that.

I just need to speak to him before it's too late.

It's not too late... is it?

36

There's something so beautiful about the beach at night –
something that really changes the vibe, like a daytime beach and
a night-time beach are two completely different places.

The sun has gone but the moon is shining bright, lighting up
the water below it. I suppose it comes with not being trapped on a
boat in the middle of the ocean, but the dark water doesn't seem
quite so scary or bottomless from the safety of the shore. Everything here is just so calm and peaceful. Everything except me
anyway.

I'm strolling along the shoreline, letting the sea breeze tangle
my hair and the water lap over my bare feet. I'm still looking,
scanning the darkness for that broad frame and messy brown
hair, thinking I'll bump into him any minute and he'll flash me
those dimples and let me know everything is going to be okay.

I can't find him anywhere though, and all I want is to talk to
him. To explain. To tell him everything, but properly this time,
leaving nothing out. I'm sure, if he just hears my side of things, it
will all make sense. I just need to bloody find him first though,
that's turning out to be the hardest part.

I'm so lost in thought that I almost miss the sound of someone calling my name.

'Jessa! Jessa! Oi!'

I turn and see Kelsey jogging toward me, her long dress fluttering around her and her hair blowing in the wind like she's in an eighties music video. If she could have done that in slo-mo, it would have looked epic.

She looks relieved to have found me – and a little out of breath. It takes her a few seconds to get her words out.

'There you are,' she says, pulling me into a hug that feels both grounding and suffocating. 'I've been looking everywhere for you!'

'Sorry, I didn't mean to freak you out, I was just looking for Brody,' I tell her. 'But... no luck.'

'I thought I was going to have to get the Italian coastguard to go look for you,' she jokes. 'Have you seen the lifeguards they have here? Every single one of them looks like a Dolce and Gabbana model.'

'You're not making me not want to throw myself in the sea,' I reply.

'Come on,' she insists, hooking her arm with mine, gently pulling me along. 'You're coming back to mine. Neil and I are doing the separate rooms thing, so I'm home alone anyway. You look like you need a bed and some snacks. Trust me, you'll feel much better when you've eaten a bunch of Italian crisps and drunk a lemon soda.'

I smile. She always knows just what I need.

We head up to her room, and true to her word, she's got an impressive stash of Italian crisps, biscuits and cans of pop. We crawl into bed like we're sixteen again, feet tucked under the covers as we break out the snacks.

'Right, okay,' she says, once we're sitting comfortably. 'Talk to me.'

So I do. I spill everything – how Brody and I were pretending, from the very beginning. That it was all meant to be just this little game, a little petty revenge, and that I didn't think it would matter, but of course, it did. I tell her about Nikki and how I had no idea it was her I was talking to when I said those things through the cubicle wall at the wedding. In fact, I'm so relieved when Kelsey mentions that at the time I did tell her I had been talking to a crying girl, but hadn't seen her face – not that she needed proof to believe me, of course.

'I was just trying to help,' I continue. 'Trying to be honest and helpful… but I just should have kept my mouth shut, minded my own business.'

'What kind of place would the world be if we didn't try to make it better?' Kelsey replies.

'That would have been so bloody profound if you had said it without the biscuit in your mouth,' I joke.

She picks up a crisp and throws it at me. I eat it before carrying on.

'You know, in a weird way, it was my fault Todd dumped me,' I say. Noticing the look on her face, I try to get to the point much quicker. 'Not like that. I just mean that when I spoke to Nikki and I told her to dump her boyfriend, to be with someone who makes her happy, I had no idea that someone was Todd. I drove her into his arms. I didn't just help their relationship come to an end – I was sealing the fate of my own too.'

Kelsey sits up straighter. She dusts herself off, like she can't make a serious point with biscuit crumbs on her top.

'Okay, first of all? None of this is your fault. Not one bit,' she insists.

I let out the huge breath I didn't realise I was holding.

'Thanks,' I reply.

'I mean it,' she insists. 'And the other thing – I've known that you and Brody were pretending to be a couple since day one. It was so, so obvious – to me anyway. I'm your best friend, you can't keep anything from me.'

'Really?' I practically squeak.

'Oh, yeah,' she says, grabbing another biscuit, almost like she's earned it.

'But I thought you said the two of us were clearly in love, or whatever,' I reply. 'You said we were great for each other.'

'Just because I knew you were both pretending to be together doesn't mean I think you were both pretending to be in love,' she replies which, again, would have sounded even bigger and more beautiful without the biscuit. 'You clearly love him,' she tells me. 'And he loves you too. Just because the two of you haven't realised it yet, or just don't want to admit it, doesn't change the facts.'

Every time she says the L word I don't know how to feel. I'm somewhere between wondering whether it's possible or whether I've blown it.

Do I love him? Can I love him yet? I mocked Todd and Nikki for getting so serious so quickly, but – if I'm being really honest with myself – maybe it is just a case of: when you know, you know? I think of Brody's hands on my body, the way he kisses me like he means it, the way he looks at me, how he always has my back. The way he calms me. The way he makes me laugh when I'm trying to be mad. God. Maybe I do. And if I don't yet, then maybe I will, if I just let myself.

'I really hope I haven't messed up your wedding,' I say quietly, almost in a whisper.

Kelsey leans her head against mine.

'All I care about is that you and Brody are there with me,' she says. 'I love you both. I just want you guys to be happy.'

'I want that too,' I admit.

'Then tomorrow, we'll make it right,' she says gently. 'Give him a little time and a bit of space. He'll talk to you when he's ready, and you'll smooth it all out, I promise. Talk to him. Tell him everything. It'll be okay.'

'Thanks, Kelsey,' I reply. 'I don't know what I'd do without you.'

'You'd be back in Yorkshire, in the rain, miserable,' she tells me. 'I hear it's been pissing it down all week.'

'Then I guess I'll be grateful for small mercies,' I reply.

Small mercies and great friends. That's a great start.

37

I wake to a gentle shake at my shoulder, a soft but persistent nudge that pulls me from my sleep – well, what little I was getting.

For a brief moment there I thought I was back on the ship, in my cabin with Brody, him waking me up to ask if he could share the bed with me, or to tell me it's 6 a.m. and we're going to the gym.

But it's not him, it's Kelsey, and seeing her reminds me of where I am, why I'm here, the whole messy situation I have found myself in.

Can I just go back to sleep, please? I can't face another crisis.

'Shit, what's wrong?' I whisper urgently, my heart pounding in that way it does when someone wakes you up in the middle of the night. I feel all woozy.

'It's nothing bad,' she reassures me quickly, her voice purposefully soothing. 'Someone is here to see you and I didn't think you would want to wait until morning.'

I sit up, groggy, my eyes still sore from crying, giving them a moment or two to adjust to the darkness. I see a shadowy figure standing at the end of my bed, its familiar outline, and yet somehow I would probably be more equipped for dealing with him if he were Nosferatu, not Brody.

'Brody?' I blurt, my voice catching in my throat.

'Hi,' he replies simply.

Kelsey glances between the two of us, a smile gracing her lips that somehow manages to be smug, satisfied and knackered all at once.

'I'll leave you two to it,' she tells us.

'No, Kelsey, where are you going?' I ask. 'You're getting married tomorrow, you need to sleep, this is your room. Don't go anywhere. We can leave, let you sleep...'

'I'm going to sleep in Neil's room,' she says with a smile and a bat of her hand. 'Screw silly tradition. We've got good men – both of us – we shouldn't spend a minute apart, especially now.'

Kelsey leans over and kisses my cheek.

'You've got this,' she whispers into my ear before disappearing out the door, leaving Brody alone in the dark.

'Mind if I sit?' Brody asks.

'Go for it,' I reply, sitting more upright, making sure there's a space next to me on the bed.

He sits down, the mattress dipping under his weight, and for a moment there's nothing but silence. One of us needs to say something, but neither of us knows who should go first. Then, breaking the tension, we both speak at once.

'I'm sorry,' we say simultaneously. Then we both laugh and suddenly everything feels easier.

'No,' I say, turning to face him. 'You don't have anything to apologise for. I do. But you have to believe me, I had no idea it was Nikki I was talking to that day. We were in cubicles, in the toilets, and I heard her crying, and I honestly didn't know she was dating you. I didn't even know you existed.'

I look down, twisting the corner of the blanket between my fingers, because I always fidget when I'm nervous. But it's now or never, I need to let him know how I really feel. The whole truth, no staging.

'I don't know, maybe I'm supposed to say that I wouldn't have told her to dump you if I had known she was dating you, but that's not true. I would've said it with even more certainty, because she's not right for you, Brody. I am.'

I'm not sure I intended to say that last part, it just slipped out with the rest. It's true though.

'I mean... if you want me, that is.'

I started out so strong but now I'm panicking again. Perhaps I shouldn't have said that.

Brody smiles, and the second I see his dimples I know it's all going to be okay.

'Whether you knew or not, I really don't care,' he tells me. 'You did me a favour. Nikki and I weren't right for each other. Not even close. I'm sorry for storming off earlier. People were watching, and I didn't want to cause a scene – just in case there were any Italian cricket fans around. I went for a run to clear my head, came back to the room thinking maybe you'd be there... but you weren't.'

His tone shifts slightly. I think he was worried that I was avoiding him, all while I was worrying that he was avoiding me.

'I wasn't,' I reassure him. 'I was looking for you. I was worried you might have believed Nikki, that I told the press about your break-up...'

'I know you didn't say anything to the press,' he says, taking my hand in his. 'It was Nikki. She was always trying to raise my profile – but really, it was hers she wanted to boost.'

He places his free hand on my face and looks deep into my eyes.

'This is new to me,' he admits, actually sounding a little bit nervous.

'It's new to me too, pretending to be with someone, we were never going to get it right,' I reply.

'No,' he says, shaking his head lightly. 'Feeling this way about someone. I've never felt like this before.'

'Neither have I,' I admit.

Whatever this is, it's something special. I don't think either of us can deny that any more.

'So,' I start, my voice barely above a whisper. 'What happens now?'

'I guess we just start again,' he says. 'From square one – the real square one, not the fake one. No secrets. No stories. No staging. Just you and me, making it up as we go along – or not, technically.'

I laugh and it's the wild kind that bubbles up from a mixture of relief and happiness.

'Let's just give the old-fashioned way a go,' he suggests, stroking my cheek. 'No pressure. Let's just see how it goes?'

'I'd really like that,' I say.

I yawn, not because I'm bored, but because with things between us back on the right track, I finally feel like I might be able to sleep.

Brody leans back on the bed, arms open wide, an invitation that I can't resist.

'Come here,' he says softly.

I don't need asking twice. I place my head on his chest, snuggling up to him, the slow steady rhythm of his heartbeat making me feel even more sleepy.

'This is nice,' I murmur sleepily, allowing myself to sink into his embrace even more.

He kisses the top of my head.

'It really is,' he replies. 'Get some sleep, you sound shattered. I'll be right here in the morning.'

And, safe in the knowledge that he will be, I allow my eyes to get heavier, to allow myself to fall asleep in his arms. Because I just know that while I'm here, nothing bad can happen to me.

38

It is surely a faux pas, to be this happy, and this loved-up, at someone else's wedding.

And yet here I am, with Brody, having one of the best days of my life. I know, that sounds dramatic, but considering how the last wedding I attended went down – and the one before that, actually – let me have this one.

This really is a perfect wedding though, my happiness aside. The fairy lights strung between the stone pillars, the faint roar of the ocean – and the food, my gosh. I hate to dunk on British tapas, because I love me a big plate of beige, but surely arancini and cannoli have sausage rolls and Party Rings beat?

If you can't get yourself a man who looks at you the way Brody looks at a silver platter covered with mozzarella and salami, then get yourself a man who looks at you the way Neil is looking at Kelsey. Seeing your best friend marry the man she loves – a man worthy of her love too – is like reading a love story with the most perfect ending. Neil looks like he's just won the lottery – I suppose he has, because the odds of getting a gem like Kelsey must be slim. I'm so lucky to have her as a friend. I mean, come on, this is her wedding, and she took time out from focusing on herself and her happiness to make sure I was okay, to bring me and Brody together, so that I could be happy too.

And I am happy. I'm smiling so hard my face aches – more than my arse did after my morning in the gym.

'I'm glad they decided to do the dance without the rest of us,' Brody says. 'It's their moment.'

'Yeah, their moment that you would have stolen with your exceptional dance moves,' I tease him. 'Are you actually trying out for *Strictly Come Dancing*?'

'I'd never rule it out,' he says with a laugh.

'There's only so many ways you can carry me, it's probably for the best,' I say with a sigh.

'Okay, okay, everyone else come and join us,' Kelsey calls out after having her moment with her man in the spotlight.

Brody takes me by the hand, leading me to the dance floor. With everyone else up on their feet we just sort of blend in, but we're in a world of our own anyway. We smile, and we dance. And I don't mess it up. Not a step.

I take a moment, from my little bubble of happiness, to glance around the room. Todd and Nikki came, but not together – presumably giving the wedding planner (or was it the coordinator?) one last heart attack, making her shift the seating plan one last time.

I wonder if they'll figure it out. I mean, they went through all of this to get together, what would it all be for, if they don't work things out?

It's funny, how genuine happiness changes your perspective, because I don't have a bad thought or feeling towards either of them. Truly, I mean it, I hope they work things out. I'm over Todd, over the betrayal, over Nikki's games – all of it. And Brody clearly is too.

Whether they do or don't work it out, you know what? It's not my problem. I'm letting it all go and I feel so, so much lighter.

With the dance over, Brody and I saunter out onto the terrace, to take in the view as the sun sets. As the sky cycles through the colours, we sit on a bench. I rest my head on Brody's shoulder and sigh.

'It's funny how things work out, isn't it?' I say.

'I know not all of it was ideal but... we're where we want to be now, right?' he replies.

'We are,' I tell him.

'If I hadn't been dumped, and you hadn't been, you know, publicly humiliated in front of everyone at Al and Kira's wedding...'

'Thank you for the reminder,' I say, deadpan.

'...then we wouldn't have ended up here. Unless this was your plan, all along – I'll bet you threw yourself into that fountain, on purpose, and when Al pulled you out instead of me, I'll bet you were gutted.'

I smile because now, when he teases me, it feels like foreplay.

'I'm not in the habit of throwing myself into water features to get men,' I tell him.

'And yet every time I've seen you fall into one – which is three times, by the way – I've fallen for you a little harder,' he replies.

'Well, in that case, I'm grateful for each impromptu dip,' I tell him.

And I mean it, I really am.

The road to the two of us getting together may have been messy – and incredibly embarrassing for me – but true love is never plain sailing, is it?

I've never really bought into the idea that everything happens for a reason. Well, why can't good stuff happen without bad? Why do we have to pretend to be grateful for shitty things if we ultimately end up in a better place? But whether I believe in fate or not is by the by.

If Todd and Nikki hadn't got together, if they hadn't broken up with me and Brody at the same time, then what are the chances that Brody and I would have met? We were thrown together at Al and Kira's wedding, whether it was by fate or circumstance, and maybe it would have happened anyway, who knows? But there's no way I would be here, with my head on his shoulder, if it hadn't been for the valet mix-up, the bouquet incident, my dip in the fountain, sharing his room that night... and so on and so on.

I look out at the ocean and smile. The view from here looks great.

Who cares if all of this is down to fate, luck or coincidence? The past is the past, and I'm so, so happy with the present. And as for the future? Suddenly that seems much brighter too. I'm not sure exactly what it looks like, but I'll send you a postcard when I get there.

39

TWO YEARS LATER

The floor beneath my boots is dusty and covered with rogue screws and bits of plasterboard. It smells like concrete and cuts of wood and outdoors. And like home, because it is, it's my home. My dream home – well, almost. It's the bones of it, the walls, the best part of the roof, some rooms plastered, some not. But it's coming along and, when I'm in here, my imagination runs away with me. Not only thinking about how I'll style it, but how I'll live in it. It's almost like I can see my life playing out in front of my eyes, but in the best possible way.

I can picture the living room, where the sun will pour in through the windows on lazy Sundays, the two of us curled up on the sofa with cups of tea and something easy to watch on the TV. Or in the kitchen, where I'll attempt overly ambitious dishes, emboldened by all the fancy appliances I'm going to have. And then there's the upstairs – not that we have the stairs to get up there yet, but I'm already getting excited about having a big bedroom, and en suite, the dressing room of my dreams.

But for now it's still a shell, and a dark one at that, because it's late and dark and the only light is coming from the work lights dotted around the place.

'I hate watching you walk down that thing,' I say, watching Brody navigate the ladder back to the ground floor.

'I just wanted to see the roof,' he replies. 'You worry too much. Here, listen to some music, chill out. We're home.'

I can't help but laugh as he scrolls through his music library, eventually settling on an REO Speedwagon song.

'You have the music taste of your dad,' I tell him.

'Thanks,' he replies. 'I suppose you would prefer a boy band...'

'Don't tempt me,' I tease him.

He holds out his hand, a glimmer of something cheeky in his eye.

'May I have this dance, princess?'

I roll my eyes, unable to stifle a grin as I take his hand anyway.

'Because it's a perfectly normal thing, to slow dance in your partially built house, late at night, to music playing out of a phone,' I reply.

'Stranger things have happened,' he says.

'Yeah, usually when I'm around you,' I remind him.

'And yet,' he says, twirling me on the spot, 'you're in love with me.'

I laugh, stepping closer until there's hardly any space left between us. We start to sway gently to the music, our bodies casting our shadows on the concrete floor. I'm sure I look more graceful in silhouette.

'Okay, I'll give it to you, this is kind of a perfect moment,' I whisper into his chest.

'I thought so,' he says with a grin. 'Because one day, when the house is finished, we'll remember tonight, we'll remember it was like this, and how far we've come. That we did all of this together.'

'We've done a great job,' I say with a sigh. 'Or rather, we've had tradespeople do really great jobs for us.'

'You always said you'd build your own home one day,' he reminds me. 'I just feel lucky I get to do it with you.'

He pulls back just enough to look into my eyes, suddenly more serious.

'In the interest of remembering the house like this, and remembering this night, I've got an idea,' he says. 'I thought this might help.'

And then he stops moving altogether. He lets go of my waist and drops to one knee. And there's a small green box in his hands...

Surely everyone in the world knows what this means and yet my brain just can't compute it. Surely not? Brody Ryan? Proposing?

'Jessa,' he says, as chill as ever. 'Will you marry me?'

My jaw is on the floor. This is the last thing I was expecting tonight. Not that I'm disappointed, I'm over the moon but... wow!

'I'm sure it's only been a second or two but it feels like you've been frozen and silent for an hour,' he says with a laugh. 'Am I going to get an answer?'

'Oh my God, yes,' I say quickly. 'The most certain yes of my life.'

He scoops me up in his big arms, a laugh escaping him as he buries his face against my neck.

'You had me going for a split second,' he tells me. 'I was sure you would say yes but... I'm glad it's over with now.'

'Just what every girl wants to hear,' I reply. 'So, what are you thinking for the wedding – cruise ship or island?'

'It's got to be both, surely?' he jokes.

'Oh, of course,' I reply.

He pulls me close and kisses me and there isn't a doubt in my mind that I'm now exactly where I'm supposed to be.

I don't know if I believe that everything happens for a reason. I suppose, by that logic, sometimes you have to go through bad times to get to good ones. If Todd and I hadn't broken up, would Brody and I have ever met? Sure, we would have kept crossing paths at the same parties, but would we have caught each other's eye? Maybe we did need to break up at the same time, to be hurt at the same time, to find ourselves trapped at sea together but... I don't know. I like to think we would have found our way here eventually.

Anyway, who cares, life is what you make it. Fate decides nothing. We make a million decisions a day, whether it's something small like what's for dinner or the decision to not cheat on our partners, even if it seems like you might get away with it, or be happier with someone else. If there is something magical that keeps us on track then it's love, as corny as it sounds. Brody and I aren't together because of fate, we're together because of love. Without it our fake relationship wouldn't have worked, or it would have fizzled out – like normal relationships do, I guess, when you're not in love.

But now Brody and I are exactly where we're supposed to be, and we plan to keep it that way.

* * *

MORE FROM PORTIA MACINTOSH

The next book from Portia MacIntosh is available to order now here:

https://mybook.to/PortiaNewBackAd

ACKNOWLEDGEMENTS

Big thanks to Megan, my editor, Amanda and the rest of the team at Boldwood HQ, and Ross, my favourite proofreader, for all of their wonderful work on *Going Overboard*.

I had so much fun writing it – thanks so much to everyone who takes the time to read and review not just this book, but all my books. It means so much to me.

Shout-out to the group-chat girlies – Laura Carter, Leonie Mack, Camilla Isley, Sandy Barker and Olivia Spring. So lucky to have you.

I couldn't do any of this without the support of my wonderful family. Thanks so much to the amazing Kim, Pino and my incredible gran, Aud. Shout-out to my brothers – James and Joey – for all of their love and support and to Rach for all her help. Thanks as always to Darcy for being by my side. Finally, huge thanks to Joe, my husband, for all of his love, support and hard work. I love you all so much.

ACKNOWLEDGEMENTS

ABOUT THE AUTHOR

Portia MacIntosh is the million copy bestselling author of over 20 romantic comedy novels. Whether it's southern Italy or the French alps, Portia's stories are the holiday you're craving, conveniently packed in between the pages. Formerly a journalist, Portia lives with her husband and her dog in Yorkshire.

Sign up to Portia MacIntosh's mailing list for news, competitions and updates on future books.

Visit Portia's website: www.portiamacintosh.com

Follow Portia MacIntosh on social media here:

facebook.com/portia.macintosh.3

x.com/PortiaMacIntosh

instagram.com/portiamacintoshauthor

bookbub.com/authors/portia-macintosh

ALSO BY PORTIA MACINTOSH

Off The Record

Love On Tour

Always The Bridesmaid

Drive Me Crazy

Truth or Date

It's Not You, It's Them

The Accidental Honeymoon

Never The Bride

Summer Secrets at the Apple Blossom Deli

Snow Love Lost

Here Comes the Ex

Honeymoon For One

My Great Ex-Scape

Make or Break at the Lighthouse B&B

The Plus One Pact

Stuck On You

Faking It

Life's a Beach

Will They, Won't They?

No Ex Before Marriage

The Date Escape

Snow Place Like Home

Just Date and See

Your Place or Mine?

Better Off Wed

Long Time No Sea

The Break Up Plot

Trouble in Paradise

Ex in the City

The Suite Life

It's All Sun and Games

You Had Me at Château

Wish You Weren't Here

Too Hot to Handle

Going Overboard

Boldwood